DEATHLESS KING

BOOK FIVE OF AURA HEALERS HALL

THOMAS K. CARPENTER

Deathless King
Book Five of Aura Healers Hall

Paperback Version

by Thomas K. Carpenter

Published by Black Moon Books

Cover design by
G&S Cover Designs

Opening Chapter Image by Grand Failure
Chapter Heading by Kristina0702

Discover other titles by this author on:
www.thomaskcarpenter.com

ISBN-13: 9798335010351

DEATHLESS
KING

The Hundred Halls Universe

Season One

THE HUNDRED HALLS
Trials of Magic
Web of Lies
Alchemy of Souls
Gathering of Shadows
City of Sorcery

THE RELUCTANT ASSASSIN
The Reluctant Assassin
The Sorcerous Spy
The Veiled Diplomat
Agent Unraveled
The Webs That Bind

GAMEMAKERS ONLINE
The Warped Forest
Gladiators of Warsong
Citadel of Broken Dreams
Enter the Daemonpits
Plane of Twilight

ANIMALIANS HALL
Wild Magic
Bane of the Hunter
Mark of the Phoenix
Arcane Mutations
Untamed Destiny

STONE SINGERS HALL
Song of Siren and Blood
House of Snake and Tome
Storm of Dragon and Stone
Sonata of Shadow and Thorn
Well of Demon and Bone

THE ORDER OF MERLIN
The Order of Merlin
Infernal Alliances
Tower of Horn and Blood

The Hundred Halls Universe

Arcanium loves books
Coterie adores power
Assassins will kill you
Stone Singers has a stone flower

Animalians is a zoo
Alchemists, you'll devour
Tinkers loves gadgets
Protectors makes you cower

Aura Healers wants to fix you
Blue Flame has a tower
Dramatics loves the spectacle
Oculus has grown sour

One Hundred Halls
Each with their own magic
The Patrons protect
Because faez madness is tragic

In the city of sorcery
Invictus is the Head
His students are many
But the foolish end up dead

- A Children's Rhyme

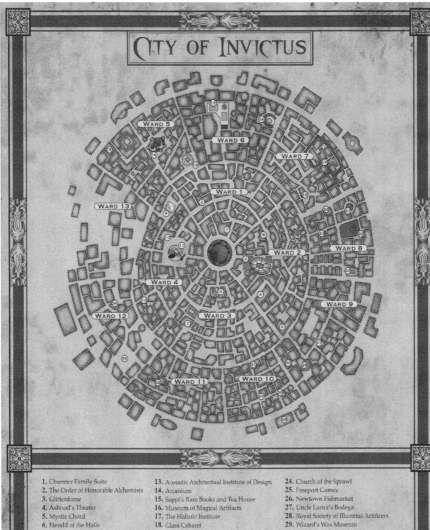

City of Invictus

ONE

Manuel could smell hot, hungry pheromones waiting to be picked out of the packed bar. The Tattered Tome wasn't his usual hangout spot, but he was on the other side of town tracking a mage who had killed his wife for accidentally throwing away an important reagent—or that's what the story was. Manuel really didn't care as long as her parents were good for the money, and he was certain they were, given their address in the first ward.

He leveraged his way past a group of college-aged guys in collared shirts drinking from mugs made to look like they'd been used in the Middle Ages. The biggest turned to make something of his passing, but when they saw his staff, they turned away, no longer interested in confrontation.

When Manuel had first joined Justicars, he'd thought the staff was an outdated sigil of their Hall. A gun or something more immediate was to his liking, but over the five years of schooling, he'd come to appreciate the staff in both use and symbology.

A whiff of floral perfume mixed with a heady scent had him diverting to the bar, elbowing the big man on the way just for fun, to find a sleek honey sitting all by herself in a painted-on white dress.

He casually leaned the staff next to her spot as he gestured towards the bartender, who was filling a trio of mugs. Manuel purposely didn't make eye contact, even when the honey glanced his direction.

"Compensating much?"

The barb caught in his throat, but he cocked a smile and casually answered.

"Working."

She started to ask another question but the bartender came over.

"Two fingers of nightshade-infused whiskey. Bone Fist, if you have it."

The bartender frowned.

"I can only serve it to—"

Manuel tapped the staff with an index finger, and the gemstone at the top flashed with eldritch energies, which put out a soothing aura that would make those around him more pliable.

The bartender stared at the fleeting light, then shrugged.

"Your funeral."

"You really a mage?" asked the honey with an eyebrow raised. "Or just cosplaying as one?"

Manuel produced his card, flicking it into her lap. She lifted it up.

"Manuel Iniesta. Private detective slash bounty hunter. Bonded by the Bank of the Arcane. Justicar Hall. This real?"

The whiskey was delivered in a chunky glass that could have doubled as a fallen meteor. Manuel swirled the amber liquid, gave it a sniff, then downed it in one go. The nightshade burned through his neural system, lighting up his senses and giving him a warm sense of invulnerability.

"Another."

The bartender walked away shaking his head.

"I guess it's real," said the honey. "You after the demon dragon?"

Manuel furrowed his brow.

"That's just a rumor."

The honey shook her head, making her blonde tresses dance around her heart-shaped face. She looked like the kind of girl who hadn't realized she was hot until after high school and wasn't going to squander an ounce of her newfound power.

"I saw it last week near the Cryptozoo. Nearly stopped my heart and I was two blocks away. Smashed a car and fled the other way, thank Merlin, or I think I would have fainted. Or is something like that too big for you?"

"I killed the Harpy Twins when they tried to come for one of my clients using vorpal wire and a come-hither bell. I doubt a demon dragon, no matter how fierce it sounds, would be much of a problem."

The honey lifted her shoulders.

"It was pretty big."

A second glass of whiskey appeared. He swirled it once before taking a sip and letting the warm liquid run down the back of his throat.

"You ever heard of Big Mag'thanan?"

"Should I?"

Manuel grumbled under his breath.

"A big ol' hob. Was squatting in some buildings on the edge of the thirteenth and scaring the daylights out of the people living in the fifth. When he wouldn't move, I melted his innards and sent him to the sewers."

"You killed a squatter?" asked the honey, seemingly not too impressed.

"He was dangerous. He could have hurt somebody."

"It's no demon dragon."

Manuel finished the whiskey, slamming it down next to the honey and making her jump.

"If the demon dragon showed up, I'd take care of it. Easy as Pi."

She recoiled, blinking and shaking her head.

"Not the thing I saw. Had nightmares every night since. It's killed a half dozen people already, and those are the ones they know about. My mom didn't even want me to come out tonight, but it's lonely sitting in my apartment alone all the time."

"I could keep you company," he said with a wink.

"I just met you and I don't know if I trust mages. Never know when one might enchant you, or slip something into your drink."

"I'm a bonded Justicar. I'd lose my license if I did something like that. Even if I was just accused." Manuel put a hand over his heart. "I wouldn't even do that if I could get away with it."

The honey lifted her glass of what looked like chardonnay, the official drink of annoying, self-righteous women. His interest was rapidly fleeting.

"It doesn't matter. You couldn't kill the demon dragon anyway."

"I could do it with one hand tied behind my back. I'm not even sure I'd need my staff."

"Guys like you always need your staff."

A ripple of alarm shot through the crowd. The festive atmosphere took a nosedive and people were moving away from the entrance. Manuel heard their concerns long before the honey, but he didn't react until she turned.

"Did you hear that?"

"Of course. I heard the bouncer when he spoke to the cop outside. They wanted everyone off the streets until the danger passed."

It was a bit of a fib as the bouncer had been inside, but it wasn't a falsehood either.

"Are you going to kill it?"

Manuel huffed.

"It's probably not the demon dragon. That thing isn't the only dangerous creature in the city. Why, just the other day, I saw the Whistling Man—"

"Oh, I see," said the honey, rolling her eyes. "Big talk until you have to perform. Figures."

He squared off.

"You don't know what you're talking about."

She raised an eyebrow.

"Oh, guys like you are a dime a dozen. You're not the first to ask yourself back to my apartment and you won't be the last. But I don't date guys who can't walk the talk."

His mood improved rapidly.

"So you're saying if I take care of this so-called demon dragon, you'll invite me back to your apartment."

The honey put a sharp fingernail under his chin and gave him an open-mouthed smile with her tongue resting on her bottom teeth.

"With pleasure."

He grabbed his staff.

"Then follow me and enjoy the preshow."

She grasped his hand on the way through the crowd, buoying him with a sense of fate. The bouncer tried to stop them, but Manuel flickered the eldritch lights in his staff and they were allowed on the street.

The warm Invictus evening brought a bead of sweat to his forehead. Manuel leaned the staff against the brick wall and replaced the weather enchantment that had faded since he'd been inside the bar.

The honey craned her neck in both directions while not moving too far away from the entrance.

"Do you think it's still out here?"

A crunch in the distance had him turning his head.

"Three blocks that way, and another to the north."

He grabbed her hand and placed his lips against the cool back of it.

She smelled even more ready than when he'd found her at the bar.

"When I return..."

The honey licked her lips.

"I can't wait."

Manuel jogged towards the sounds of destruction, his heavy boots ringing across the concrete. He spun the ring on his right pinky finger, waking the protective enchantment, and considered pulling out the Taka Charm.

His adrenaline soared as he approached the corner. He'd heard a muffled scream a short time ago, but that could have been anyone.

The first thing Manuel saw was a crushed cop car with one faint blue light spinning. It looked like a giant had stepped on the front. He was certain anyone inside was dead.

He thought the creature might have moved on until he saw the shifting of shadows in the park past the apartment buildings. The suggestion of movement had him reaching for his Taka Charm from a hidden pocket. He snapped the bracelet around his wrist. The activation sent out a high-pitched buzz before modulating to silence. He was protected from anything short of a major explosion. Activating the charm would cost him later, but he sensed this was a bigger challenge than he was letting on with the honey.

"You'd better be worth it," he said as he padded down the street, staying in a hunch even though he was walking down the center line.

Manuel crouched by the low wall that went around the park. A lamp-post snapped and sent up a geyser of sparks about fifty meters away.

"Okay, what's the plan? It's probably the size of an elephant. Best to blast out one of its legs, reduce its mobility, and then whittle it down to size."

He tilted his head, hearing the bevy of police sirens and at least two helicopters headed his way. Manuel jogged into the park, determined to take care of the creature before the cavalry arrived.

A thick oak tree provided a good hiding spot. He peered around it to see the next one over had been severed in half.

"Maybe it's bigger than an elephant," he whispered to himself.

Manuel channeled faez into his staff, charging it up until he was certain he could blow a hole through a warship if required.

"Come on, baby, come to Daddy Manuel."

He saw movement through the trees, and stepped out near a freshly painted jungle gym. The first thing he saw was a scaled leg, wider than the tree trunk. He thought the helicopter had somehow flown over the park without sound until he realized the movement above the trees was an enormous head.

Glowing, fiery eyes peered at him like a bug in a glass, sending ripples of fear through his midsection, but he was no stranger to tough fights. Manuel slammed his staff on the concrete, sending out sparks and warning the creature that he would not be an easy kill.

"Come on, you oversized worm! I'm not afraid of you!"

The announcement brought the demon dragon into the open, massive and serpentine, the scales shimmering with a dark iridescence that was both mesmerizing and frightening. The sounds of approaching copters felt distant, even as he could see their lights reflecting off the nearby skyscrapers.

Manuel held his staff tilted forward as if he were about to fire a mortar. He prepared to trigger the pent-up energies and teach the demon dragon what it meant to tangle with a Justicar.

"Come on, come on..."

The dragon shifted forward like a dark, swirling river overflowing its banks and rushing after him. Manuel screamed with battle rage as he fired his staff. The blast filled his vision with white light. As it faded, he saw the deflection of his fell energies off the scintillating scales. The realization of his grave mistake lasted half a second before a talon took his head off.

TWO

The tension headache at the base of her skull was climbing up the Richter scale. Remi massaged her temples as she leaned against the nurses station and tried to remember where she'd left her elixir.

The ER looked like an ant farm had been dumped onto the ground, with patients, families, and staff all moving through the crowded space in a semblance of order. Dr. Morrison was shouting instructions to the group of first years that had arrived a couple of weeks ago.

The rustle of paper had Remi turning to find Nurse Mandy searching through the incoming files.

"Have you seen a red energy potion? I left it on the desk, I think."

Nurse Mandy screwed up her face.

"Oh crap. I'm sorry, Remi. I thought it was mine from earlier. I'll send down to Jeb's for another round. I think we're gonna need it, being a four-beller and all. It's a good thing you and Lily are doing time down here—this latest batch of newbies is nothing like your class."

"Thanks, Mandy, though I'm ready to be done with my punishment and get back to full time in the Hospice. I barely feel a part of the ward when I'm there."

All the nurses and doctors in the ER lifted their chins while the group of first years looked around as if they were trying to find the fire.

"Oh no, what is that, five howlers?" asked Remi.

Nurse Mandy tilted her head.

"Six. No, seven. What the hell?"

She leaned over and switched on the television, which was always tuned to the twenty-four-hour City of Sorcery news channel. Reporters were standing on a darkened street next to a burning helicopter and a half dozen destroyed police vehicles. A building in the background looked like it'd had a bite taken out of it.

"I really wish I had that potion now."

The patter of sneakers was followed by Lily and Boon coming around the corner, the latter looking like he'd just woken up.

"Alright everyone, listen up," said Dr. Morrison from atop a chair. Her hair had been braided into tight rows and wrapped around her head like a crown. "We had a major event in the ninth ward. Details are still coming in but we have a lot of life-threatening injuries. We're on full triage. Turf any elbow scrapes to general, and the surgery team has their sorcery on standby. If I have to tell you what to do, I'm not going to be happy. Go."

The first of the howlers arrived. Remi grabbed a screaming police officer with a mangled arm and with Lily's help wheeled him into a curtained area, immediately applying a pain blocker enchantment. The arm looked like it'd been caught in a press and nearly all the bones were broken.

"We got an AE amputation. I'll call up to surgery," said Lily.

"No," said the police officer, grabbing her arm with his working hand. Even with the pain blockers he looked distressed. "I'm a mage. I need that hand, or I'll be useless."

Remi shared a worried glance with Lily.

"If we don't cut it off, you might die from the injuries. We have great limb cutters. They'll do their best to make sure you have as much of your arm as necessary for prosthetics. The enchanted ones are out of this world."

"But not good enough for spells. Please, don't take my livelihood from me."

When Lily gave her a look, Remi shrugged.

"I'd want the same."

A phone call, two charms, and a gurney team later, the officer was on his way to surgery with instructions to save the arm.

The next hour was a whirlwind of emergency care. Remi sent three more to surgery, a half dozen to general, and called time of death on three more. The migraine lingered at the base of her skull, making it hard to concentrate on the constant spell work, but she knew even a few seconds of hesitation could cost someone their life.

When the rush finally started to subside, Remi found herself checking on an officer who had strange burns on his arm. She'd placed his injured limb into a runed glass tube and filled it with an elixir that would help the skin grow back quickly.

"How's the pain, Officer Sam?"

He returned a glassy-eyed stare, but nodded.

"I got off easy, considering."

Officer Sam only looked a few years out of Protectors, especially with his newly grown mustache. A set of enchanted guns sat on the table.

"What's the word on my arm?"

Remi tapped on the glass.

"The skin isn't healing as quickly as I'd like. Any idea what it was that did that? It'll help us with the recovery plan."

Officer Sam ran a free hand through his dirty-blond hair.

"Never seen anything like it, not since the Event anyway. When the call came in, they said it was a demon dragon, which I thought was a bit overblown. Until I saw it."

The curtains moved aside, revealing Lily, who'd been working next door. Her mass of curly auburn hair was pulled back with a cord and her scrubs had bloodstains on the front.

"What kind of dragon?" asked Lily.

"There are different kinds? You know, we mostly focused on humans in Protectors, since they're the worst perps."

Lily shifted her mouth to the side.

"Was it big chested with wide wings? Or long and sleek like a serpent? Or something else?"

"The second. Damn thing was like a freight train once we engaged with it. I emptied both clips into its chest with barely a scratch on its scales."

"What about the color? Of the scales," said Lily.

"Dark iridescent green."

Lily paused with thought.

"What are you thinking?" asked Remi, but her friend shook her off.

"And what happened with your arm? Tell me true, as best as you can. This is important," said Lily.

The officer pursed his lips.

"After I unloaded my guns into its chest, it rose above me and un-leashed a glowing mist from its mouth. The only thing that saved me was my protective wards and a last-second force shield I learned from my girlfriend. Never thought an Animalians trick would save my life. I think I owe her an extravagant vacation."

"You do, you definitely do," said Remi.

Lily patted on the runed tube.

"You should be fine, Officer Sam. It was a bloody close one, but that shield saved your life and this tube will do the rest."

"Yeah, but we lost far too many of our own trying to take that thing down," he said, staring at the floor.

"What happened to it? Did you kill it?" asked Remi.

"I wish. Would make me feel like it was worth it, but the damn thing just disappeared. After I got knocked down, it fled east, but then when the backup arrived, thinking they'd surrounded it, they found the street empty and not a witness alive."

"Thank you, Officer," said Lily.

Remi joined her friend in the hallway. She was going to ask a question, but Lily led her to a corner of the ER where a row of covered bodies waited to be picked up by the morgue.

When Lily pulled back the sheet covering one, Remi recoiled, not in disgust, but surprise.

"No head?"

"This poor fool was the first on the scene. A Justicar. Took his bloody head right off."

"Merlin's tits," said Remi, shaking her head. "Multiple Protectors, a Justicar, and countless other mundane personnel. What the hell was this thing? I heard people call it a demon dragon, but that doesn't make any sense to me."

"It does to me," said Lily, lips squeezed white.

"I don't like that look."

Lily rubbed the spot where her hair met her forehead.

"It's not a dragon. Not in that sense."

"Then what is it? Is it like the big snake thing that was guarding Koschei's soul?"

"Not a serpent either. A wyrm is a better description, but that doesn't even tell the tale. As much as I understand. Aye, everything they said—

the shape, the scales, even the mist breath—matches the legends of the Caoránarch."

"The Caoránarch," repeated Remi, stumbling over the Irish name.

"It's a type of Olliphéist. A river dragon. Some call the Caoránarch the mother of demons, but it's not a demon in the infernal sense. More of a very angry wyrm that was birthed by mistake over a millennia ago. It's a particular wyrm, given the descriptions. I heard stories of it when I was a wee lass, but most thought it either dead, or confined to the Summer Fae where it came from."

A heavy weight shifted onto Remi's shoulders.

"Of course, the Summer Fae."

"My bloody thoughts exactly. Though this seems a little larger than the normal critters that sneak through the barrier between realms."

"I don't think it's a coincidence that it's here in the city of sorcery rather than anywhere else."

"Nor do I," said Lily.

"Where do you think it went?"

Lily frowned.

"That's a good question, but I don't think now is the time for mysteries. I've got to check on my patients."

Lily left her alone with the bodies. Remi covered up the headless body of the Justicar.

"Bad night, my headless friend," said Remi, patting the corpse's chest. "Should have stuck to the bounty hunting."

THREE

The spot behind the filing cabinets at the nurses station was as quiet as any for reading. Lily had found a tome from a private dealer a few days before about the history of the Summer Fae. She'd been sneaking passages in between patients, but so far the material had been things she already knew, or had read in other books.

A stern voice alerted her to the presence of Dr. Broomfield. He was asking the nurses where she was. Lily shoved the tome behind a plant and stuck her head around the wall.

"Did I hear you say Lily?"

Dr. Broomfield's lip twitched with disgust when he met her gaze.

"Come with me."

Under normal circumstances, his footsteps were quiet, because he liked to sneak up on the staff and remind them of all the things they were doing wrong. This wasn't one of those times. His soles rang against the tile like thunderclaps. Anger in every step. They were a warning.

She followed him into one of her patients' rooms. Delilia Cross. The woman had been in the wrong place at the wrong time, leaving a clothing boutique in the third ward only to get hit by a curse from two dueling mages that had gotten in a fight over a parking spot. Neither of them had been punished and the woman had been suffering from uncontrollable shakes for days until Lily had prescribed a solution that had dialed them down to a light tremor, allowing her to rest.

Dr. Broomfield grabbed the clipboard and jammed his finger into the paper as Delilia watched from her bed with a slight quiver in her jaw.

"Did you authorize this hemlock potion?"

"I did."

He marched into the hallway. Lily closed the door behind her.

"You are aware that hemlock is on the restricted list and needs my approval to be given to a patient?"

"I am."

The veins in his forehead bulged.

"Then why did you ignore my orders? You could have killed Miss Cross."

Lily lifted her chin.

"The restriction is for the hemlock potion, not for hemlock extract, which I combined with nightshade and an elderberry solution. The final mixture required an additive charm, but it's been greener than gold in helping out our unfortunate bystander."

Dr. Broomfield chewed his words as he stared her down, but then he looked over her shoulder and gave a forced smile.

"Dr. Fairlight. Thank you for coming down. I know you're a busy woman."

When Lily turned to greet the head of the hospital, the words died on her lips as she saw Dr. Fairlight's expression. Normally, she wore a kind smile, even if she looked perpetually exhausted. Most said she was one of the best doctors to ever have this difficult role.

"What kind of mischief have you been up to this time?" asked Dr. Fairlight.

The accusing tone caught Lily off guard. She'd never heard words like that from Dr. Fairlight.

"I found a solution to my patient's curse, without puttin' her in any danger, I might add. I'm not a bloody hack."

"Marcus informed me you prescribed a restricted potion."

"I'm sorry, Dr. Fairlight, that you had to come down here for this considering your busy schedule, but I didn't prescribe a restricted potion. There is hemlock extract in the solution I gave her, but it's in a less dangerous form. It's something my sisters and I—"

"What is your location?" asked Dr. Fairlight menacingly.

"My location?" asked Lily, taken aback.

"I don't think my words were confusing."

"Not confusing, but didn't understand the reason."

"I don't think you should be questioning me under these circumstances, Miss de Meath."

Lily felt like she was standing on quicksand. She caught the alarm in the expressions of the nurses behind the station and the unrepentant glee in Dr. Broomfield's brown eyes. Lily knew something was wrong when Dr. Fairlight called her by her last name, something that she never did, but was more common from Dr. Broomfield's lips.

"Aye, my apologies, Dr. Fairlight. What I meant to say is that we're in the Curse Ward at Golden Willow hospital."

"Is this Ireland?"

"No, ma'am."

"Then I don't want to hear about your bog witch solutions again. You're to follow Marcus' instructions without fail. Any further digressions will be punished severely."

"Linda. I thought we agreed she should be expelled," said Dr. Broomfield.

If Lily hadn't been standing there, she might not have believed it had someone told her, but when Dr. Fairlight reacted to the question, her eyes glossed over and went black for a half second before returning to their normal hazel color.

"I… she… did not violate the rule. But next time she'll face expulsion."

The way Dr. Fairlight's jaw pulsed wasn't in anger, but as if she were waging an internal fight.

"You've been warned, Miss de Meath. Let there not be another," said Dr. Broomfield before marching away, leaving Lily in stunned silence.

Dr. Fairlight stood there like an automaton waiting for her next instruction until she snapped to and with a confused look, wandered back towards the elevators.

"What in bloody hell was that?"

The interaction left her feeling cold enough to wrap her arms around her chest. Lily couldn't say for sure without doing a full inspection, but she was nearly certain that Dr. Fairlight was under some sort of compulsion. Not a lock-tight one, or she'd be expelled already, but enough that she was strongly influenced by Dr. Broomfield's suggestions.

FOUR

The lights in the open space buzzed on, flickering slightly before resuming their luminance. Half the big room was covered in stationary workout equipment with another corner containing free weights. Rubber mats were placed in front of the machines, but the open space was smooth gray concrete.

"We're not a fancy gym, but we get the job done," said Engelhardt.

Damon unshouldered the huge duffle bag, which clanked on the hard floor.

"That should be a big enough space," he said, jutting his chin towards the open corner, then his gaze trended upward. "And the ceiling is high enough."

"I don't know what a doc has to do with swordplay, but you saved my life, so I'm not going to pepper you with the questions I normally would."

Damon put a hand on the owner's solid shoulder. Engelhardt looked like a fireplug, with arms as wide as most people's thighs.

"Just a hobby. After four plus years at Aura Healers, I need something physical."

"Yeah, whatever. Just don't put a hole in my wall," he said with a wink, then his jaw angled sideways with a yawn. "You've got the code now, so I'll let you do your thing. I'm getting back to dreamland. Even this is too early for me."

After the owner was gone, Damon set his phone alarm for five a.m., which would give him two solid hours of work before he had to shower and get back to the hospital for his shift.

Unzipping the duffle bag revealed the weapon known as the Shining Sword, or Claíomh Ag Lonrú. He was big enough to wield it as a one-handed weapon, but he grasped it with two as the weight felt uncomfortable, despite his strength. Damon swung it awkwardly a few times before setting the point carefully on a rubber mat and examining the pommel, which contained a Celtic knot. The hilt was wrapped with thick leather and the guard was in the shape of two lions.

Examining the famed weapon reminded him of Connor's last command, to bond with the sword and become its Keeper. He had yet to perform the ritual, mostly because he felt unworthy of the weapon, which was why he was in the gym so early for training.

Damon knelt on the concrete and rested his forehead against the pommel. He knew the theory of how to bond, but as he was faced with the prospect, he felt silly, like a child playing games in the woods alone.

"I pledge myself to you, sword."

The words felt feeble and empty. He closed his eyes and willed himself to connect with the sword, but the closest he got was a strange tingle in his hands that went away the moment he noticed it.

Damon sighed and stood.

"Alright, let's see how I use this thing."

He pulled a second object from the duffle bag, a smooth round stone the size of his fist. Damon set it in the open space and breathed the activation word with a bit of faez.

A tall, athletic blond with his hair pulled back in a tight knot and shaved on the sides appeared from the stone, making Damon jump back with surprise. For a brief second, he thought him real until Damon realized he could see through the man.

"Hei, Warriors. Today is the first day of the rest of your life. You have come to the right place to reclaim your right to bear arms!"

Damon rolled his eyes.

"I didn't realize cheese came with the lesson."

The illusionary teacher leaned to the side and when he shifted back a similarly sized sword was in his hand.

"I'm Karl Johansen, your new favorite weapon instructor, and today you begin your first lesson in the two-handed weapon style. Sometimes called a Zwëihander in German, or broad sword, or a Scottish claymore."

The next part of the lesson was the illusionary instructor showing basic stances and moves for the two-handed weapon. Damon followed them as best he could, but the Shining Sword was heavier than expected, which made all his movements pass the expected stopping point.

He felt like a child with the weapon. By the time he'd repeated the basic lesson twice, he was drenched in sweat and his arms quivered from the effort.

"The twins would die laughing if they saw me now," he said to the empty gym. "Maybe I should have given the sword to Nat. I bet they train with weapons in Protectors."

After chugging his water, he returned to the stone and activated the sparring routine.

"Hei, Warriors! Feeling a little cocky now, I see. Want to test your swordsmanship against the stone. Be warned, there are twenty-eight random sparring patterns, so don't think you can just memorize my actions.

When you're ready, speak the command word and the battle will start."

"Slass."

As soon as the word left his lips, Instructor Karl surged forward in a High Vom Tag Stance. Damon lifted his weapon to block the high attack, but the instructor shifted his hips and brought his blade around, right through Damon's midsection. The stone flashed red and Karl returned to his original position.

"You lie bleeding on the battlefield with your intestines hanging out. Ravens will feast on your failure. Congratulations, you're dead."

"Blood and bone," said Damon, returning to his starting spot. "Slass."

The next attempts went almost the same as the first, except for the description of his death. Disemboweled. Beheaded. Disarmed. He found new ways to die with a sword in his hand.

"What am I doing?" he asked himself after the tenth failure. He barely lasted one pass with the illusion, which always seemed to know where he was going to strike, or block.

But he knew the answer. When he'd been in the Hall of the Dead in the Veil, he'd encountered his uncle Connor Black. The apparition had told him to find a teacher. That the sword would be necessary in the coming battles. The illusionary stone was the best he could find without giving away that he was the owner of the legendary weapon.

"Fat lot this does in my hands," he said after the umpteenth failure. "Come on, Damon. It shouldn't be this hard."

He triggered the start to the stone, using a Plow Stance in hope of catching the illusionary warrior with a quick thrust. The instructor Karl appeared with a smirk, which seemed new, and purposefully offered as a slight to his weapon handling.

"I've got you this time," he said, noticing that Karl was in a Side Stance.

Damon slammed his foot on the ground, feinting a lunge to the right, and then extended his arms. The sword tip sailed towards Karl, but at the last moment, the instructor twirled past the blade and brought his weapon through Damon's midsection.

"Cut in half, ladies and gentlemen. Our warrior would like to extend his entrails to all the carrion birds in the sky. Bon Appetit, my winged friends."

Frustrated by the mocking tone and his lack of progress, Damon grunted and spun around, intending to bring the sword through the illusionary instructor, but his palms were covered in sweat and the weapon slipped out of his hands.

The screeching and tearing of metal was followed by a heavy thunk into the wall. Damon watched in horror as three stationary machines collapsed as their steel girders had been sliced in half by the spinning weapon. Wires and weights, unleashed from their tension, spilled onto the mats. Then as he slapped his hand against his forehead, he heard a great gush of water shooting from the hole in the wall around the blade. The sword had hit the main water line.

As a great pool of water began forming near the wall, Damon heard a whooping noise from across the room as the alarm that signaled when he needed to return to Golden Willow went off.

FIVE

The gravestones had been scrubbed clean, their etched lettering gleaming in the distant lamplight. Remi bit her lower lip and enjoyed the way the soft soil cushioned her feet after a long shift in the hospital. Near the back of the graveyard, she saw faint movements, the washed-out colors of a lost soul lurking. He looked like he'd been in his late teens, with a buzz cut that belonged in the '80s.

While she was in the hospital, the wards kept them at bay, but out in the city where there were few protections, and more encouragements, she saw apparitions lingering. She'd found they were attracted to her, but thankfully did little more than watch from a distance.

"I didn't think there'd be a graveyard in the city."

Dr. Morsdux strolled behind her with his hands behind his back, in his long white coat looking like an apparition on an evening walk.

"It existed before the city was founded, though you can see they replaced the headstones recently."

"No, but we shouldn't waste it either."

"Seven hells," she muttered to herself.

It wasn't the lesson she was expecting, but it was the one she was going to have to learn.

As the bald man tentatively walked forward, examining the mist for dangers, Remi reached into the Veil, silently calling for anything nearby. There was no guarantee that Buzz cut or any other apparitions would still be in the area.

The bald man took a long swig from his bottle as he approached, his confidence growing with each step. The others were drawn forward, but were more wary of the green mist, which was up to her knees.

"What have you got on you, little girl?"

"I'm not a little girl, and I suggest that you not touch me."

He patted the knife on his hip.

"I don't respond well to authority."

Remi chuckled at the idea that *she* was the authority in this situation.

"What's so funny?" he demanded.

"Roles."

She sensed the nearness of Veil beings as he closed the distance.

"Don't touch me."

"Don't touch you, or what?"

In her past interactions with the Veil, like the time they'd helped her at the spirit ward, she'd had to talk with them to explain what she wanted, but as she stared at the menacing expression of the bald man the words felt unnecessary.

"What was that?" he asked, his head shifting to the side.

"I said not to touch me."

"I haven't yet, but I will soon. Real soon," he said, tossing his potion to the grass and reaching for his blade.

Remi could have blasted him with a force bolt, but that would have only incited the others to reveal their guns. Besides, she wanted to see what was going to happen.

"Just fucking tricks," said the bald man as he reached out his hand to grab her arm.

His fingers never reached her as a something pale slammed into his cheek, knocking him backwards.

"I told you not to interfere," said Remi.

The bald man's eyes were wide as he held his knife defensively, his gaze shifting around the mist-laden graveyard.

"What touched me?"

Another figure lunged from the Veil, hitting him across the jaw, followed by a skeletal hand grasping his wrist, which he quickly broke free. His lip started bleeding immediately.

"They're drawn to blood," said Remi with a smirk.

Cries rose from his friends, who appeared to have similarly been attacked. One of them pulled out a gun and pointed it at Buzz cut, who'd shifted through the gravestone.

"Make them go away."

"I can't. They were here already. But we're protected and you're not. You should have listened and stayed an observer. Now they see you as fair game," said Remi.

A gunshot startled Remi. She reached for her stomach thinking she'd been hit, but saw Dr. Morsdux fall instead.

Anger rose up as she rushed to his side. The words were merely a vocalization of her fury, but in retrospect, she felt like it was what triggered the response.

"You bastards! Get out of here!"

Remi slapped her hands to the blooming crimson around his shoulder. She glanced back to see one of the men aiming his weapon at her back, but then something pale and frightening engulfed him. The screams were primal and filled with pain and fear, followed by the men trying to escape the graveyard as more incorporeal figures went after them.

"Are you okay?"

Dr. Morsdux grimaced.

"It hurts, but thankfully I have an experienced healer here," he said with a wry grin.

Remi pulled the ruined jacket back as screams followed the men back to their vehicle. She examined the wound while Dr. Morsdux's mouth contorted into a slash.

"Looks like the bullet went all the way through. I'm going to close up the holes. Do you want a pain blocker first?"

He shook his head with his eyes shut. They both knew it was going to hurt.

After a summer in the ER, the spell was simple. She closed the wound on both sides. Someone would have to come back later and verify there was no internal bleeding, but the worst of the danger was past.

They both looked up when the vehicle squealed onto the road, followed by more gunshots, which lit up the inside, backlighting the frightened men. It went fishtailing down the road, and as it passed the next block and started to turn, red and blue flashing lights appeared behind it.

"Looks like they found a friend," said Remi as she helped Dr. Morsdux to his feet. "Shall we get out of here?"

"Dismiss your connection first."

Remi closed her eyes and pinched off the flow of faez that was keeping the connection open. Faint ghostly figures flashed briefly before disappearing.

"You know, I thought you might have planned that until they started shooting."

Dr. Morsdux held his wounded shoulder as he limped towards the gate.

"I must confess that I knew they frequented this place around this time. I live two blocks from here and I know the complaints of my fellow residents."

"You could have been killed."

He smiled.

"But I wasn't, thanks to you. Both your Veil powers and your healing ones. A potent combination."

She spun on him.

"This wasn't about exploring the Veil. You wanted me to hurt them," she said.

"Not hurt, but scare. Mostly I wanted you to learn to defend yourself."

She looked into his gaunt face. Try as she might, she couldn't see malice.

"Why?"

His chin dropped towards his chest.

"I do not know the kind of trouble you're in, but I know when things are coming to a head. I've heard the things that Dr. Broomfield has said about you and your friends. They're not the words of a doctor. Something has changed in him."

"Then tell Dr. Fairlight. Or the board."

"She's changed as well."

Remi sighed. She knew he was right based on what Lily had told them about her interaction when they tried to expel her.

"They want you dead."

Remi checked over her shoulder.

"You want me to learn to protect myself using the Veil."

"It would be wise. And I believe I was correct. You managed to summon your spectral guardians with relative ease. Eventually you should be able to learn how to do it without establishing a connection first."

"I don't know."

"I do, Remi Wilde. Since your trip to the Veil, I've seen much change in you. You might not see it, but it's there. The Veil lurks close. You need only to open the way to access it."

"I wish I felt the same."

"It will become easier in time." He grimaced. "Now, let's get back to the hospital. I feel dizzy."

Remi put her arm around Dr. Morsdux's midsection and helped him to his car. She took the wheel as he leaned back into the passenger seat.

"No dying on me, Dr. Morsdux," she said with a weak grin.

"You can't get rid of an old man that easily."

Remi put the car in drive and pulled out of the parking spot. She thought back to the graveyard as they headed down the road, wondering what could have happened to her to give her those powers.

SIX

The clinic in the twelfth ward didn't feel as alien as it had upon Lily's first few visits. Most non-humans didn't give her the stink eye, or pull out their very long and sharp knives when she passed.

The attendant at the window smiled when she saw Lily.

"Dr. Marcie is in the blue room."

"I need to see her too, but I came for my sister. Alice."

"Oh," said the woman in surprise. "She's in the back area getting a transfusion."

The heaviness of lingering fear weighed on Lily as she thought about the condition of her sister. As the youngest, she was best suited to resist the effects of the corruption, but even that hardening wasn't proving enough.

Lily was surprised to find a Fomorian shaman chanting softly over Alice in a bed while her boyfriend, Mag, looked on with concern. The shaman wore colorful leather strips tied around her arms and legs, with bits of metal and bone connected to the wrappings.

The entirety of Alice's body was covered in small runes making her look like a piece of living parchment. Pale smoke blew over her from the brazier while the shaman stomped her feet and smacked her hands together, creating crackling sparks.

When the ritual was over, the shaman bowed before Alice and Mag, then marched out of the room, giving Lily a nasty look on the way out.

"What are you doing here?" asked Alice.

"You said you were getting treatments. I wanted to see how they were done. I also need to talk to Dr. Marcie."

Her sister's eyes fluttered with exhaustion before snapping open.

"Are you sure you don't want to come by Golden Willow?" asked Lily. "The treatments have been helping."

"I can hardly tell with all the runes. And wouldn't our Hall magic be better?"

Mag cleared his throat as he stepped to Alice's side.

"They've been working. She feels better for the few days after a cleansing. Nothing else we've tried was working. Not even the things Lady Nimueh suggested."

"I'm sure the cleansings are helping, but we need a solution, not a band-aid. Maybe we can figure out more with our advanced equipment."

"You don't trust Fomorian magic," said Mag.

"It's not that, I swear."

"Lily," said her sister, reaching out. "I know you want to help, but I'm comfortable with my treatment plan. It's not like the sickness is going to go away no matter what we do."

"I've tried. I'm trying. I don't know what else to do," said Lily.

"I talked to Nyx the other day. Mother passed out in the middle of the Eó Ruis ritual. It's not the first time. Some of the other elders are doing worse. It's only a matter of time now."

The frustration in Lily's chest felt like a forest fire was burning there. She'd hoped the Horn would be a solution to the corruption, but the artifact had refused to produce a liquid, which told her the answer wasn't a simple cure.

"What did you need to see Dr. Marcie for?" asked Alice.

"The corruption."

"I'm sure she would have volunteered a solution if she knew of one."

Part of Lily didn't believe that, even if that was the reason she'd come to the clinic. The Fae and the Fomorians had been at war for millennia. Why not let your enemy die to a strange affliction? But she wasn't about to let any opportunity pass by. Especially after the failure of the Horn.

Lily gave hugs and went in search of Dr. Marcie. She found her outside of a patient's room reaching from her phone.

"Healer Lily..."

"Dr. Marcie."

"Are you here for—"

Lily shook her head right away.

"No. It's best that it stays hidden."

"Then how can I help you?"

Lily exhaled.

"I've run out of ideas about the kalkatai. Nothing has worked. You know Alice's condition. The rest of my family is worse."

"Maybe it's not a medical solution."

"If you have an idea, I'll go after it. I'm open for bloody anything, even if it's stupid dangerous. They're running out of time."

Dr. Marcie chewed on her lower lip.

"If there's something I could do I would have done it already."

"I know. But I'm desperate. Is there something that you've been holding back because it seems outlandish or dangerous?"

"There is a new arrival in the enclave. A Fomorian shaman. But not like the others. An elder. Danger haunts her every breath. Even the others of her kind have stayed away in fear. I'm not sure she would talk to you..."

"I'm willing to try. Luck's opportunity is blinded by ambivalence."

Dr. Marcie motioned for her to follow. She told the window attendant they'd be back shortly.

They headed deeper into the enclave, which had been built up in an old factory. Lily hadn't been in these parts, and was surprised at how many makeshift huts filled the space. But as they went into the darker confines of the enclave, the living quarters grew more infrequent.

Stepping through a gash in the wall, they entered an old generator room, except most of the equipment had been ripped out except the concrete pads with rusted bolts sticking up.

"Tread carefully."

A ground fire put out thick smoke from the corner near a set of old tents. Bones and other trinkets hung from wires. The place smelled like rendered fat.

Dr. Marcie called out in Fomorian. A rumbling answer returned, and after a brief conversation, in which Lily heard her name spoken twice, the elder shaman appeared.

Lily wasn't sure what she was expecting, but it wasn't what she saw. This one reminded her more of Balor of the Evil Eye, than the other Fomorians she'd met. She was tall, but hunched, covered in thick, overlapping robes that looked as though they could have been made out of human skin. She couldn't see the shaman's face except for her lips, blackened and scarred as if her flesh had been cut and let heal hundreds of times.

"This is the witch?" came a rasping voice from beneath the robes as though she'd been expecting her.

Lily girded herself as she looked into the shadowy cowl, already sensing the gathering power within the shaman. She exuded danger.

Dr. Marcie bowed deeply, spat in her hand, and wiped it into the dirt. When she stood again, the shaman chuckled.

"She wishes to speak to you about the kalkatai, the corruption of the Summer Fae."

"And why would I care about the decline of my enemies?" asked the shaman.

"Because whatever is happening in the Summer Fae is affecting the city of sorcery, and if these lands fall, then every realm is at risk of collapse," said Lily.

"You speak too confidently for someone who knows nothing."

"I admit, some of this is bloody-thin speculation, but since I've been here, we've battled a corrupted Green Man who was trying to influence the elites with mind-control worms, made a sojourn into the Summer Fae ourselves to confirm the corruption, and recently the Caoránarch was spotted in the city killing those that got in its way."

"And still I do not see why I care."

"Because whatever happens to us, and this city, will be worse for you. The rich, the powerful, these changes, whatever they are, will affect them least. I know it's a shite deal, but I can't change the way the city works."

Dr. Marcie stepped forward.

"Lily has helped our people despite the risk to herself. Her sister is a friend of the enclave as well, working for Lady Nimueh, a known ally."

The elder shaman hissed and cackled, her enormous hands rubbing together.

"Are you willing to pay the price?"

"Anything, up to and including my life," said Lily.

The shaman continued laughing.

"Desperation does not suit you."

"Yet I offer it."

The shaman stilled in thought. Lily knew she might have erred in not negotiating, but she didn't want to risk the elder's rejection.

"There is one thing you might do."

"What is it?"

"For this, I require a favor in return. Not now, but in the future."

"What kind of favor?"

"You said you'd do anything."

Lily nodded.

"I would, but knowing my fate would at least help me prepare."

"It gives me pleasure to know that you would be squirming on the spit, forever in my debt. I will not tell you my intentions."

"Then I accept your proposal."

Dr. Marcie inhaled sharply, but Lily was determined.

"Come forward and seal your promise," said the elder shaman as she held out her palm.

Lily thought she would need to kneel, but the shaman was even taller than expected. She took the hand, which was covered in calluses and scars, and in one long motion, licked the palm from base to fingertips. She repressed a shiver of disgust and stepped back next to Dr. Marcie.

The elder shaman cackled with amusement.

"Oh, if my sisters could see me now, with an Irish witch groveling at my feet for unspecified favors."

"Your answer, please."

The shaman cracked her neck with a practiced tilt of her head. It sounded like bones being crushed beneath a heel.

"In the town of Hog's Breath, not far from the city of sorcery, a woman of sorrow pretends to be a caretaker for the town's historic buildings."

Lily hissed out surprise.

"A leannán sídhe?"

The Fomorian shaman coughed, a rumbling rattle in her chest.

"I sensed her when we passed through the town. We did not stay long."

"She would be no danger to you," said Lily.

"This one is known as the Bhróin."

Lily cursed under her breath.

"I've heard of this one."

"Then you know why we did not stop. But you may receive answers from her. If you're willing to pay *her* price."

Dr. Marcie was staring at her expectantly. Clearly, she did not know what dangers a leannán sídhe presented.

"You have met your end of the bargain," said Lily. "I thank you and hope that in the future our two peoples can coexist peacefully."

"Such are the words of the overlords."

The Fomorian shaman turned back towards her tents and charms, leaving Lily to follow Dr. Marcie back to the more populated areas of the enclave.

"A leannán sídhe? Why would a Fae woman be a danger to you?"

"A woman of sorrow is a danger to anyone, even other Fae. They come from Spring and are called fairy lovers. They prey mostly on men or the occasional woman who seek their good fortune, but it comes at the cost of their shortened lives. It is said some of the great artists of history made a deal with a woman of Sorrow in exchange for their talent. But that day comes faster than they expect."

"You will seek this fairy lover out?"

"I must, despite the dangers."

"Can you get your answers safely?"

Lily turned and grabbed Dr. Marcie's hands.

"I beg of you, please do not speak a word of the leannán sídhe to Alice. It would put more strain on her weakened heart."

Dr. Marcie nodded.

"You've been a friend to the enclave. I can do that simple thing for you."

Lily's thoughts already turned towards the woman of sorrow, calculating how she might survive such a fateful encounter.

"Thank you, Dr. Marcie. I'll see you again, soon enough I hope."

SEVEN

The text message had informed Damon to meet Dr. Broomfield in the Supernatural Ward. Dr. Vista hadn't been happy to have one of her students get pulled away again with so much going on in her ward, but there wasn't much she would do about it.

Damon wasn't happy either. Dr. Broomfield had been tormenting his friends all summer and fall. Damon had mostly been left out of it, but now it seemed he was going to see his turn.

The soft-soled approach had Damon expecting another doctor, but was surprised to find a smiling Dr. Broomfield with his hand out.

"Damon, thank you for joining me for rounds today. I know you prefer Dr. Vista's ward, but I thought you'd find today a special treat."

Damon stammered out a response, thrown off-kilter by the pleasant turn.

"I'm looking forward to it."

"Come, come. Let's get started."

Dr. Broomfield swung by the nurses station to pick up a clipboard full of papers and headed straight to a room down the hall. He knocked on the frame before walking through the open door.

"Jeremiah," said Dr. Broomfield with a warm smile.

The lanky young man on the bed had been thumbing through his phone, but looked up at their arrival and returned the grin. He had blond peach fuzz on his cheeks and a thin mustache that looked like a dusting of chocolate milk.

"Dr. Marcus! I didn't think you could come by."

He approached the bed and gave Jeremiah's arm a squeeze.

"I have a special treat for you today."

Damon had been standing in the doorway, mystified by the doctor's unusually amiable behavior, but he managed to sniff the air and figure out that the young man on the bed was a fellow therianthrope.

"Healer Damon, this is Jeremiah Vindal. He's a cougar. And our talented healer here is a wolf from the Zev Clan."

"Hey, Jeremiah," said Damon, holding out his hand. "It's nice to meet you."

"Zev Clan?" asked Jeremiah, lips coming to a point. "I'm sorry."

"It's okay. I've come to terms with it. The beauty of time and perspective. May I ask why you've come to Golden Willow?"

Jeremiah's cheeks blushed as he stared into his lap.

"I can't change. Or if I do, it's really painful. The worst thing ever. I don't want to be a therianthrope any longer."

The coil of uncertainty around Damon's chest unloosened. He'd been worried about Dr. Broomfield's intention, but for once, they were working together as doctor and healer.

"Did something happen recently to cause this, or have you always struggled to change?"

Jeremiah swallowed as he continued staring into his blankets with watery eyes.

"It's embarrassing..."

"You can't shock us," said Damon. "You'd be surprised the things that happen to people that have to come to Golden Willow."

"Like what?" asked Jeremiah, lifting his head with eyes rounded.

Damon leaned forward conspiratorially.

"You ever heard the song by the Krakens called "Give a Load of This"?"

"Yeah," said Jeremiah, his forehead knitted with confusion.

Damon checked back to Dr. Broomfield, expecting a stern expression, but he was watching with silent approval.

"You, uhm, get the innuendo in the song?"

Jeremiah rolled his eyes.

"Duh, I'm thirteen, not six."

"The lead singer of the Krakens wrote that song about one of the staff members after she helped him with his problem."

Damon wagged his eyebrows as he made air quotes around problem. The kid burst into laughter.

"No way."

"Way."

"Okay, like, what else has happened here?"

Damon leaned against the bed like they were old friends and told the kid about other events like the time a woman had somehow eaten twenty-eight bats alive and when they found the right spell, she vomited them all back up. Still alive.

Or when a contagious curse that made people's clothes see-through spread amongst the staff one day until they found the counter.

Damon told more tales while Jeremiah was enraptured.

"Wow, there's a lot of weird shit that happened here." Jeremiah put a hand to his mouth. "Sorry. I'm not going to get in trouble, am I?"

"No, but it would be super helpful if you tell us what happened."

Jeremiah exhaled deeply.

"My story sounds pretty stupid compared to those."

"No story is stupid when you're in the middle of it. Emotions can be difficult to deal with, especially for a therianthrope going through puberty. We've got more to deal with than the average kid your age. It's not easy."

"There was this girl I liked. I thought she was out of my league, but one day we were seated next to each other during study hour. We started talking and then we continued on the phone later. I thought she liked me, but then she asked if I would change for her. We were in the woods behind my house. After I changed, I sat in her lap and she played with my ears and was rubbing my back."

Jeremiah closed his eyes, the shame coming to the front. His cheeks were bright red.

"I can hide it when I'm wearing clothes. I should have never let my guard down..."

"I understand," said Damon. "I really do. This is normal. It's especially hard to control your reaction when you're changed at that age. Once, when I was hunting deer, I got a little too excited and cut myself when I jumped over a barbed-wire fence. Let me tell you, I was afraid to look at a cute girl sideways for months after that."

"Oh, wow."

"What happened with the girl?"

"We haven't talked since. She hasn't told anyone or anything, but she freezes up whenever I'm anywhere near."

Damon leaned in conspiratorially.

"Do you want to know something? She's probably even more interested in you after that. And if she's not, then she wasn't the one for you. But if she knew you were a therianthrope already, then I'm guessing it's the first one. That she has the hots for you and doesn't know how to act around you now that she knows the truth."

"You think? Are you sure there's not something wrong with me?"

"There would be something wrong with you if you hadn't gotten excited. And if you're worried about puberty, we can proscribe an elixir, but in my opinion, professionally and as a fellow shifter, I don't think you need it."

Jeremiah nodded.

"I guess I could try it."

"That's the spirit."

Dr. Broomfield cleared his throat. "Thank you, Healer Damon. We have to get to another patient, Jeremiah, but I'm glad we could work things out."

The next four hours, Damon worked with the doctor on a number of therianthropic cases. While shifters were a minority in the general population, there were few places other than Golden Willow to go for treatment.

When they were finished, Dr. Broomfield led Damon back to his office. The walls were covered in pictures of the doctor with many famous people including numerous patrons. He reached into a desk drawer and pulled out a bottle of reddish liquid.

"Is that…?"

"No wolfsbane here. Just a mild distilled elderberry drink. Less alcohol than a light beer, but perfect for celebratory moments."

"What are we celebrating?" asked Damon.

"You, Damon. I know these last two years have been difficult, especially the unfortunate absence, but between the alchemical solution and your overall performance as a healer, I'm proud to be thinking of you for a recommendation."

"A recommendation?" asked Damon, accepting the glass of pinkish liquid.

"The Institute of Therianthropic Studies. You're still interested, right? I'm strongly considering putting in a recommendation for you. I haven't completely decided, but if I do, you know my word goes a long way."

Damon nearly fell over in surprise.

"Really?"

Dr. Broomfield laughed.

"Yes, really. Today's performance just proved what I'd already suspected. You're a natural for the role. You have the healer chops and the personal touch that can be an issue for some. But you managed to help Jeremiah without resorting to an alchemical or arcane solution."

Damon glowed from within. He could hardly feel his face. It wasn't what he was expecting when Dr. Broomfield had called on him.

"Cheers," said Dr. Broomfield, holding out his glass.

Damon clinked his glass and placed it to his lips. He was about to throw it back when he saw how eagerly the doctor was staring without looking like he was intending to drink. A light sniff revealed something foreign in the distilled elderberries.

As the pinkish liquid touched his lower lip, he let the glass slip from his fingers and crash onto the desk, spilling it over the papers.

"Oh no!"

The next few moments were a mad rush to contain the spill, but when he looked up, he caught a searing glance that only confirmed his suspicion. The day's events had been an attempt to get his guard down.

"Here," said Dr. Broomfield, grabbing the bottle. "Let's try that again."

Damon froze when he realized he wouldn't be able to pull the same trick a second time. He reached for the phone in his pocket.

"Oh no. It looks like Dr. Vista needs me. I should get going. She really needed me today, but I'm glad to have helped Jeremiah and the other patients."

Dr. Broomfield had the glass held at arm's length.

"You *really* should drink this."

"I'd better not. But thank you. Your kind words mean the world to me."

As Damon's hand collapsed around the door handle, Dr. Broomfield spoke in a low voice.

"You'd better get on the right side, Damon."

He turned his head.

"The right side?"

"You heard me. I don't need to explain. Do you want to help people? Or do you want to go down with your friends?"

Damon ignored the question and pushed out of the door, marching quickly away until he was at the elevators. To his relief, the car was empty, and once the doors were closed and he was on his way back to Dr. Vista's ward, he leaned against the wall and closed his eyes, knowing how close he'd been to catastrophe.

EIGHT

Remi knew something was wrong when Nurse Juniper wouldn't meet her gaze and then again when she found her clipboard but there were no follow-up sheets attached.

"June? Am I supposed to be off today?"

The older nurse shook her head and winced.

"I'm supposed to send you to Dr. Morsdux when you arrive."

A cold hand wrapped around Remi's heart.

"What's this about?"

"I'm sorry, Remi. We're all gutted. It's not fair."

Remi had an out-of-body experience on the way to Dr. Morsdux's office. She'd been enjoying the last few weeks of focusing entirely on her preferred ward and started believing that Dr. Broomfield had given up on punishing her.

"What's going on?" she asked when she stuck her head into his office.

Dr. Morsdux had been scribbling in an old diary. He liked to keep handwritten notes of his daily routine. The devastation in his normally unshakable gaze had her assuming the worst.

"What happened? Who died?"

"No one died. But I'm afraid I have very bad news."

Remi wracked her brain for what might have caused the upheaval, but came away with nothing.

"You've been moved to EMT services."

She furrowed her forehead.

"Like the double shifts I was doing in the ER?"

Dr. Morsdux ran his hand along the edge of his desk.

"No. Moved. You're one hundred percent dedicated to the EMT department, and it's my understanding you're being embedded with our toughest teams. The ones that deal with the worst problems."

"I don't understand. I didn't think that was an option for students. Too dangerous."

"Dr. Broomfield had it approved with Patron Jenner."

"What? He's back? Can I talk to him? Plead my case. I don't understand why this is happening."

"He's not back, unfortunately. But his message was delivered directly to my door. I'm sorry, Remi. I already spoke to Dr. Fairlight, but she refused to hear my opinion on the matter. The entire ward is devastated by this news. The patients, the nurses, the orderlies...everyone. The only good news I have is that once your fifth year is over, you can choose your own path, which could include coming back to the Hospice Ward."

Remi felt like she was standing on quicksand.

"Of course I'm coming back, but seven months feels like a life sentence."

"I know this is disappointing, but you're a talented healer and a variety of experiences always makes one even stronger. While the EMT is not the best learning environment, I think someone of your caliber will find a way to shine even in this difficult situation."

"When do I report?"

"Right now, I'm afraid," he said, handing over a piece of paper with a couple of names on it.

Remi left without saying another word. She felt like when her supposed parents hadn't picked her up after Utica. Every time she thought she'd found a home, she got kicked to the curb. And while she had intentions of returning, she knew that diversions like this sometimes completely changed people's lives. She feared she'd never get to return.

Remi left the hospital through a side door and headed across the parking lot to the EMT shed, which was a separate building. Most EMT services were hospital agnostic and run entirely by the local government, but due to the unique problems that occurred in the city of sorcery, Golden Willow ran its own ambulances that worked in tandem with the regular system.

The lonely walk across the hot concrete felt like last rites. A group of EMTs were outside the shed gathered in a circle, shouting and whooping as if it were a party. She caught a few furtive glances, but most of their attention was focused on what was going on where she couldn't see.

"Ten! Ten! Ten! Ten!" they were chanting.

Remi had to wedge her way into the circle to see what was happening.

A woman with short, spiky black hair and a red bandana was standing in the center with her muscular arms flexing. The sleeves of her EMT shirt had been cut off and the dark blue jumpsuit with the Golden Willow badge was wrapped around her waist.

Opposite her was a hulking guy wearing a similar jumpsuit. He had a shaved head and tattoos on his neck that shifted. He held a black baton in his right hand. Near his feet was a pile of crumpled bills.

"What's going on?" she asked the black guy with glasses next to her.

"Shush. I don't want to miss this."

The woman cocked her mouth to the side as she stared at the big guy with the baton.

"Okay, ten."

The crowd erupted in cheers, which was even more confusing to Remi. Then the big bald guy clicked the base of the baton and advanced on the woman, who had her arms wide. Without warning, he jammed it into her gut and she went over like a stiff board, landing on a piece of foam that had been lying behind her. She convulsed for a few seconds before finally lying still. Another EMT ran to her side and started checking vitals.

"What the...?"

"Okay, what's your damage, green skin?"

"Green skin?"

He tugged on his shirt, which made her realize he was referring to her scrubs.

"Got it. I'm looking for an ambulance crew."

"Drugs?"

"What? No. I've been assigned to EMT services."

He burst out laughing.

"You serious? Whose cereal did you piss in?" He narrowed his gaze. "Wait. You're a student. Merlin's tits, girl, you must have really pissed in a *lot* of bowls."

"You're telling me."

Their conversation was interrupted when the woman on the ground popped up like a spring.

"I'm good, I'm good."

She climbed to her feet without help and then snatched the wads of cash on the ground to applause and jeers from the rest of the EMTs.

"Who have you been assigned to?"

Remi pulled the piece of paper out of her pocket and handed it over.

The black guy snorted and handed the paper back while shaking his head.

"Somebody *really* doesn't like you."

"Which crew?" she asked.

He jammed his thumb towards the woman counting bills.

"That's your crew. They call 'em the Kamikaze Kids."

"Why?"

"You'll see. Good luck," he said, walking away laughing.

Remi approached the woman and the big bald guy.

"Vasquez?"

"I don't sell to Green Shirts."

"I'm not here for drugs. I can get those on my own if I wanted."

"Not what I have, but what's your damage?" she asked while continuing to count.

"I've been assigned to your crew."

Vasquez checked over her shoulder, then looked between her legs, then back to Remi.

"Is this a joke?"

"I wish it was. But I've been assigned to your crew, starting today and for the foreseeable future."

"Dammit. A Green Shirt? I guess there's nothing we can do. Come on. Our shift starts soon."

"I'm Remi, by the way," she said, holding out her hand as she hurried to keep up.

"I'm Vasquez, this is Paxton. Our driver is Ansel, but don't talk to him. He doesn't like people, but he keeps us safe."

Remi followed them past the ambulances in the huge vehicle shed. Other crews were putting new gear and supplies into the back of their ambulances.

"What were you doing back there?"

"Earning money, what does it look like?"

As soon as Remi saw the ambulance in the back of the shed, she knew it was the one she'd be riding in. Along the side of the normally white and red wall was a painting of a dragon with explosives strapped to it gliding into a small building with men shooting automatic weapons at it.

Neither Vasquez nor Paxton spoke to her as they loaded bags into the back, so she jumped in and carried some on her own. Once they were inside, the pair started unloading supplies into the drawers built into the walls.

Remi reached for a box of syringes only to hear the clucking of a tongue.

"Don't even think about it," said Vasquez. "You don't know where shit goes, which means I won't be my normally speedy self. It's life or death every night for the Kamikaze Kids. I can't afford even a second's delay."

Remi nodded and stepped back, watching the pair refill their drawers with surprising efficiency. When they opened what Remi thought was going to be a clothing closet, she saw a miniature alchemy lab instead.

"No one gives us the stuff we really need."

A few minutes later, they were speeding away from the hospital. Vasquez was seated on the gurney while Paxton sat on the floor cross-legged, playing with a fidget cube.

"What's your specialty?" asked Vasquez as she pulled her jumpsuit on.

"Do I get one of those?" asked Remi.

"Yeah, right," said Vasquez, jumping down and reaching under the driver's seat to produce one in a plastic bag. "This is one of my backups. You're a touch shorter, but it should work."

"Hospice ward," said Remi as she climbed into the baggy jumpsuit.

"Merlin's hairy tits, are you kidding me? They really hate us as much as they do you," said Vasquez.

"I like the death ward," said Paxton, nodding.

"You would, big man, you would."

"What's the route?"

Vasquez snorted softly.

"The ass-end of the city. Eleventh through thirteenth ward. Unless there's a particularly messed-up case nearby, then they send us wherever."

Vasquez leaned back and yanked down a calendar that was on a pull cord.

"Let's see. What's on the schedule? Oh, that harbinger cult in the eleventh is having their end of times celebration tonight. Can probably expect some of those idiots to blow something off. Looks like we got a Monta parade in the fifth. You can be sure someone will take a shot at them. Let me mix up a few Monta coagulators just in case."

Before Vasquez could open the alchemy closet, the radio crackled to life.

"Rig 69, there's an 819 with an 888 at the corner of Turner and Allanon in the eleventh. Be warned there might be a heater."

"Copy that," said Vasquez, shaking her head. "Dammit. Not a good way to start the night. Green Shirt, grab that piece of PVC pipe above the door."

The sirens on the vehicle spun into life, startling Remi. She went for the tube, but kept getting thrown into the walls. The sudden high speed turned the back of the ambulance into a shake machine.

"You'll get used to it," said Vasquez as she nimbly moved around the drawers, collecting gear that she shoved in her fanny pack while Paxton sat on the ground as calmly as if he were meditating.

They arrived outside of a run-down bar called the Faez Demon. Remi had been in the eleventh a few times, but this was clearly the older section that most people avoided.

"No cops?" she asked.

"They might be along eventually, but they generally like to let things work out naturally, if you get my drift," said Vasquez as she threw a duffle bag over her shoulder. "Bring that PVC tube."

To get into the bar, they had to step over a woman passed out on the sidewalk. Her left hand and around her lips glowed with a faint nimbus.

"Witching powder?" asked Paxton as he knelt by the unconscious woman's side.

"Looks like it," said Vasquez. "Keep those muscles of yours on the ready."

Once they were inside, the bartender met them and pointed into a back room where whooping and hollering could be heard along with the occasional smashing of a glass or drywall.

"I don't know what Jesper and Sam got into, but there's a lot of blood and Jesper won't let anyone in."

They moved towards the back room, close enough to see through the door that had been ripped off its hinges. A stringy-haired man in a gray tank top was marching around the pool table whooping and screaming with his hands and lips glowing. Sitting against the wall was a second person covered in blood, poking inside their belly with similarly glowing hands.

"What do you want me to do?" asked Remi.

Vasquez kept her gaze on the room beyond.

"Stay out of our way unless I tell you." She turned to Paxton. "Think you can hold 'em?"

He pulled an asthma inhaler from a pocket.

"Hit 'em with the stun cannon first."

Vasquez reached into her duffle bag and pulled out another piece of PVC pipe and held out her hand for the one in Remi's possession. A few connections later it looked like a long firing tube. Then she pulled out a small heavy bag, unzipped it, and poured a blue powder into the center, then shoved it into the end of the pipe, pushing it all the way to the middle with a rod that had been fixed on the side.

"Ready?" asked Vasquez, receiving a nod from Paxton.

She held the PVC cannon on her shoulder, pulled a can of hairspray from a pocket, and sprayed it into a small hole on the side. A lighter appeared in her hands and she nodded at Paxton.

The big man put the inhaler to his lips and hit the button. As he expanded his chest, his eyes lit up.

"Hey Jasper!"

The guy in the pool room turned towards the door. He looked like a maniac.

"I am a living god!"

"You're a lunatic," muttered Vasquez as she sparked the lighter and shoved it against the hole.

A heavy thump was followed by a projectile speeding out of the end and slamming into Jasper's chest, throwing him onto the pool table. Before he could get up, Paxton went running into the room and grabbed him, yanking him around.

Vasquez threw the PVC cannon aside and followed, so Remi did the same. The EMT pulled a syringe out of her bag and jammed it into Jasper's thigh, which made him scream. The two wrestled even harder, and Paxton looked like he was barely holding on.

"Help me..."

Remi looked over to the man sitting against the wall with blood leaking out of his stomach. Her healer instincts kicked in and she moved towards him, readying a wound closure spell around the same time she heard Vasquez say, "Don't."

As she leaned down to tell him not to worry, he grabbed her by the shoulder and threw her across the room. Remi hit the wall upside down, the impact knocking the air out of her lungs. She landed in a heap and knocked an ashtray onto her face, but she was too stunned to move.

"Damn Green Shirt," said Vasquez, pulling a dart gun from her pack, aiming it at Sam, and firing into his thigh.

The injured man screamed for a few seconds and then slumped over. Vasquez took one look at him before jogging over to Remi, who was struggling to get upright.

"You okay? Do you need medical help?"

Remi wheezed out a response while shaking her head.

"Alright, Green Shirt, you get better while I tend to him."

It took a few minutes, but eventually Remi managed to sit up. By that time, Vasquez had removed Sam's shirt, exposing the wound in his belly.

"Alright, Green Shirt, it's your time to shine. Think you can close this?"

Remi grimaced, as her whole body still hurt from the impact, but she didn't want to look weak in front of them, so she fought through the pain and closed the wound with a spell.

As they were cleaning up the mess, a trio of uniformed officers of Invictus PD strolled in.

"Hey, the Kamikaze Kids. Looks like you had a fun one," said a mustached cop with his hands on his belt. "Need us to take them off your hands?"

"Up to the owner," said Vasquez. "But they're stable now. The antidote is mostly working."

The mustached cop tilted his head.

"I didn't think there was an antidote for Witching Powder."

"That's your problem, Justin. You don't think," said Vasquez, brushing past them. "Come on, Green Shirt. Let's get back to the rig."

When they were back in the ambulance, Vasquez said, "Come here. I need to do a concussion check."

After shining a light in Remi's eyes, she said, "All good. A little rattled, but I think you'll be okay. And hopefully next time you'll listen to me. This isn't like the hospital. By the time you're seeing a patient, they've already been calmed, or you have the ropes team to deal with them. We only have Paxton and our wits out here."

"Noted," said Remi, rubbing her ribs where she'd landed on the metal ashtray.

She barely had time to get situated before another call came in for their rig and they went speeding off to the next job, which was a near over-dose on the latest rave drug. Then they were off to another. And another.

Remi felt like she was simultaneously in a drag race and a four-beller ER double shift. Her bones felt loose from the constant rattling and while she wasn't thrown into a wall again, she was spit on, kicked, and almost stabbed. Twice.

It wasn't until a faint nimbus covered the horizon and the tip of the Spire at the center of the city reflected the rising sun that she had a sense of time. Their driver, Ansel, headed back to the EMT shed, and Remi felt like a soldier returning from the front.

After unloading the ambulance and wiping everything down with a cleaning solution, Vasquez gave Remi the okay to return to her dorm.

"That wasn't terrible, Green Shirt. For your first day in the rig."

"Is it always this bad?" she asked.

Vasquez raised an eyebrow towards Paxton, who was openly grinning.

"This bad? This wasn't even a bad night. I'd call it a good night."

"Merlin's tits, what's a bad night like?" asked Remi.

"You'll find out eventually," said Vasquez. "Anyway, enjoy your rest. We've got a fourteen-hour shift tonight. I'll have some energy elixirs mixed up and ready to go for us."

Remi gave them a little wave and snaked back through the other rigs, half of which were preparing for their next shift or having just returned from a long night. No one looked particularly rested.

As she crossed the parking lot and returned to Golden Willow, she had a sense that she was coming back to a different world than the one she'd just existed in for the last twelve hours.

Nurse Mandy was standing on the sidewalk, hitting her vape, when Remi limped past.

"Hey."

"You look like someone stuffed you in a barrel and rolled you down a mountain."

"Twice."

"Twice?"

"Yeah, twice."

"Good luck, Remi," said Nurse Mandy, her eyes betraying her worry.

Remi thought about taking a shower, but by the time she got back to her room, she couldn't keep her eyes open and passed out on the bed.

NINE

Hog's Breath had the feel of a tourist town, with signs detailing the various historical buildings on every other street corner. Lily spotted at least three candy and T-shirt shops, which was a sure marker what kind of folks the town made its money from.

Lily thought it might take time to find the Bhróin, but almost as soon as she got out of the taxi she felt a sense of impending fate. The entirety of her skin itched as if she'd run through a field of nettles naked.

"This is a proper Fae," she said to Neko, before she remembered that she'd left the changeling back at the hospital.

A family with two small children eating cotton candy passed her. The taller girl looked up from her treat.

"This looks just like her hair."

"That's not nice to comment on people's appearance," said the mother, corralling the girl down the sidewalk.

Lily stuck her tongue out once the mother had turned her back, which made the girl giggle.

It took a trip up the main drag to figure out where the woman of sorrow was located. The pull was strongest outside a building with a historical marker. The Madams of Hog's Breath. A sign on the front door said that it was closed for renovations.

Lily stared at the old 1800s era building with trepidation. She wasn't afraid of the Bhróin, but caution was warranted. There were different types of Fae. The relatively harmless but annoying tricksters like the Clover sisters, the regal Lords and Ladies of the Court, and then there were the wilder Fae. The ones that plied trades of deceit with a pleasant smile. Lily had always been told to stay far away from the leannán sídhe. They were too wild, too dangerous for even the most cautious soul. To talk to one was to invite disaster, let alone strike a deal. But that hadn't stopped humans from trading their lives for a taste of greatness. It was said that Frank Orpheum, the head of Dramatics Hall, had made a deal with a leannán sídhe to become the most famous entertainer in the world, and he'd died in the middle of his prime about ten years ago. Lily wasn't sure she believed it, but it made for a cautionary tale.

She went inside.

The Victorian-era interior had a player piano in the corner next to a stocked bar. Scaffolding around the half-repaired stairs made it a one-floor building, unless she wanted to climb one of the ladders leading to the balcony.

The steady clop of high heels had Lily turning towards a hallway. A beautiful woman in a velvet crimson dress with her black hair coiled into an updo stalked into the bar across the hardwood floor. She stopped across from Lily, staring back with the intensity of a loaded gun.

"The brothel is closed."

"You and I both know I'm not here for the brothel."

The corner of the woman's ruby lips curled before she waved her hand casually. A shimmer revealed the true form beneath the glamour. Sharp cheekbones, angled alien curves, and a feral grin that betrayed her true hunger.

"You stink of the Eó Ruis tree."

"What should I call you?"

She shifted into a Wild West accent.

"They call me Belle Powers."

Lily didn't want to take her eyes off the leannán sídhe, so she nodded towards the bar.

"This was yours before, wasn't it?"

Belle smirked as she strolled past Lily, licking her lips and staring hungrily. She ran her fingernails down Lily's back on the way around.

"I miss those times, but thankfully, my meals come to me fully aware of the cost these days. I haven't had a witch in quite some time. This should be interesting."

"I haven't agreed to your terms, leannán sídhe. Or Bhróin."

Belle lifted a single shoulder.

"So what, you know what I am. You wouldn't be here if that wasn't the case." She placed a fingernail under Lily's chin, the edge feeling sharp enough to cut her throat. "What is it that you want? To become the greatest witch ever to live? Oh wait, I smell the awful stench of a hospital. Is that your desire? To become a renowned healer? No, it's close, but that's not it. Not entirely. You seek something darker, more personal. You seek great power."

A hitch in her chest told Lily there was some truth to that last comment. She stared back at Belle.

"I seek an answer."

"An answer is so boring," said Belle, letting the last part draw out like a petulant teenage girl as she rolled her eyes. "Maybe I should cut your throat and drink your blood. It's not my preferred meal, but you're no fun."

Lily knew the Bhróin would do no such thing. It wasn't how they operated, but the comment was meant to corral her towards the decision the fairy lover wanted her to make. After years of hanging out with Remi, she easily saw the way some people tried to manipulate her.

Belle angrily stomped towards the bar, reached over, and grabbed a bottle and two small glasses.

"It's not fairy magic, don't worry. But you need to loosen up. That stick in your ass is going to cause sepsis."

Normally Lily would have declined, but this was part of the negotiation. She took a glass and after Belle poured what smelled like whiskey, Lily cast a spell over the amber liquid to confirm it hadn't been tampered with.

"Not very trusting."

"I don't trust the bloody Fae, even under the best of circumstances."

"Yet here you are, at my door, begging for answers."

"Some things are worth the price."

Belle held out her glass for a toast and then they threw their drinks back in unison. The whiskey burned down Lily's throat, but the light pain was enjoyable.

"What does your heart desire?" asked Belle.

"Tell me the price."

"Not until I know what it is you seek. You don't ask a salesman how much a car is before you tell him which one."

"Are you not affected by the kalkatai?"

Belle's gaze narrowed.

"I left that awful place centuries ago. I draw my sustenance from the willing souls here now, which has mostly protected me from its effects."

Lily grimaced internally. She'd hoped that Belle would want the end of the corruption as much as her, but at least on the surface, it appeared she wasn't as compromised.

"I need to know how to stop it."

Belle laughed in Lily's face, her cheeks matching the crimson of her lips as she cackled for a long minute, until she finally settled.

"You're serious," said Belle, pouring two more shots.

"Serious as your black heart."

Belle arched an eyebrow.

"That's proper serious."

"Can you help me?"

Belle downed her shot and then grabbed Lily's and drank hers too.

"This isn't the usual request. I typically hear from desperate men who want to become golf pros, or rock musicians. Or women who want revenge on a rival, or to become pop stars. Why?"

"I am a de Meath. If I don't fix the corruption, my whole bloody family is going to die."

The corner of her eyes creased at the name, but she showed no other reaction.

"I can give you an answer. For a price, of course. But you're not going to like it."

"Do you know something?"

Belle pursed her lips.

"Intuition. When you dabble in my crafts for as long as I have, you have a sense for the direction things are going to go. It was like when I made a deal with that damned Siad. I knew it wasn't going to go as I expected. A rare failure on my part."

"What's your price?"

"Your life, of course."

"How much of it?"

Belle leaned close and sniffed Lily's neck, inhaling deeply as if she were sampling a fine vintage of wine.

"Oh my, your life thread goes on for a long, long time. I can smell that latent power. If you let your family go, ignore the kalkatai and focus on yourself, you can become a great witch. One of the greatest, with power that could warp realms. That awful pain would drive you to become godly."

Belle leaned back, appraising her differently.

"What a meal you've brought to me. Unexpected in its richness. I don't think I've ever been offered so much. Most of the fools that haunt my doorstep are chancers with nothing but a few half-assed years of finance or family man to trade."

She stuck a finger down her throat mockingly.

"Gross. But a girl has to feed on what comes to her door. That's how it works. But you, darling Lily, you're a magnificent feast. I could dine on your bounty for a long, long time. I might expand after that, regain some of my lost territory. That sounds marvelous. Or maybe I should turn you down to prevent what you eventually become."

Belle was lost in thought, imagining the glories of her future, while Lily felt the walls of her decision closing in. She'd said she'd do anything she could for her family. Even sacrifice her life. And now she had the opportunity to prove it.

"How. Long?"

The leannán sídhe put a fingernail on her chin.

"For an answer this dear, I'm afraid I need almost all of it."

Lily knew she should have bargained better, but she didn't want to lose the chance at her family's redemption, and leannán sídhe were known for their cunning in negotiations.

"You can guarantee that the information will lead me to fixing the kalkatai and saving my family."

"I can do no such thing. I can give you the answers that lurk on the horizon, but I cannot guarantee that you'll like them. If there is no solution, then there's no answer to give. But I can see it in your eyes, that dying not long after your family would be a blessing."

"How. Long?"

Belle blinked and looked into the distance.

"A year, maybe two, at most. It won't be pretty either. You'll wish you'd died along with your family from the corruption. A more noble end in comparison."

Lily felt like she was standing on the edge of a cliff with the endless expanse threating to pull her into a rapid descent. Her knees buckled slightly, but she girded her resolve and stared back at Belle.

"I accept your offer."

Belle daintily clapped her hands in front of her like a child excited for birthday cake.

"How do you want to do it? They don't call us fairy lovers for nothing. I can at least make the bargain taste as sweet as possible."

"No," said Lily, shaking her head. "I would not soil this moment with that kind of revelry. Take your cursed silver and give me my answer."

The shrug from Belle could have knocked her over.

"Your funeral."

Belle held her palm out, and after a moment of staring, Lily placed her hand where it was expected. Then Belle curled her hand around Lily's neck, pulling her closer. The act was sensual, but made Lily sick to her stomach.

When Belle's wet lips latched onto her neck, Lily cried out in surprise and a little pain. True to her word, she didn't make it pleasurable. Lily felt like her soul had been bound with steel cords, covered in barbs, to make it bleed for hungry mouths.

When Belle pulled away, Lily forced herself not to collapse, while the leannán sídhe in front of her looked like she'd ingested the sun.

"What a meal."

"The answer."

Belle's lazy-eyed stare made her look drunk.

"I suppose I shall give it, even if you're not going to like it."

The vise closed around Lily's heart in anticipation as Belle's eyes narrowed in thought.

"How can I say this in the best way for you to understand. Ah yes, that's how it's shaped. Hear this, witch. You can't treat a cancer with a potion. You have to cut it out with a sharp enough knife at the source to keep it from feeding on the body."

Lily stared at Belle, expecting more, but the fairy lover stared back with amusement lurking on her lips.

"What else?"

"That's it," said Belle, smirking.

"You're lying."

"I never lie. Not when it comes to a bargain well struck. I gave you the answer. I even warned you that it might not be what you wanted, but here it is."

Lily needed to throw up. The whiskey in her belly gurgled and she rushed out of the building, stumbling onto the wooden walkway with her hands holding her stomach until the contents splashed into the bushes.

She'd been conned. She could see it now. Desperation had blinded her. The answer was the same kind of bullshit that one could get from an online medium. Vague enough to sound real without giving a true answer.

Her life for nothing.

Lily wandered drunkenly down the sidewalk, wanting to set the world on fire. She passed a candy shop. The girl from earlier gave a little wave of greeting, but Lily scowled and kept going. It was strange to know that she'd given up a powerful future. But maybe Belle had been right. Better to die with her family than know she was the only survivor.

TEN

Acolorful bird flew past Damon, making him duck as he entered the
lush garden. He wasn't expecting the thick foliage in the fourth-ward
building, especially with the plain glass front. The employee working the
retail area had sent him back with a smirk.

"Hello? Master Chi? It's Damon Wolfhard. I spoke to your assistant
a few days ago."

The plants swallowed his voice and he had the urge to head back to
the hospital and forget the whole thing. This was the sixth sword trainer
he'd found in the city since the disaster with the training stone in the old
gym, but he felt compelled to continue trying since the apparition of his
uncle Connor Black had told him that the Shining Sword was the key to
his problems. Damon was beginning to wonder if his uncle was mistaken.

Hearing nothing but birdsong, he continued exploring until he came
upon a small pond with poles at uneven heights sticking from the water.

On the center pole was a man with stark white hair, suspended upside down and balanced on his sword point. It looked like he'd fallen from the ceiling and gotten his weapon impaled in the wood.

"Master Chi?"

The white-haired man in black robes gave no indication that he'd heard. Damon left the duffle bag near the path and took another step forward. And another, until he was next to the pond. The display of stamina and supernatural skill gave him hope that Master Chi might be able to teach him how to use the Shining Sword.

"Master—"

The old man balanced on the sword flung himself through the air to land on the next pole, then flew across the water, slapping his blade against the still surface, which propelled him straight at Damon, who nearly fell over trying to get out of the way.

"Master Chi."

"Silence!"

The old man made a complete circle around Damon, noises of disapproval in the back of his throat. Damon felt like a poorly raised cattle at a state fair.

"You don't look like a warrior."

"I'm a healer, I work at Golden Willow."

The old man frowned.

"Where is your weapon?"

Damon hurried back to his bag, unzipped it, and produced the huge sword in the runed sheath. He jogged back, holding it out for Master Chi to inspect.

"It's too big for you," said Master Chi with another frown.

"Too big? I'm more than strong enough."

Master Chi put a finger in his chest. It felt like pure steel.

"Strength is not the most important attribute when it comes to using a sword."

"What is?"

Another disapproving noise in the back of Master Chi's throat.

"Show me what you can do."

Damon pulled the Shining Sword out, which he thought might receive an encouraging comment, or at least an acknowledgement of the weapon's make. The other trainers he'd visited had at least been impressed with his sword, even if they'd declined to work with him.

Master Chi flicked the blade with a fingernail.

"It's not much of a weapon."

Damon choked on his response.

"It's...not?"

"Show me what you know."

Damon felt most comfortable with what he'd learned from the training stone, so he went through the maneuvers of each stance, swinging confidently while focusing on maintaining a firm grip. It'd taken a chunk out of his bank account to get everything fixed in the gym.

When he was finished, Damon let the sword rest on his shoulder and approached the master.

The deepening frown was worse than the comment that came right after.

"You fight like someone expecting praise after each maneuver. I'm sorry. You're too old. To become a master, you must start very young and dedicate your life to it. You're a hobbyist at best, which is nothing to be ashamed of, but I do not want to teach you."

"Please, Master Chi, it's imperative that I learn how to use this sword."

"This is a family heirloom, no?"

"It is—"

"It does not matter if you learn how to use it. If it was, you wouldn't be moving from trainer to trainer trying to find one that can help you."

The ache in his heart had him grimacing.

"This isn't about me. I cannot say much except that the city is in danger."

Master Chi raised a bushy white eyebrow.

"And you are going to save it with this sword? I've met many delusional aspirants, but you have to be the most delusional of all of them."

"I swear to you this is true. This isn't just any sword, it's the Shining Sword. It was once owned by King Nuada, who pledged himself to the King of the Summer Fae, the Oakfather, King Oberon."

"A sword is not a sword without someone to wield it. Maybe you should give it to someone else."

"There is no one else. My extended family was murdered to get to this sword."

For the first time since Damon had entered the garden, he sensed a softening of Master Chi's stance.

"Please, I'll do anything you ask. I'm a mage of Aura Healers, if that helps. Maybe I can use my faez to an advantage. I heard the gangs in the Undercity are using faez to do crazy things like run up walls."

"I will consider your apprenticeship under one condition."

"What? Anything."

Master Chi swept his arm towards the pond.

"Cross the water without touching it."

Damon furrowed his forehead.

"I can, like, use the poles?"

"Of course." Master Chi grinned. "But do not get even a single drop on you."

Damon stared at the poles in the pond. It didn't look that difficult. There were about fifteen poles that crisscrossed the water and he'd probably have to use half of them. The elevation change would be the hardest part, but it wasn't like he couldn't manage.

"Okay. I can do it."

"Show me."

Damon started to put down the sword until he saw Master Chi's frown.

"Right. Got it. With the sword."

He approached the pond, holding the weapon near his side, without getting too close and cutting himself. He'd have to keep the Shining Sword away from his body while he was jumping. He started to take his phone out of his pocket, but thought that would be admitting that he might fail, so he kept it on his person.

The first pole was a short hop. He balanced on top easily, using the long weapon as a tail of sorts. Damon almost looked back to Master Chi, but he instinctively knew he would be frowning.

The second and the third poles were further apart and took more concentration to land safely, but he was already a quarter across and feeling more confident about his chances.

"Come on, Damon, you got this."

The next few jumps required big elevation changes. He summoned his animal spirits to make the leap and landed easily.

But then he saw the gap between the next two poles. Master Chi had used a sword slap to bounce off the surface, but there was no way Damon could manage that. He'd have to make a standing jump. It was a big distance, but not impossible for a therianthrope.

Damon let the change extend his fingernails until he felt the power thrumming through his body. Holding the Shining Sword tight in his fist, he visualized landing the leap. If he could make it, the last three poles were relatively easy.

He rocked a few times and then pushed off hard, using the edge of the pole to propel himself through the air.

The first few feet Damon was sure he was going to make it. Then his altitude arced downward faster than he expected.

In a last-second desperation move, Damon brought the blade downward hoping to bounce off the water like Master Chi. The tip sliced though the still surface and Damon followed it into the pond.

Submerged instantly, Damon flailed to regain the surface so he could breathe, and then with the weapon making his paddling awkward, he made his way to the edge.

Dripping wet, Damon pulled his phone out of his pocket, cursing under his breath.

"Can I try again? I think I could get it a second time."

The stone-like expression of Master Chi gave him an answer.

"Right. One try."

Damon smoothed the water from his face and after wiping down the sword with a cloth, put it back into the sheath.

Master Chi walked him to the front door.

"Is there any hope for me?" asked Damon.

"I'm afraid not. You might become a passable swordsman, but you'll never become a master. You don't have a warrior's heart. But I can see other strengths in you. Those should be your focus, not this distraction imposed by your family's expectations."

Damon thanked him for his time and headed to the train station, leaving a trail of puddles and regrets on the sidewalk.

ELEVEN

The three-tailed feline was sitting outside Ruby's door, looking like an old petitioner having a smoke before returning inside. The cat rose to its feet and stretched.

Remi glanced down the hallway where she'd seen an apparition shift through the wall when she'd ascended the stairs. The little girl in a long T-shirt that went down to her knees was peeking around the corner.

"'Allo, luv, fancy the door handle for me?"

Remi shifted her mouth to the side, trying not to be distracted by the ghost.

"You're not in trouble, are you?"

The cat stared back with hazel eyes until Remi sighed.

"Is she recording?"

"She is."

The door was surprisingly unlocked. She was wondering if Ruby knew she was coming again when the illusionary head of her host appeared in the middle of the room.

"Grab a drink, I'll be with you shortly."

The kitchen was meticulously clean. The refrigerator was filled with various colors of Mage Blast, but nothing else. Remi grabbed a Lemon Shock and headed to the couch. She could hear the melodic voice of Ruby speaking to her stream. While she waited, Remi investigated the ebony skull filled with candy on the table.

"I wouldn't eat that," said Ruby, coming through the door as Remi picked up a piece of the individually wrapped candy.

"Poison?"

"Cat treats. They taste like smoked salmon or fried liver."

"Oh," said Remi, dropping the treat and leaning back into the couch. "It's okay that I came by?"

Ruby winked and pursed her thick, crimson lips.

"Anything for my personal savior. Speaking of the cat, you didn't happen to let him in, did you?"

"Is it bad that I did?"

Ruby crossed her arms and called out to the rest of the apartment.

"If you shit anywhere other than the litter box, I'm going to sell you to a real bog witch. Then you'll see how good you have it."

A faint meow came from another room, which had Ruby muttering.

"Familiars are such a pain. I should have gotten a talking turtle instead." Ruby sat across from her, crossing her legs. "I assume this isn't a social visit."

"I'm sorry I only come here when I need something. I don't really have much of a life outside the hospital."

Ruby tilted her head and gave the air a healthy sniff.

"You managed the trip to Autumn, didn't you? And the Veil. How unusual. Did you find what you were looking for?"

"Yes and no. But that's not why I came."

"And why is that?"

The words failed to form. Except for her friends, she hadn't spoken to anyone else about what had happened to her parents.

"Take your time."

Remi clenched her hand into a fist.

"I let my parents die in the Veil. Or the people that I thought were my parents."

Ruby raised an exquisite eyebrow.

"That wasn't what I was expecting you to say. That sounds terrible. I'm sorry, Remi. May I ask what happened?"

Without revealing the Horn, Remi told Ruby about the final hours in the Tomb. Whether or not Ruby was actually sympathetic, Remi couldn't tell, but it felt nice to talk to someone besides her friends about it.

"You need a therapist, not a hag," said Ruby, pursing her lips.

"I'd be a horrible person if I didn't feel guilty, but that's not why I came. You just needed to know the backstory."

"You want to know who your real parents are?" asked Ruby.

"It would help me make sense of who I am and where I came from."

"It's not really my expertise."

"You were able to point me to the Autumn Fae for the pendant."

"That was different. The magic of that powerful magical item had worn off on you. Enough that I could see the imprint."

"There's nothing you can do? People have been telling me for years that I have trickster blood. When I was in the Fae, I thought that it was because Greta had birthed me there, but now that I know that's not true, the trickster comment doesn't make sense anymore."

Ruby leaned forward, making Remi nervous as she stared intently. After a half-minute of unrestrained eye contact, Ruby returned to her casual siting position.

"You're not a trickster."

"What? I thought you couldn't tell."

Ruby waved a hand randomly in the air.

"I can't tell you who your parents are but I can tell you you're not a trickster. You might have an aura of Fae to you. Which I think is confusing the others, but you're clearly not a trickster."

"What tells you that?"

Ruby smirked.

"That you saved me. And went after the pendant, which you knew would be dangerous. Those aren't acts of a trickster, despite what you've been led to believe."

"You're not using your crone magic at all?"

"Nope. Sorry, Remi. I know you want me to be the all-knowing hag for you, but my powers are limited. Powerful in their own way, but I cannot just snap my fingers and give you the answers you desire."

"I'm sorry, Ruby."

"You shouldn't be sorry. I would do the same if I were in your shoes."

Remi rose from the couch.

"I should head back. I'm probably keeping you from another streaming session."

When she reached the door, Ruby said, "Be careful. You're being watched."

"I'm being watched?"

Ruby shook her head.

"I can't tell you anything more than that, but my senses went on high alert the moment you arrived, and now that you're about to leave, I'm feeling them fade."

"I'll be careful. Thanks."

Remi almost forgot about the little ghost girl until she was leaving the apartment. She looked back to see her wagging a finger. It was unusual for the ghosts to try and communicate, but the apparition faded from view before she could think to ask a question.

The October night air was cool on Remi's face. The laughing and constant chatter of the Canal District rose above the blocking buildings. She headed the other way towards the train station.

The quieter the noise from the Canal District got, the more she checked over her shoulder.

The station was two blocks away. Remi watched a northbound train rumble over the elevated tracks while sirens wailed in the distance. She smelled old hotdogs and sewer steam, and then—the rot of vegetation.

It smelled like the kalkatai.

Her entire body went on high alert. That scent was permanently ingrained into her nose from the battle with the White Worm and her trip to the Summer Fae. It was unavoidable.

Remi suddenly had the urge to run all the way to the station.

Then she heard a huff.

A slow turn revealed something enormous behind her in the street.

Remi could scarcely believe it when she was faced with the triangular head of the giant wyrm. It was the Caoránarch. Questions of how it could have snuck up without her hearing it was lost beneath the fear ricocheting through her system.

"You're not going to do anything..."

The Caoránarch reared back its head and roared, swampy material flying off the dark green scales around its mouth. Remembering the story of the decimated police force, Remi ran the opposite way.

The pounding of heavy feet, cracking concrete, followed her. In that moment, she wished she'd been from another Hall, one that could give her supernatural speed.

The impacts grew closer.

She felt hot, swampy breath on her backside.

A parked car went screeching out of the way when the Caoránarch hit it, nearly taking out Remi's legs, but she managed to avoid it and cut around the corner.

The turn gave her space as the huge river dragon had to keep to the center of the street.

A car with blinding headlights came the other way and veered onto the opposite sidewalk, crashing into the concrete steps of an apartment building to avoid the Caoránarch.

When Remi realized that she wouldn't make it to the station, she instinctively reached out to the Veil and called for help.

It wasn't until she was another hundred feet down the street that she realized her call had been answered.

Half turning, she spotted the Caoránarch, halted in front of a spectral being. Remi stumbled to a stop, mystified by the success of her request. A ghostly woman with her hand out had placed herself before the river dragon.

"Keep running, you idiot," she told herself before turning back to the mad sprint.

She made it another hundred feet before glancing back again to see an empty street and slowed to a light jog. Neither the ghost she had summoned or the Caoránarch were anywhere in sight, which made her wonder if she'd seen anything at all.

But fear still coursed through her veins, so she kept up her run until she reached the station. The turnstile guard gave her a funny look when she pushed through covered in sweat.

"Late for a meeting."

Even when she reached the platform, Remi kept checking back to sky above the building to make sure that the Caoránarch hadn't followed her. She didn't know why any of it had happened, but counted herself lucky that she wasn't dead.

TWELVE

Lily was finishing notes on her last patient for the day when Dr. Broomfield appeared. She tried not to stiffen but the head of instruction made her nervous, especially after Damon had told them the story about the spiked drink.

"Healer Lily."

"Yes, Dr. Broomfield. How can I help you?"

"You've heard about the problem in the city?"

"Which one?"

His forehead furrowed as if he were trying to figure out if she was being disrespectful.

"A new disease. Something we've not seen before, but it has leadership in Golden Willow worried."

"That is concerning," said Lily, resisting the urge to add a few Gaelic curse words to her response. "Let me know if there's anything I can do to help."

"I'm glad you feel that way, because I'm reassigning you to the Super Curse Ward."

"What?"

The Super Curse Ward was the place they sent patients when their afflictions were extremely dangerous or could easily spread. It was one of the most dangerous places in the hospital to work.

"Did I stutter?"

"No, Dr. Broomfield. I just thought that the Super Curse Ward was off-limits to students."

The smile that spread across his lips felt like a dagger blow to the chest.

"You've told me time and again how talented you are. This shouldn't be a problem for a healer of your caliber. Right?"

"I'm here to serve."

"That's good. You're relieved of your patients here," he said, holding out his hand for the clipboard. "You can report to your new ward right this moment."

"But I—"

The complaint that she'd just finished an extra-long shift died on her tongue. He wouldn't care and the complaint would only give him satisfaction.

"—can't wait to get started."

"That's the spirit."

When she passed the nurses' desk, they gave her sympathetic looks but could say nothing while Dr. Broomfield was in range. She shouldn't be surprised, she told herself. After all, Remi had already been shipped to the EMT group. Dr. Broomfield had probably been waiting for an excuse to send her somewhere equally dangerous. The request from upper management for more help for the Super Curse Ward had probably been that trigger.

The Super Curse Ward was protected by an airlock system. Lily had to get badged into the chamber, which blew air all over her while vacuums sucked out any potential contaminates. Then she stepped into a machine with a circular wall of runes surrounding her. The equipment spun into motion the moment she was in the center, while the runes glowed brightly, making her squint.

"All clear. You can step through, Healer Lily."

The Super Curse Ward looked nothing like the others. Lily thought she'd stepped into a space station by the smooth white walls and most of the staff walking around in moonsuits.

A short balding man in a white doctor's coat and wearing glasses walked towards her with his hand out.

"Healer Lily. I'm Doctor Niles. Head of the Arcane Infectious Disease Ward, though feel free to call it the Super Curse Ward like everyone else."

"I'm happy to be here," said Lily, accepting his handshake.

Dr. Niles raised his eyebrows.

"I happen to know that's not true, but given our situation, I'm pleased to accept the help. While I know Marcus isn't a big fan, I've heard enough good things from the nurses that we came out way ahead on this deal."

"The new disease in the city is that big of a concern?"

The long pause put a stone in Lily's gut.

"Come with me."

He led her to his office, which was barren except for a laptop, three medical certificates on the wall, and a picture of his smiling family of six. After typing in a password and navigating his computer using a mouse, he spun the screen around revealing a familiar face.

"That's Aleksandr Grimm, Head of Arcane Phytology," said Lily.

"He took a look at some samples for us," said Dr. Niles. "Let me hit play."

"—personally examined the piece of mortua folia you sent. It has high faez markers, which is very unusual for any plant material, let alone one pulled out of a corpse."

"Wait," said Lily, jamming the stop button. "Plants pulled out of a corpse?"

"There's a lot to go through to get you caught up. Let's play through and then you can ask me all the questions you want."

Lily's finger hovered over the button as she thought about the kalkatai. Could it be coming to their realm? Lily didn't think that was possible, but she hadn't thought the corruption of the Summer Fae was possible either.

"I took a piece of the sample and left it in a sealed container with a living mouse. This is what we found the next morning."

The camera panned to a glass cage connected to an oxygenation machine. At the center was a brown mouse lying on its side with a piece of vine material snaking out of its mouth. The belly was distended.

"It's contagious. Not in all situations. We repeated the test with three other mice and the rotting plant material didn't spread. We're trying to isolate the conditions which help, but so far we've been unable."

The next part of the video was Patron Grimm going over other analysis of the plant, but most of it was too specific to his Hall and went over her head.

"How many cases in the city?"

"Thirty-three that we're aware of. Only a few of those can be attributed to contagion spread. The rest came from other vectors."

"That's bloody scary."

"More than scary. Under the right conditions, it could be apocalyptic. We've informed the mayor and the city emergency services to be on the lookout and exercise caution if they encounter it, but until we can come up with a solution, we're at its mercy."

Dr. Niles stood and headed out of the room, motioning for her to follow. He led her to a room with an airlock. The interior was covered in runes she knew meant it was a kill room. The purpose of the arcane design was to destroy anything in the room if certain conditions were met. The runes were a dull gray. At the center of the room, lying on a bed, was what had once been a human body before the stomach cavity had exploded with plant material. Black, leafy vines burst from the midsection like replacement intestines.

"It happened this morning. Thankfully, no one was in the room with the patient. The runes killed him and the plant, but we're giving it more time before we do an autopsy."

Dr. Niles turned toward her. The deadness in his eyes betrayed the deep-seated worry.

"Now you know why we requested help and the normal prohibitions against Aura Healer students in my ward were revoked."

"Whatever you need me to do," said Lily.

"Thank you. I appreciate your willingness to jump in, because I won't lie to you. This is a dangerous situation. We're on the front lines of this battle. If it gets out of hand, I expect casualties."

"I understand."

"Good. Now I need one of the nurses to help you through with the on-boarding paperwork. You know, next of kin, notarized will, that sort of thing."

Lily nodded and followed him back to the central area.

"Oh, and we have great post-death benefits. Especially if you get stuck in the Veil. We spring for exorcisms and other death counters. The hospital really does a bang-up job with making sure we're compensated in the next life."

THIRTEEN

The Arcade Parade looked different in the daytime full of screaming kids and parents staring at their phones looking like inmates on death row. Damon strolled past the machine that they'd taken the glowy balls from during their escape from the Full Moon Killer, wondering if his sisters knew how this place had figured in the events of that year.

He found the twins at an arcade game called Ninja Kaiju. They were using plastic swords to swipe through illusionary monsters that were coming at them from all sides of the dome-like machine.

Fighting back-to-back, they kept up their defense, racking up another high score while whittling away at their enemies. Then the lights flashed red and they faced towards a glowing mountain in the distance that rose into a formidable kaiju that looked like an armored turtle with spikes as big as hills on its back. The action lasted for a good minute while tiny turtle beasts dropped from the kaiju's belly until an earthquake stomp made Nat miss a block, and once she went down, Talia soon followed.

"That was impressive," he told them when they came out and gave him a hug, each slightly sweaty but grinning ear to ear.

"We haven't gotten past Turtle Mom yet, but we're getting close," said Nat, still wearing her camo pants and tan shirt with a Protectors badge on the front.

"Come on, you're buying us pizza," said Talia, hooking her arm around his.

"Pizza? I don't think my bank account can take that," he said, grinning.

He picked up three extra larges with everything, including anchovies. They sat as far away as possible from the birthday party of ten-year-old boys who'd been given novelty wands that shot harmless magical sparks and were busy spraying them over everyone around them.

"That was you two at that age," said Damon, smirking as he glanced back with a piece of pizza in his hand.

Nat rolled her eyes.

"We'd never get caught dead with those stupid wands. I recall Talia modified those more expensive ones to shoot actual fire. At least until Mom found them and threw them away."

Talia frowned.

"Some of my best work. I was so close to turning one into a bomb. Those stupid wand makers put too much resident faez in them."

"How's the hospital?" asked Nat.

Damon finished chewing his bite before he leaned back in the plastic chair while a sparkling disc went flying over their heads.

"That's what I wanted to talk to you about."

"Uh-oh," said Nat, grinning at her sister. "Big brother talk. Something serious is going down."

Talia gestured at him.

"Real serious by that look. Our poor brother has aged ten years since joining Aura Healers."

Damon leaned forward and spoke quietly.

"I'm not messing around. There's a really bad affliction going around town. It's turning people's insides into contagious plants."

"The Death Rot," said Nat, nodding.

"You know about it?"

"Of course. Second and third years have been put on the regular beat because they need officers with magic to deal with the infected. Sanchez had to roast a body with a full-on flame blast like a funeral incinerator last week. He smelled like burnt hair for days."

Heat rose in Damon's chest thinking about his sisters in danger.

"Hey, wolf boy," said Talia, gesturing towards his right hand.

"What?"

The pizza slice he'd been holding was now a ball of crust and toppings because he'd squeezed it with his fist.

"Blood and bone," he said, using a napkin to wipe off his palm. "At least one of us isn't exposed to this, what did you call it? Death Rot?"

"Not true," said Talia. "They've been quietly checking people coming into the theater for signs. I'm playing to a packed house three nights a week."

"It's worse than that," said Nat. "The mayor is considering a lockdown on the city. I've heard rumblings from the instructors. It probably would have happened last week, but that cold front really put a damper on it. Or that's the theory."

Damon shook his head and stared into the distance. He couldn't help but think about how the Horn could help the city, but getting it would only put the artifact at risk of being stolen.

"You look like you're plotting," said Nat.

"Considering all options. I hate that we never get peace and quiet in the Halls. One crisis to the next."

"That's why we joined up. It wasn't to sit on our hands and do nothing," said Nat.

"Just be careful. We've lost enough family. We can't lose each other."

"We're more worried about you, big brother. Trouble seems to follow you and your friends. You still haven't told us where you were when you disappeared last spring," said Talia.

"The less you know the better."

"See," said Talia. "It's a good thing we like Remi, because she seems to attract trouble."

Damon checked the time.

"Shift soon?" asked Nat.

"I should get back. You can have the rest of my pizza."

"At least *we* get some free time," said Nat, smirking.

They exchanged a round of hugs.

"Be careful," he told them on the way out.

It took half a block before Damon thought he might be followed. The late-afternoon sun was reflecting off the Spire and he half turned to avoid the glare and caught sight of a man with his head down and his hands in his coat pockets. Damon's hackles immediately went up and while he had no obvious reason to mistrust the individual, he knew to have faith in his instincts.

Damon thought about texting the twins to help with the guy, but decided he was too far away from the Arcade Parade and didn't want to get them involved if the Death Rot had a human origin.

Crossing traffic ahead of the light put some distance between him and his follower. Damon made a show of hurrying and checking his watch as if he were going to be late.

When he neared the train station, Damon stepped behind an outbuilding in the parking lot. The guy appeared thirty seconds later. Damon grabbed him by the collar and slammed him against the wooden building.

"Why are you following me?"

Even before the guy answered, Damon saw the sickness in his pale face. Flop sweat covered his forehead. Damon dropped him immediately and stepped back.

"I got paid to follow you," said the guy, swallowing hard.

He had a distended belly and dark circles around his eyes. Damon took a second step back.

"By who?"

"I...I don't remember," said the guy as he knitted his brow. "I mean, I should remember. I don't understand."

"If you tell me everything you know, I might not tear your arms from your body," said Damon, holding out his claws.

The guy rocked on his heels and exhaled with effort.

"I'm sorry, I know I should. No offense, but I needed the money. I thought it was an easy job."

He put a hand to his mouth and belched, which smelled like a dead swamp. Damon took another step back.

"I need to get you to the hospital."

"What?"

"You've been infected."

"Infected? With what?"

Damon was pulling out his phone when the guy collapsed to one knee. He put a hand to his forehead.

"He was tall..."

A gurgle was followed by him falling over on his side and hugging his midsection. Knowing everything that Lily had told him about the precautions from the Super Curse Ward was the only thing that kept him from rushing to the man's side. He hated seeing someone suffer.

"Hold on, I'm calling the ambulance."

Damon had barely finished punching in the numbers when the guy released a low rising moan than was slowly strangled from within.

"Hello, yeah, I need—"

Before he could get the words out, the guy started convulsing and his eyes rolled into the back of his head. A couple walking nearby started to move towards him, but Damon yelled at them to stay back. Then dark, crusty vines climbed from the guy's mouth and he stilled with his back arched and staring at the sky.

After Damon identified himself as a member of Aura Healers, he finished giving instructions, which included deploying the hazmat team and directing that he be put into isolation when he returned to Golden Willow. Then he performed a self-cleanse enchantment he hoped would be enough to protect him from the Death Rot while he waited for the ambulance to arrive.

FOURTEEN

The back of the Kamikaze Kids' rig bounced as they rumbled over the broken streets of the thirteenth ward while Remi texted with Damon, who had just gotten out of isolation the day before. It'd been over a week since the exposure, which was longer than anyone else had stayed in isolation, but the order had come down from Dr. Fairlight. They hadn't wanted to risk his patients given the severity of the affliction, but Remi wasn't sure that was the only reason.

"Hey, Green Shirt, a 669 just came in," said Vasquez as she was assembling another one of her contraptions. It looked like a kid's water pistol combined with a pressurized air tank. "I need you to grab the powdered camazotz membrane from the alchemy cabinet."

Remi went straight for the closet, rocking with the rig as it went around a corner. Her knees were bruised from constantly running into the walls. The drawers slid open easily, but after the first two tries she had to ask Vasquez which one they were in while Paxton looked on with silent amusement.

"Not C, but A for apparition."

"Apparition?"

"Didn't you hear the call? Got two injured at a fourth-ward apartment building near the ring road. Sounds like an energy ghost. We're going to be first on scene, so we'd better be ready."

With directions from Vasquez, Remi mixed the camazotz powder with a neutral base solution and a jar of fresh cinnamon. When it was ready, Vasquez loaded it into the squirt gun and attached the air cannister.

Ansel banged on the wall between them.

"Arriving in twenty seconds."

It was about as much as she'd heard him talk. Their driver mostly kept to himself with headphones on, but she'd come to appreciate his skill behind the wheel.

"Hey, Vasquez, when we get in there, I might—"

Remi never got a chance to finish her comment, as the rig slammed on the brakes, sliding into a parking spot sideways. Vasquez was out the door with Paxton right behind carrying one bag of emergency supplies while Remi had the other. Unlike most of the EMT teams, the Kamikaze Kids didn't wait for the police or other emergency services to make the scene safe.

A group of residents was standing outside the apartment building. An old woman in a flowery housecoat pointed upward.

"It's on the fifth floor."

"Elevator?" asked Vasquez.

"What does this look like, the Royal Grand?"

Vasquez led them into the stairwell. She paused at the bottom.

"I hate stairs."

Halfway up the first flight, Remi tried again.

"About the ghost, you know in the Hospice Ward I—"

The rending of metal from above had them slowing and staring up the center of the stairwell.

"Does that sound like an energy ghost to you, Big Guy?"

"No, but that doesn't mean it was the ghost."

"Come on," said Vasquez, charging upward.

Remi's third attempt at notifying Vasquez of her experience died in her throat from running up three flights of stairs carrying a giant red duffle bag of emergency supplies.

"Blood and bone," said Remi at the bottom of the fourth as her thighs screamed for relief.

"No time to rest, Green Shirt. Get a move on!"

The weight of the duffle bag grew heavier with each step. Remi wished she could have drank one of Jeb's specials, but she didn't have access from the EMT shed.

The ground trembled when Remi caught up with the two EMTs. Remi was covered in sweat while the two EMTs looked unfazed.

"Got eyes on it?" asked Vasquez, peeking around the corner.

Paxton tilted his head down the hallway.

"Something went sideways fast."

"You going to make it?" asked Vasquez, smirking. "You look like a tomato."

Remi raised her middle finger, because she didn't have the lungs to speak. Vasquez chuckled as she checked down the hallway again.

"I like you, Green Shirt."

"What about protocols?" asked Remi.

Vasquez frowned then reached into her pocket for the enchanted mask. The hospital had implemented a new round of safety measures until they could figure out what was causing the Death Rot. They put their masks on and then Vasquez jogged down with her modified squirt gun until she peered into an open door.

"They're in here."

Remi reached them right after. Two people lying limbs akimbo on the carpet, moaning softly with feet kicking.

Vasquez dropped to her knees, tossed the squirt gun to the floor, and started checking pulses and other vital signs while Paxton dug into the first bag.

The sensation that they were being watched had Remi on high alert. She stayed in the hallway, but close enough to hear any of Vasquez's requests.

"I think they're going to be okay. Nothing seems too wrong, even though I don't know why they're unconscious."

"No bad smells?" asked Remi.

"No Death Rot here," said Vasquez, furrowing her forehead. "First thing I checked."

The cold had kept the spread of the strange disease down, but cases popped up from time to time. They had yet to run into any, but Damon in isolation had made them all abundantly cautious.

The building rumbled again.

"Any construction nearby?" asked Paxton.

"I didn't see any cranes."

"I think we can move them back to the rig," said Vasquez. "Green Shirt, you stand guard. We'll take the woman down first."

"Roger that."

After they unfolded the stretcher, they loaded the unconscious woman and disappeared down the hall while Remi stood in the doorway with the squirt gun feeling a little ridiculous.

Without the rest of her team, she felt the walls close in. The hair on the back of her neck was at full attention. She swore she could detect something just beyond her senses, but she had no proof.

Remi knelt by the unconscious man and after a moment of quiet examination, she set the squirt gun down and cast a quick spell over him. She was expecting greenish mist to form over him, which would indicate the Veil, but what she got was flashes of dark pulsing purples and the smell of pine. The conflicting information had her confused as to the origins of the affliction.

The beat of footsteps had Remi rising to find Vasquez returning with the stretcher. They loaded the second patient and the three of them headed down the stairwell. Remi had both duffle bags, but at least she didn't have to carry the stretcher.

Around the time they exited the building, three police cars arrived with swirling lights and no sirens. The mustached officer named Justin strolled up with his hands on his belt.

"Ghost problem?"

"Dunno, didn't see any," said Vasquez, as she applied a stim tab to the woman's arm. "But you should probably check. I don't think anyone wants to go back in."

The crowd at the base of the apartment had grown in size as they stared upward.

Officer Justin saluted them before yelling to his team about grabbing their ghost hunting equipment. The rig was about to close the back doors, but Remi jumped out, much to Vasquez's annoyance, and ran over to the police cars.

"Hey, I don't think it's a ghost."

Officer Justin raised an eyebrow.

"I don't take suggestions from wet-behind-the-ears EMTs."

"I normally don't work in the rig. I'm an Aura Healer and I was in the Death Ward before this. I know the Veil. Whatever took them down wasn't from there."

"Better get back to your rig. Your mommy and daddy are waiting," said Officer Justin, eliciting laughter from his fellow officers.

Remi mumbled curses under her breath as she returned to the team.

"How'd that go?" asked Vasquez with a smirk.

"Bunch of wankers."

"No worries. We got what we came for. Let's get 'em back to GW, and let someone else figure out how to wake them."

As the ambulance sped away, Remi couldn't help but feel like she was missing something.

With two loaded beds in back, there wasn't much room, so she wedged herself against the wall and repeated the spell on the woman. The signs came back even stronger than with the man.

"What the hell is that?" asked Vasquez, frowning.

"I don't know."

As the rig went around a corner, Remi noticed black threads shifting opposite of their direction. She peered out the small side window at a parking garage and saw movement on the second floor. Something large and shifting.

"Stop the rig!"

The vehicle started to slow until Vasquez said, "Keep going, Ansel."

"Seriously, stop."

When the rig sped up, Remi grabbed the handle and opened the door, which brought swirling chill winds into the back and screams from her teammates. The change got Ansel to slow down until she could jump out the back and run towards the garage, which was covered in scaffolding and construction signs warning to stay out. She heard the ambulance skid to a stop but she was already heading after the gut feeling.

"This might be a bad idea," she told herself as she found the stairwell and sped up to the second level, removing her mask halfway up because it was making her mouth hot.

The parking garage was empty of vehicles, but there were piles of unbuilt scaffolding and other machines stationed inside. The late afternoon and lack of interior lighting cast thick shadows, making it hard to see.

"What in the hell are you doing, Green Shirt?" asked Vasquez angrily when she reached the second floor.

"Hush," said Remi, staring into the darkness.

"What's going on?" asked Paxton when he arrived.

Vasquez gestured towards her and shrugged, but Remi was too busy trying to figure out what she'd seen before.

"There," she said, extending her hand.

The darkness had shifted over the opposite edge. Remi ran across the concrete, feeling her lungs burn and promising to do more cardio in the future. When she got to the opposite side, she saw a river of shifting dark green scales snaking down the alleyway away from the parking garage.

There was no stairwell in sight, so Remi vaulted over the edge, landing hard enough to clack her teeth and twist her knee slightly. She limped into the alleyway, but there was no sign of the Caoránarch.

Remi repeated the spell she'd used on the patient, which revealed streaks of darkness leading further into the alley. She hauled herself forward despite the pain in her knee until the black threads led her to a closed sewer lid issuing steam.

"Have you gone mad?" asked Vasquez when they arrived out of breath.

"Can you open it?" she asked Paxton.

He dug his fingers into the small holes on either side and with a grunt, yanked it upward. As soon as the way was open, Remi scurried down the metal ladder, hating the way it clanked in the darkness.

The other two followed her down. Before Remi could go further, Vasquez grabbed her arm.

"What are you doing?"

"Did you see it?"

Vasquez screwed up her face.

"I saw something. What was it?"

"The Caoránarch, but it somehow went down here, which doesn't make any sense."

"The big dragon, wyrm thing that everyone's scared shitless about in the city?"

"Yeah, that one."

"Then why are we following it? Do you have a death wish?"

"If it were really the Caoránarch, it wouldn't have been able to squeeze past a sewer lid. Which means it's something else that I don't understand. It's not the Veil. It sort of has hints of the Fae. But there's something else, more rotten, more...oh shit."

"What?"

"The corruption. That's what that weird black stuff is. Like what Lily saw in her Greenwalk. Which means, oh no. We have to get back to the rig."

When Remi couldn't run fast enough because of her knee, Paxton let her climb on his back and they ran all the way to the street, where they found Ansel with his headphones around his neck, staring at the ambulance from the sidewalk.

The open doors revealed a mass of rotting vines that had exploded from the two—now dead—patients.

Vasquez put a hand to her mouth.

"We're not...?"

Remi gathered them together and cast the same spell she had on the body and in the sewer. The auras revealed were normal. She cast it again towards the ruined ambulance, and blooms of purple darkness appeared in the air.

"I think we're safe. Good thing we had our masks on, but we're gonna need a new rig."

Vasquez had her hands on her head as she stared at the plant-based destruction.

"Hey, Green Shirt."

"Yeah?"

"Good work."

FIFTEEN

The moonsuit made it difficult to analyze the body on the stainless steel table. Lily felt like she'd been wrapped in bubble wrap. It didn't help that she was wary of the mass of plants and vines that had exploded out of the man's midsection like a host of angry snakes.

"Stop bein' a bloody eejit and do your job, Lily."

The voice echoed in her helmet.

Lily grabbed a scalpel from the tray and used it to slice a section of black, rotting vine. She still couldn't believe how close this person had gotten to Remi. The EMT team had just gotten out of observation this morning once it had been confirmed they weren't infected.

When she'd spoken to Remi, she'd told her about the Caoránarch, and how the great wyrm had disappeared down a sewer entrance, which made no sense for many reasons. Remi had also reported the presence of a greenish-black aura, but Lily's initial investigation hadn't given her the same information. She wasn't sure she believed Remi's suggestion that it was the same thing as what she'd seen in the Greenwalk, but since neither of them had witnessed what each other had seen, it made it hard to corroborate.

The section of blackened vine fit beneath the faez analyzer, which was a fancy magical microscope that could help see enchantments, curses, and other artificial spells.

Using the one-way tube, Lily breathed faez into the machine, which helped activate the runes. The apparatus heated up as it bombarded the plant material. It was the same thing she could achieve with a series of spells, but since she was in the moonsuit, casting them would be extremely challenging.

With her own eyes, the plant material looked like it was rotting, but under magnification, the vine looked like the surface of an alien planet. The sections of living material appeared healthy and normal while the cracks of black goo looked like oil coming up through fissures in the surface of the planet.

"What are you?"

It wasn't anything like she was expecting. Lily pulled away and mentally revisited her plan. Then she clicked the analyzer one rune over to shine different lights on the subject.

The competing auras wavered like the Northern Lights over the sample. She caught the greenish-black spots sizzling at the barrier between the two materials, and when she looked closer she thought she saw a pulsing purple-black glow.

It reminded her of the chaos-shaped hole she'd seen in the Court of the Summer King. It was the same, she was sure of it. But what did that have to do with the Death Rot? Was it as simple as the corruption was leaking over to the City of Sorcery?

That might make sense if Remi hadn't seen the Caoránarch disappear into the sewers. Nor did it explain the virality of the cursed plant material.

Lily couldn't help but think the two people who'd been infected had been left for Remi like a trap. If she'd stayed in the ambulance a little bit longer, the bodies would have exploded and infected her and the rest of her EMT team, and no one could have done anything about it.

Using the clicker, she shifted the analyzer to other runes so she could try to figure out where the foreign material had come from and possibly what the chaos-shaped hole she'd seen in the Summer Fae might be.

It was hard to focus on the purple-black glow because it appeared fleetingly, but she managed to catch the edge of it a few times. It wasn't from the Fae. Nor their realm. In fact, as Lily cross-referenced the information into the chart, it didn't appear to come from any known realm. As she contemplated the new information and how she might tease out where the strange energy was coming from, Lily leaned sideways against the table.

It was probably the only thing that saved her.

She spotted the vine moments before it wrapped around her ankle. Lily threw herself over the analyzer table.

A half dozen vines snaked from the dead body, reaching after her with spiked ends that looked hard enough to rip through the moonsuit. Lily grabbed the scalpel that she'd used to slice a piece away and slashed at the grasping vines.

She managed to cut the thorny end off one vine, but then she watched as it regrew with new sharp edges. Trapped in the corner with no way to reach the exit, Lily kept up her defense using the tiny knife. If she didn't have the suit on, she could unleash a fury of flame. As it was, she'd be likely to burn a hole in her suit even if she could pull off the spell in the protective gear.

Seeing only one chance to escape, Lily put her shoulder into the heavy table with the expensive analyzer on it and shoved it over. It tipped over and landed on the vines, trapping them enough that she could vault over the ends and make it to the door.

Lily threw herself into the airlock as new vines slammed against the barrier behind her. She watched as they undulated like tentacles from an angry octopus. When she hit the cleaner cycle, thick white fumes sprayed into the chamber, cleaning the surface of the moonsuit with corrosive elixirs and then again with human-safe washes.

When it was finished, she stumbled out of the chamber and ripped off the helmet for fresh air, which released her mass of curly locks around her face.

Lily peered through the window to see the vines banging on the door. More plant material was snaking out of the inner cavity as if it were a portal to another realm.

Still recovering from the burst of adrenaline, she didn't hear the heavy footsteps until Dr. Niles appeared. He took one look at the interior of the safe room, then shifted over to the keypad at the outer lock.

The reason for all the beeping wasn't apparent to Lily until it was too late. She saw the flashing red letters that spelled out "KILL" right before he hit the execute button.

"Don't!"

Dr. Niles mashed the command and the entire space she'd escaped from flashed crimson with annihilation runes followed by white smoke pouring in.

"I was so bloody close to finding the answer."

Dr. Niles grimaced.

"I'm sorry. It's protocol. You're lucky you survived it. I got an alert and turned on the video feed around the time you flipped the table. Good thinking, but we couldn't let whatever that was try to get out."

"The other body!"

Dr. Niles yanked out his phone and dialed the morgue.

"Randy, I need you to...what? Really? Dammit. Okay. Well, it's what you had to do. Thanks. We'll send a team down later to see if there's anything left to analyze."

When he pulled the phone away from his ear, she said, "Let me guess. The body exploded with vines and they had to burn it."

Dr. Niles sighed.

"Better than the whole hospital getting infected."

"Aye, true. But I felt like I was getting somewhere."

"Anything good?"

Lily was about to give Dr. Niles her theory about another realm, but then she thought about how quickly he'd appeared to destroy the body and how it appeared Dr. Fairlight had been corrupted somehow.

"No. I was bloody close, but not close enough. Everything we might have learned was in that room."

As she finished speaking, the smoke cleared, revealing a pile of ash on the table and in river-like lines across the floor. The equipment was charred black.

"Don't worry," said Dr. Niles. "I fear that it won't be long before we have another sample to analyze. Maybe too many. You should take the rest of the afternoon off. You earned it."

Under normal circumstances, Lily would have taken Dr. Niles up on his offer, but she no longer trusted anyone in the hospital except for her friends. After stripping out of the moonsuit, Lily texted Damon and Remi and told them to meet her on the roof.

SIXTEEN

The rooftop picnic table was relaxing after the busy shift. Damon cradled a beer as he watched the colorful illusions in the second ward reflect off the Spire.

"Got any more of those?" asked Remi when she appeared.

He nodded towards the bucket of beers on ice. She grabbed one then rubbed her hands together as mist blew out of her mouth. Remi cast a weather enchantment then took a spot next to him.

"What do you think Lily wants to talk about?" he asked.

"Find out soon enough, but I bet it has something to do with the exploding body."

Damon hadn't heard, so Remi told him about what had happened.

"Too close. Again. I feel like we're running out of good luck."

"Yeah," said Remi, frowning then taking a long swig.

"Any luck with your parents?"

Remi exhaled deeply.

"Nothing new."

The scuff of footsteps alerted them to Lily's arrival. Her hair was shaped weird, which Damon assumed was from the moonsuit.

"Heard you had a close one."

"Too bloody close. And that eejit Dr. Niles burned the body. I was near an answer."

"Good enough to share?"

Lily grabbed a beer from the bucket and joined them at the picnic table.

"You remember when I told you about the weird thing I saw in the Fae Court? I think I saw signs of it in the vines. I was trying to narrow down which realm it might have come from, but it wasn't anything that was in the reference books. Or at least the hospital ones. They only cover the common realms. If it was anything strange or exotic, it wouldn't be there."

"I wish Dr. Decker was here," said Remi.

Damon nodded as he finished his beer and grabbed a second, popping off the cap with a twist of his wrist.

"Speaking of Decker," said Damon, "I got a postcard in the mail the other day. It was from Costa Rica."

"What did it say?"

"No one knows anything and the ones that do are lying. Follow the facts, listen to your gut, and don't forget to breathe, or you'll never find the answer."

"Ha, breathe," said Remi, tugging on the mask around her neck. "He got that one wrong this time."

Damon lifted his beer in the air.

"He's not wrong, but I don't know if we're going to have enough time to find the answer before it all goes to shit."

"We've got until the winter is over," Lily said grimly.

"You think?"

She nodded.

"It's affected by cold weather. Right now, it's really only spreading by whoever is creating it. But if it gets warm again, it'll be able to spread from person to person, and that's when things are really going to get bad."

"It's early December, so we've got a few months until spring," said Remi.

"I hope it's long enough," said Damon.

Remi tilted her head.

"Do you think what's going on with the hospital staff is connected to the Death Rot?"

Damon frowned.

"Possibly? Why else were you sent off to the EMT squad and Super Curse Wards where it was easier to come in contact with the Death Rot, and why did Dr. Broomfield try to poison me, or whatever it was he tried to give me. It's all connected, we just don't know how."

"Whatever happened to the alchemy project that you helped him with last year?" asked Lily.

Damon hung his head.

"Haven't heard a word about it since. Yeah, I've been thinking the same thing. That we actually helped them somehow. But I find it hard to believe that Dr. Broomfield is behind the Death Rot. For all his bluster, he does care about his patients."

"I'm going to disagree with you on this one," said Remi. "He's as rotten as those plants that tried to kill me and Lily. Face it, Damon. You just want to believe he's good because he's the one you need to get into the Institute."

"We should get the Horn," said Lily suddenly.

"It won't fix the corruption," said Damon.

"Not the corruption. This Death Rot. If we don't find a solution fast, it could take the whole city down."

"We have time."

"Not that much time," said Lily.

Remi shook her head.

"It's not safe. We're being watched. I'm afraid if we tried to use it, they'd figure out where we hid it. I'm just not ready to take that chance yet."

"Yet?" asked Damon.

Remi set her empty bottle on the table and leaned back as a helicopter flew overhead to the hospital landing pad.

"I agree with Lily. It's only a matter of time."

No one spoke for a long time after that while they finished the rest of the beers. Damon was the last to leave the roof. He stared across the nighttime city. How many millions of people were at risk if they couldn't find an answer? He shuddered and went back inside.

SEVENTEEN

The streets were covered in a slushy brown snow. The ambulance fish-tailed around corners, but Remi had grown to trust the driver, so she sat in the back throwing darts at a board they'd fixed to the ceiling. One of Paxton's throws hit a wire and flew back down, nearly catching Remi in the leg.

The radio lit up with chatter. Everyone held their breath while a number of emergencies in the city were given to the other rigs on duty.

"It's a mess out there," said Vasquez.

"They're saving the worst ones for us," said Paxton.

Vasquez grinned.

"Kamikaze Kids, ba-bee," she said, smashing knuckles with Paxton.

"How's your kid?" asked Remi as she thumbed the flight on the dart.

Vasquez got a faraway look with her mouth shifted to the side.

"She's a good kid. Nearly straight A's. Couldn't be prouder. Her Merlin scores aren't too bad either. She's considering the Halls, but there's plenty of time for those kinds of decisions."

The radio lit up again with a new round of assignments. Remi thought they'd been left off again when they were assigned a 269 in the second ward.

"Second ward?" asked Vasquez aloud. "Is someone on Glow Juice back at dispatch? We haven't seen the eastern half of the city since the Event."

"What's a 269? I don't recall that one," said Remi.

Paxton pulled out a stack of laminated sheets held by a metal ring. He ran his finger down the information before looking up with a perplexed expression.

"There isn't a 269."

Remi's entire body tightened up as if someone had wound the spring.

"I don't like this."

"Yeah, Green Shirt," said Vasquez, frowning. "This is strange. I don't even know how to prepare for this one."

"What's the address?" asked Remi tersely.

"It's for the Twilight Theater, right near the ring road opposite the seventh. It's a music venue."

The name sent alarm bells in Remi's head. The Horn of Bran Galed was also called the Twilight Horn. Was this a warning?

"I think we should treat this one as a hostile," said Remi, shifting to her knees to apply protective enchantments.

"A hostile? This isn't some twelfth ward pop-up bar run by one of the gangs, Remi. This club is legit. We can't go rolling into it like we're headed into a war zone," said Vasquez.

"You know I've been straight up with you about my past and how I think those bodies last month were left as a trap, right?"

Vasquez narrowed her gaze.

"You've been honest about the danger, but not the why."

"I wish I could. I really do."

Paxton lifted his shoulders, which was almost comical with his thick neck.

"If someone gets in our way, I'll give 'em a stone biscuit," he said, holding a fist.

"One minute," said Ansel through the open door.

"Get ready," said Vasquez.

"Lock and load," said Paxton, grabbing a shock baton and a tranquilizer gun loaded with a potent homemade knockout potion.

When they pulled up, the sidewalk was packed with people waiting to get into the venue. Remi slipped on her mask, grabbed her bags, and followed Paxton through the crowd, wishing she had her hands free for spellcasting. The people were more packed in the closer they got, with fans yelling at them as if they were trying to cut in line. Someone tried to reach their hand into one of her bags, so she kicked them in the ankle.

"What's the emergency?" asked Vasquez when they reached the bouncer, a guy with a thicker neck than Paxton.

A flat stare was followed by the bouncer removing the rope so they could enter the club.

"Front of stage."

Remi wracked her brain to see if she remembered the guy. Everything about this seemed off, and more likely was a trap.

"I don't like this," she shout-whispered to Vasquez as they continued into the crowded venue.

A band was playing inside. Thrumming bass notes pounded the air while electric guitars screamed into the void. The music was vaguely familiar, but she focused on her surroundings, investigating every face to make sure they weren't going to attack.

The nearer they got to the front, the more her entire body was on high alert. She kept expecting someone with vines crawling out of their mouth to grab her.

When they finally pushed through the last knot of people to reach the front of the stage, there was no one they could see that was injured.

"What's going on?" asked Vasquez, turning in a circle.

Remi had dropped her bags and had her hands up, ready to cast a spell, when the house lights focused on them and the music downshifted in a light beat.

"It's a trap, I can feel the Veil somewhere near," said Remi, but her comment was swallowed by the cheers from the crowd. She tried to force her way out, but she was easily pushed back into the open circle that had formed around her.

The band was playing behind her but she was too focused on her surroundings to notice until the words leaked into her brain.

"... she got me going halfway, heartache, all day. Charms, and whips, love and hips, with a spell I dance, that half-pint hex made me blow my chance..."

The world dropped out from beneath Remi. One moment, she was worried she was going to be attacked by an animated corpse filled with rotting vines from an unknown realm, the next she was blushing from her head to her toes.

Remi turned as the crowd's cheers grew in intensity. She pulled the mask around her neck. Standing on stage was the handsome lead singer of the Krakens, Gerard Lyons, who when she saw him last had been screaming at the top of his lungs in pleasure.

He cocked a grin and held his hand out for her to climb on stage.

"Punks and Pussies, may I present to you, Half-Pint Hex!"

The crowd went nuts. Vasquez's jaw was nearly on the floor. By the time Remi turned to Paxton in hopes that he would help her escape, he was laughing incredulously, and he grabbed her by the hips and lifted her onto the stage next to Gerard, who was continuing to sing the song.

Gerard grabbed her hand and held it up as if she'd just won a prize-fight. Desperate to get out of the limelight, she turned to the band, to see them each grinning maniacally at her. There were two guitarists, a bass player, and a translucent drummer. The reason she felt the presence of the Veil became clear, even if she didn't know how the band had gained a ghost drummer.

The entire crowd, minus her stunned rig-mates, sang along to the song, "Give a Load of This." Remi even found herself singing along since she'd listened to the song a few dozen times after it had come out.

The end of the song rose to an appropriate crescendo and the entire crowd went absolutely nuts, throwing beer into the air when it finished.

"We'll take a short break and be back soon!" shouted Gerard into the mic.

The next thing Remi knew she was being led backstage, still holding the lead singer's hand. She'd forgotten how handsome he was. Not the normal kind, but the almost supernatural version that made you wonder if he was part siren.

A minor ruckus behind them revealed Paxton and Vasquez, who'd forced themselves backstage.

They ended up in a small room filled with ratty lime green couches. The table was filled with empty bottles of beer, a half-eaten pizza, and a bucket of fried chicken.

"Hey," said Gerard when he turned around. "Thanks for being a good sport about that. When our tour was coming back through town, I knew I wanted to do something, but when I inquired about you at the hospital, they said you'd been transferred to the EMT group, so that's when I pulled some favors to get you here."

"I'm flattered..."

The rest of the band had thrown themselves on the couches, except for the ghost drummer girl, who stood near the back by the mirrors.

Someone handed Remi a fresh beer. She wasn't going to drink until she saw Vasquez and Paxton pounding down theirs.

"We really shouldn't stay long," she said.

"I think we can take a short break, Remi," said Vasquez with her arms around the back of the couch. "It's not like this happens very often."

When Remi looked up, Gerard was staring at her. He had nice eyes and the kind of mouth that was made for kissing. She felt a pang in her gut.

"You know, I haven't stopped thinking about that day."

Remi took a long drink as she was painfully aware that everyone in the room was trying to listen without making it obvious they were.

"It was an accident."

"Look," he said, leaning close. "It's not just about the pleasure, which was otherworldly, but I don't know, there's something about you that I haven't been able to find anywhere else. It was like I met this badass warrior from times past, but in the middle of a hospital. You seem like you've led an interesting life and you don't take shit from anyone."

Remi frowned, trying to remember that day and how he could have come to that conclusion.

"I'm not sure..."

"I am. I've been thinking about you for years."

He placed a hand along the side of her face, which made her whole body break out in tingles. She'd never thought of herself as the kind of woman who might swoon, but his magnetic presence was making it hard to think.

"I...I..."

"I know, Remi. I know. I feel it strongly too."

She shook her head.

"No. I don't feel it. This is just overwhelming. We were expecting an emergency."

He pulled his hand away as if her flesh was a fire.

"If this was too much, I'd be happy to meet you for coffee or dinner sometime. Anywhere you want. I'd just love to get to know you."

Remi couldn't believe it.

"Gerard. As flattering as this is, I've got someone," she said, looking into his perfect face.

"You do?"

As she mustered the thoughts to speak, she remembered Damon's desire to work at the Institute, which wasn't in the city of sorcery. She feared they were destined to be apart. For a moment, she imagined herself kissing Gerard, but then remembered his unusual lifestyle.

"I do. He works at Golden Willow. He's a great healer, and a were-wolf too."

"Oh."

The disappointment in his face was endearing. He was clearly unused to being turned down.

"I'm sorry. But thank you for tonight. I won't forget it."

Gerard leaned forward and she thought he was trying to kiss her, but he put his arms around her shoulders and gave her a gentle squeeze.

"Good luck."

Before she could say another word, he left the green room with his chin tucked to his chest. Everyone made a show of looking the other way, or engaging in conversation even though they'd just been completely silent while listening.

Remi was going to head out, until she remembered the ghost drummer in the corner.

"Hi?"

"I'm Katie," she said, twirling a physical drumstick.

"How are you doing that?"

Katie smirked.

"It's not that unusual. There are ghost taxis."

"Yeah, but..."

"You have a connection to the Veil."

Remi recoiled.

"You can tell?"

"It's obvious for someone like me."

"How did you get like this?"

Katie looked askance.

"It's a long story."

Vasquez put a hand on her shoulder.

"Hey, sorry to interrupt, but we just got a call for an 818 in the eleventh. Seems our little side adventure has to come to an end."

Remi turned but the ghost drummer held her back. The look on her face was fraught with concern.

"Be careful."

"Why? Do you know something?" asked Remi.

"I sense Devlin..."

"Devlin? The Stranger?"

Katie screwed up her face.

"Dammit. I wasn't supposed to say that."

"Do I need to be worried about Devlin?"

Katie shook her head.

"No, but...never mind, I've said too much already."

"Katie, please, anything you can—"

The incorporeal girl faded from view, leaving Remi staring at the wall.

She let herself be led out of the music venue through a back door. When they were on the sidewalk, Vasquez looked at her and shook her head.

"The girl from the Kraken song has been in my rig the entire time and I didn't know it."

"It's not something I advertise," said Remi.

"And I can't believe you turned him down. I would have given my left ovary for a night with Gerard."

"I can recommend you..."

Vasquez pushed her towards the open doors of the rig.

"Get in, Remi. We've got lives to save."

EIGHTEEN

The machines hooked up to the second year, Daryna, wheezed as they pumped super-cooled oxygen into her lungs. Lily approached the bed in her moonsuit.

The fear in Daryna's eyes was palpable. Everyone joining Aura Healers knew they would be putting their life at risk, but everyone secretly thought that the danger didn't apply to them.

"I should have known he was going to grab my mask. There was something in his eyes..."

"Daryna. Don't," said Lily, putting her marshmallow glove on the girl's arm. "You were doing all the right protocols at the time. You didn't know he was going to rip your mask off and breathe in your face."

"Is he still alive?"

Lily was glad for the moonsuit because it hid her reaction.

"He died this morning."

The death had been like the other bad Death Rots. An explosion of rotten vines and other plant material. They'd had him in the incineration room, which made the end as neat as a bonfire.

Daryna stared into her lap as mist hit the interior of the see-through mask.

"That's not gonna be you if I can bloody help it," said Lily. "This preventative treatment should keep you safe until we find a cure. Trust me, we're going to find one."

Daryna shivered.

"I'm so cold even with the enchantments."

"It's the only thing keeping the Death Rot at bay, but I can bring you some extra blankets."

"That would be awesome," she said, though her voice didn't match the words.

"Is there anything else I can get you?"

"A cure..."

"Daryna."

She lifted up her phone.

"I've got everything I need. All the channels are boring-ass old people stuff anyway."

Lily couldn't help but chuckle despite the dire circumstances. She grabbed Daryna's hand and gave it a squeeze.

"Why would he do that to me?" Daryna asked in a voice that suggested it was an internal thought, not directed at Lily.

But Lily had an awful suspicion. The two of them looked alike. Not completely, but the second year had messy curls, pale skin, and freckles. Their facial features were different, but if someone was sick and in the throes of a compulsion, they looked close enough. The patient would have been sent up to the Super Curse Ward next, and since he hadn't exhibited signs of the Death Rot, it was likely that he could have gotten close to her.

"I'm going to go. I'll get one of the nurses to bring you some heavy blankets. Text me if you need anything. I'll be your personal healer while you're in this ward. I'll treat you like one of my sisters."

"Why are you being so nice to me? I know I was a disaster of a first year," said Daryna.

"Because you're a healer and we're all screwups our first year."

"From what I hear, that wasn't you."

Lily leaned in close.

"Technically, it wasn't my first year. I've been a healer since I was a wee lass."

Lily gave her hand another squeeze and left the isolation chamber. The faint runes on the wall reminded Lily that it was a kill room. If something went wrong, Daryna would be condemned to an inferno and turned to ash.

After she removed the moonsuit and put it into the cleaning machine, Lily leaned against the wall and massaged the bridge of her nose with her forefingers.

At the nurses station, Lily caught the patter of the weatherman talking about the next few weeks. She was expecting another snowstorm since that's what the forecast had been a few days ago.

"…the jet stream shifted north, which means, guess what, instead of snow, we're going to be seeing warmer spring weather for the next few weeks. Starting tomorrow."

Lily froze.

Her whole body went into shock. She'd thought they'd have a few more months of winter. It was only the first week of January. They shouldn't be having a heat wave, but here it was.

Dr. Niles was off today, so she asked one of the nurses if Dr. Fairlight was in the hospital. Another nurse mentioned she'd just seen her on the first floor talking to some potential donors.

Lily took the stairs rather than the elevator. Since the Death Rot, she didn't like being in confined spaces with others, especially knowing someone was trying to infect her and her friends.

She found Dr. Fairlight at the entrance having just said goodbye to a group of older men with graying hair.

"Dr. Fairlight, I'm bloody glad I found you."

The older woman's forehead knitted.

"Is there an emergency?"

"Aye. It's the weather. We're lookin' to have a warm streak starting in the next few days."

"That sounds lovely. I'd like to leave my winter jacket at home if I could."

"No, you don't understand. The Death Rot. It's not spreading right now because of the cold weather. If it warms up, it's going to find an easy time of jumping from host to host. We'll be overrun. More than my first year and maybe worse than the Event."

"Healer de Meath. This kind of fearmongering doesn't become you."

The tone of the rebuke didn't sound like the Dr. Fairlight she knew.

"Fearmongering? We're a bloody hospital in the middle of the city of sorcery. We deal with awful, magical crises all the time. This isn't fearmongering. It'll be a bloodbath if we don't start preparing."

Dr. Fairlight frowned.

"I spoke to Aleksander Grimm about this plant. Sent him some samples. He said it's not contagious and that there's nothing to worry about."

"Patron Grimm..."

It wasn't so much a question, but a stone-dead worry.

"Yes. Patron Grimm. Head of Arcane Phytology. If anyone can understand this plant, it's him."

"Always check for parasites," said Lily under her breath.

"What was that?"

"Nothing, Dr. Fairlight. I'm very sorry that I bothered you."

The Chief of Staff gave her a head tilt before heading the other way.

Lily wandered around the first floor in a daze. She knew she should be getting back to her ward, but connections were being made, and she didn't want to interrupt her thoughts. Either Patron Grimm, much like Dr. Fairlight and Dr. Broomfield, was compromised, or he was one of the people behind it. Remi's once-parents had said that a big shot was behind the pursuit of the Horn. What if it was Patron Grimm? He seemed to be lurking around the edges of everything going on in the city and related to the hospital.

She found herself near the ER when a nurse announced that three howlers were set to arrive. Three howlers. Lily's curiosity drew her towards the automatic doors at the same time the three vehicles pulled up.

The first held a man on a gurney, a manticore spike jutting from his chest. He looked like the victim of a vicious attack, but the chains holding him down told a different story. He'd been stabbed in self-defense.

The second ambulance was an older woman who'd had a stroke. She was quickly shuttled to the surgery department. The rig sped away to the next job.

The third ambulance had stopped on the sidewalk past the entrance and it still hadn't moved. Lily approached cautiously and then remembering she didn't have her protective gear, stood back.

Two gurney runners came speeding out with masks on and ran to the back of the rig.

"Hey."

They turned back to her.

"I haven't seen anyone come out. Not even the EMTs."

The two runners looked at each other. They threw hands, then the loser stepped forward and put his hand on the silver bar.

He cranked it down and yanked the door open, stepping out of the way at the same time. The rot hit Lily's nose right away. Then she saw the carnage. The entire interior was covered in rotting vines, even the two EMTs who'd had the unfortunate luck to have picked up that patient.

Lily checked back to the sky. To the west of the city was a rolling storm front. The warm weather was about to arrive.

NINETEEN

Damon watched as Lily paced the edge of the hospital roof while chewing on her fingernails. She kept staring at the brooding sky, which was threatening rain during the evening.

"Lily, are you going to tell me what's going on?"

The Irish witch glanced over then went back to her pacing and mumbling. He'd never seen her this rattled and it was spooking him.

Remi appeared a short time later still in her EMT jumpsuit.

"I came as soon as you messaged. The Kids dropped me off before they went to the next emergency."

"Aren't you gonna be in trouble?" he asked.

"They'll cover for me."

"Alright, Lily. Stop freaking me out and tell us what's going on."

She stared at the incoming storm once again before facing off with them, arms crossed, chewing her lower lip.

"We've been eejits. All of us."

"What do you mean?" he asked.

"The Death Rot. What Hall would be perfectly suited to creating such an awful affliction?"

"Coterie?" he asked.

"No, think about it. Arcane Phytology. Aleksandr Grimm's Hall."

He shared a glance with Remi, who appeared equally skeptical.

"He killed the White Worm our first year."

"The same as a mob boss would kill one of his own if he thought they might squeal on 'em. But it's not just that. There's a warm front coming tonight and I went to warn Dr. Fairlight about it so we might prepare for an explosion of the Death Rot, but she told me there was nothing to worry about. That she'd talked to Patron Grimm and he told her that it wasn't contagious."

"Merlin's tits," said Remi, shaking her head. "Even a first year would know this shit is highly contagious."

"What if Grimm was behind everything that first year and the White Worm was just his patsy? Grimm could be using those mind-control worms on Dr. Fairlight, or Broomfield, or anyone else for that matter."

"What if that's what he was trying to get me to drink?"

"There weren't any worms in it," said Remi, punching him in the shoulder.

"Unless he'd put an illusion on it, or wait, what if it didn't need the worms anymore, but it was just a potent elixir..."

Damon put a hand to his forehead.

"The extract. It would be perfect for that. Blood and bone, I gave him the solution on how to control people without the worms."

"Which means that Dr. Broomfield is in on it," said Remi.

"Not necessarily. He could have been infected by a worm, or something else."

Lily slapped her hand on the picnic table.

"As much as I'd like to debate Grimm's guilt or innocence, that's not the immediate problem."

She gestured to the bruised purple clouds, which crackled with lightning.

"When that warm front gets here, the Death Rot is going to spread like wildfire."

"What can we do?" asked Damon.

"You know what we have to do. We have to get the Horn. It's the only way. There's no way in a million years we'd be able to find a cure before it arrives."

"No," said Remi, shaking her head. "This whole Death Rot thing is probably to get us to reveal its location. We were smart by hiding it right away where we did."

"The Death Rot is pretty bad, but the Horn could be worse. We agreed not to reveal it," said Damon.

"You don't think I know?" she asked, throwing her hands wide. "They almost got me before. Which reminds me, how does the Caoránarch fit in? It's not like the Patron of Arcane Phytology comes with control of a Fae demon dragon."

"If that's what it is at all," said Lily. "But I don't care about Grimm right now. We need to get the Horn before it's too late. Do you really want the twins to get infected? Isn't Nat on patrol? And Talia has a big show coming up? They're both in danger. The whole city is."

Damon squeezed his eyes shut thinking about his sisters. If anything happened to them...

"Okay, fine. We get the Horn. Remi?"

They looked to her. She stared back defiantly then uncrossed her arms.

"We get the Horn. But we can't be seen leaving the hospital. I can make it there no problem, but you two are going to be an issue. We need a way to get you out without anyone seeing."

Lily snapped her fingers.

"I have an idea. Damon, how good are you with confined spaces?"

TWENTY

The Kamikaze Kids let Remi out at the morgue processing center in the third ward. The building was unassuming, without any obvious signs that suggested what it was. To her surprise, there were no apparitions lurking about, but since they hadn't died here—the place was for body storage and analysis—it made sense.

A scrawny guy in glasses was sitting behind the counter reading a book titled *No One Goes Home Alone*. He glanced over the pages with an eyebrow raised.

"I'm Remi."

He set the book down.

"Roger. Follow me."

The jangle of keys was followed by them heading deeper into the building where it smelled like embalming fluids.

"Thanks for doing this."

Roger looked at her sideways.

"Yeah, right."

She held out a jar filled with tiny bones.

"Are those really...?"

"Fresh from the Veil."

"Wicked," said Roger, shaking the glass before his eyes. "Are you really an Ossarii?"

"That's the rumor."

He keyed them through an inner door. The room was ice cold and stacked with rectangular wooden boxes.

"The latest shipment should be over here," said Roger, approaching a pile of six coffin boxes. "They're due to head to their respective funeral homes tonight. Is this some kind of fetish thing? Because I can leave if you want to get freaky. No extra charge."

"Got a crowbar?"

"Yeah."

Roger produced one after digging into a tool cabinet. Remi tapped on the boxes until she heard a muffled response.

"Can you help me move these?"

Using a sliding crane that moved around the ceiling, they freed two boxes from the bottom. Remi popped the top of one using the crowbar, and the coffin lid squeaked open, revealing a sweaty Damon.

"Oh, finally. That was starting to get to me."

Roger's mouth was hanging open.

"This isn't going to be a problem, is it?" asked Remi as she opened Lily's box.

"Not at all. Your gift more than covers my silence, though I am curious."

"I wouldn't be," said Lily, climbing from her coffin.

The Kamikaze Kids were waiting for them when they left the processing facility.

Remi introduced her friends to the team. Vasquez eyed Damon up and down with a smirk.

"I can see why you turned down Gerard, though I might have asked for a one-night Hall Pass if it'd been me."

Damon blushed as he took a spot along the wall.

"Be nice," laughed Remi.

The ambulance took them west to the enclave, where they were dropped off in a narrow alleyway.

"We'll be back in two hours."

Once they were gone, Lily cast a spell that theoretically would detect if anyone was scrying them.

"We're clean as a leprechaun's butthole."

Remi led them through the back way into the enclave past guards who'd been warned they were coming. When they reached a secluded corner of the old factory, Dr. Marcie stepped out from behind a rusting boiler.

"Thanks for seeing us on short notice, Dr. Marcie."

The clinic doctor had her hair in two long braids covered in bones and other trinkets.

"I thought you weren't coming back here anytime soon."

"It's an emergency."

Dr. Marcie led them down old metal stairs that rattled at every step. The basement level was covered in oil spills and leftover chemicals from the 1950s and it smelled like rat shit. A thick steel door required a spell from Dr. Marcie to unlock.

"I'll stay out here."

Remi had no idea what the room had been in the old factory, but it was a perfect hiding spot for the Horn.

The runed box in the corner had cost them a considerable sum. Theoretically, it would keep anyone from detecting the Horn's presence, if they could believe the salesman who'd sold it to them. Undoing the protective enchantment required all three of them to be present and perform the spell.

The Horn of Bran Galed was about four feet long, a black drinking horn with streaks of white and gold inlays. It looked like it belonged in a museum, not in a box in the bowels of an old factory.

"Who wants to do the honors? Lily? You did it last time," said Remi.

Her Irish friend shook her head.

"Not this time. I fear I'd just try to fix Medb again, and having that much power in my hands gives me the bog shakes," said Lily.

"Definitely not me," said Damon, right away. "Sorry."

Remi sighed as she stared at the powerful artifact.

"The surroundings aren't exactly fitting the weight of what we're doing. I feel like we should be doing this in a great hall, or at a Court of Fae."

"The hinge points of history are rarely the big flashy events, but the small decisions in the dark that create a cascade of outcomes," said Lily, crossing her arms.

Remi raised an eyebrow.

"That was heavy."

Damon stared at the ceiling.

"We should get this over with. The longer this box is open, the greater the chance that someone can find it."

Remi pulled three collapsible plastic bottles out of her pack. She'd gotten them at an outdoor store. The sales rep had extolled the product as a way to stay hydrated on the trail that could be collapsed down for easy storage when not being used.

"Feels a little sacrilegious to be putting this in these, but I didn't want to take anything from the hospital."

She handed the bottles to Damon, who would collect the liquid once she summoned it. Remi held her hands over the Horn and closed her eyes. It wasn't lost on her that the artifact could produce liquids that would make her rich and famous. Everything her parents had always wanted was now in the palm of her hands and she was choosing not to be selfish.

There was a time the decision would have been difficult, but she'd come to enjoy service for others. Sure, the rewards weren't great and the hours were brutally long, but she'd never felt as satisfied as she did in the Hospice Ward.

Remi placed her hands on the Horn. The surface was cool and sent a tremor through her arms. She couldn't decide if it was her imagination or the thrumming of untold power.

There'd been no instruction on how to use the Horn, so she improvised, speaking aloud at the same time she imagined what she desired.

"We need a safe drinkable vaccine for the Death Rot, a replicable solution that will protect people from being infected, and will cure anyone who contracts it."

At first, Remi didn't think it'd worked because nothing was happening, then she saw the surprise on Damon's face as he held the first bottle closer to the end of the Horn. A pale, milky liquid streamed out, quickly filling the first bottle. A few precious drops were lost as he maneuvered the second bottle into position and then the third in short order.

Remi was worried that the vaccine would continue flow onto the floor, but as soon as the third bottle was filled to the brim, it stopped.

"I should have bought more bottles."

Damon closed the third lid.

"If it's replicable, then we shouldn't have an issue."

Remi frowned at the bottle in her hands.

"How much does it take to make us immune?"

"Aye, good question," said Lily. "I think I have a solution. We can give a small amount to Daryna and see if she improves."

"Let's get out of here. That storm should be hitting the city in a few hours."

Returning the Horn to its protected hiding spot helped relieve the tension in her shoulders. Dr. Marcie led them back to the Kamikaze rig, which took them back to the Golden Willow EMT shed.

"I'll take this one right to Jeb for replication," said Damon, holding up his bottle.

"I'll use Daryna to confirm how much it takes for a cure, which should be the same as immunity," said Lily.

"The third one will stay with me, and once you give me the word, I'll pass this around the EMTs. They're the first line of defense for the city."

Her friends headed back to Golden Willow and Remi got back into the rig with the Kids.

"Where to, Half-Pint?" asked Vasquez.

Holding the priceless cure to the Death Rot in her hands, Remi felt like it was best to keep it separate from the others in case something happened to them in the hospital.

"Let's take a tour of the city and watch the storm roll in."

Vasquez shot her a wink.

"You got it, Half-Pint."

TWENTY-ONE

The bright blue sunny skies had Lily checking out the window every time she passed one. The temperature on her phone said it was nearly seventy outside, a record for mid-January. She kept expecting a wave of ambulances even though Remi said she'd warn her if things changed in the city.

"How are you feeling in there?" Lily asked Daryna through the speaker.

The second year gave her an enthusiastic thumbs-up. They'd taken her off the chilled oxygen that morning and the enchantments had come back negative, except for some chest crud they thought was the dead vines once the vaccine had attacked them. A round of elixirs would help clean them out.

The initial vaccine direct from the Horn had been passed around their classmates, and the staff in the Super Curse Ward. Then as Jeb synthesized new vaccine, it was given to the ER, and then the other wards in order of potential exposure.

Lily was kind of surprised at how easily they'd been able to get the staff to take the vaccine, but the stories of the Death Rot, and that the Super Curse Ward was promoting it, helped with its acceptance. It also helped her know that Dr. Niles wasn't compromised like some of the other staff.

A text from Dr. Niles told her that Dr. Broomfield wanted to speak to her in the Aura Healers common area. The location was suspicious, but she knew better than to keep him waiting.

She arrived to find the rest of her class, minus Remi, who was with the Kamikaze Kids, sitting on the hard plastic chairs that had replaced the comfy couches. The whiteboard had been scrubbed clean.

"Hey, I heard you were behind getting us the vaccine," said Boon. "I don't know how you did it, but I don't feel so exposed now in the ER. Best thing that's happened in this hospital in a while."

The rest of the class added their thanks and congratulations while she shared a look with Damon, who lifted a single shoulder. Lily wasn't sure how she got associated with the cure rather than Damon.

"Anyone know why we're here?" she asked.

An answer from Boon was cut short when everyone stiffened, announcing Dr. Broomfield's arrival. The door slammed behind him, rattling the blinds. His red-hot gaze settled on her before he checked back to the rest of the class.

"Who's behind it?"

The veins on his forehead pulsed with anger.

"An unauthorized and untested vaccine has been given out to the staff of Golden Willow without approval. Do you know the potential consequences if this vaccine is bad? It would destroy the hospital and leave the city crippled in the face of our oncoming threats."

No one spoke or made eye contact with Dr. Broomfield.

"I don't need your corroboration. I know where the vaccine origi-nated."

His gaze fell upon Lily.

"Do you have something to say?"

"No, sir."

His nose wrinkled with an internal snarl.

"Silence isn't an option. I know you're behind it. It has your grubby little bog witch fingers all over it. You've a long history of ignoring proto-cols and applying your folksy medicine despite the prohibitions. The staff has looked the other way thus far, but I can no longer ignore this blatant disregard for hospital norms."

"You're right," said Lily. "I made the vaccine. Someone had to since the hospital leadership was ignoring the problem."

Dr. Broomfield's lips curled with disgust.

"You're not smart or talented enough to create a vaccine like that. You got it from somewhere else, or someone else. You'd better tell me now or there will be grave consequences."

"There would've been grave consequences without it. Now we stand a chance against the Death Rot."

Dr. Broomfield pointed a finger into her face.

"Tell. Me. Now."

He looked to the rest of the class.

"Which one of you helped her? You? You? I can make an example out of all of you if you won't talk."

"They don't know nothin', cause they weren't involved. It was my bloody project, so don't you be slinging blame elsewhere."

"What did you say to me?" he asked as he puffed up his chest.

"You heard me well and clear. You don't have bog mud in your ears last I checked."

The corners of his eyes creased with anger. He listed to and fro before turning back.

"Tell me now," he began in a quiet, intense voice. "Tell me how and who else did it and I'll go lenient on you. There's a slim chance you can stay in Aura Healers, but you'd better spill your guts. Everything."

Lily crossed her arms and stared back, channeling Biddy in her intensity.

"Fine, if you don't tell me then I'll have to assume that the rest of the class was in on it."

The sound of chairs shifting on the squeaky tile filled the room, but Lily never broke eye contact.

"You're right, Dr. Marcus Broomfield."

He startled with genuine surprise.

"I am? About what?"

At the second part, he leaned in suspiciously.

"That I'm to blame. That I used my bog witch magic to ensorcel the entire hospital and give them an untested vaccine. And you know, I don't have a bloody bit of regret. Not one ounce. You know why? Because you're a fooking eejit with his head so far up his ass I'm surprised your hair has any gray left in it."

"Lilith de Meath!"

Before he could continue, she leaned into his face.

"I quit."

"You can't."

"You're an eejit if you don't think I can. I can and I just did. You said it yourself, whoever is to blame should face the consequences, and that someone is me. So you can end your little witch hunt because you found her. The witch is me. And I'm a *bad* witch."

His incredulous look nearly made her burst out in laughter, but she kept up her glare until he broke eye contact. He stewed in his anger until his cheeks bloomed darker.

"I should call the Invictus PD on you..."

The threat hid the quiet muttering of a spell from somewhere in the room.

Dr. Broomfield pulled his phone out.

"That's just what I'll do. We'll charge you with attempted—"

Before he could finish speaking, Lily smelled the smoke. Dr. Broomfield did too.

The bottom hem of his white jacket burst into flames.

"Ah!"

He spun around trying to put it out, which only made the fire grow.

"Quick, put him out!" shouted Boon.

As Dr. Broomfield put his hands up, the entire class unleashed a variety of fire extinguishing spells onto him. There were slimes, smokes, a spray that looked like year-old ketchup, other unusual liquids, and at least one audible fart noise that came with the onslaught of spell casting.

Dr. Broomfield ripped off his jacket and threw it on the ground, but the class continued to pelt him with their unusual and disgusting liquids until he fled down the hallway.

"Oh, bloody hell, you shouldn't have done that but I won't forget it."

The class circled around Lily.

"I can't believe you quit," said Damon.

"Not like I had a choice. He would have forced me out either way, better to go out on my terms." She looked down the hallway. "You know, he's going to be looking for revenge."

Boon winked.

"There's a lot more of us than him. He's going to regret what he did today."

The murmurings and head nods had her warm from within.

"I'd better get out of here before he comes through with his threat.

Thank you all."

After getting smothered with hugs, she pulled Damon aside and whispered, "Stay out of it with Broomfield. You're the only one left inside the hospital. We need your eyes and ears."

"Lily..."

"No arguing. Keep your nose out of it. Let Boon and the others torment him. We have bigger dragons to fry."

Damon leaned down and kissed her on the forehead. She pinched his cheek and hurried to the dormitory side of the complex to grab her things. Neko was on the bed napping when she arrived. It didn't take long to pack, and she headed out a side door as she saw a trio of police vehicles pull up front.

Lily smirked to herself before she headed into the night.

"I *am* a bad witch."

TWENTY-TWO

The young patient was staring out the window when Damon came in. Lisa barely turned her head to acknowledge his arrival, which made his heart sink.

"Hey."

"Hey," she responded without turning her head.

"I heard from a very good source that the cafeteria has chocolate ice cream today."

Lisa perked up.

"Really?"

Damon pulled two small cups out of his jacket.

"I might have even swiped some."

Lisa greedily grabbed the cup, pulled the lid off, and used the wooden spoon to scoop a hunk of chocolate ice cream into her mouth.

"Thank you," she said around a mouthful of ice cream.

He sat on the edge of the bed and ate with her in silence.

As she finished, he asked, "How are the visions?"

Lisa's eyes fluttered closed.

"The spells aren't working."

"It's going to take time to find a counter to the curse. I swear to you on my claws that we'll find one. Sooner than later."

"On your claws?"

He held out his hand and with an audible grunt, made them appear at the end of his fingers. She cooed with excitement and touched the ends.

"Can I see you change?"

Damon tilted his head.

"Maybe. If you promise to keep your chin up and let the doctors help you. I know it hurts sometimes, but it's the only way they're going to find a solution."

"Okay, Wolfboy," she said with a sly grin.

He mussed up her hair and rose from the bed.

"Promise me you'll try and I *might* let you see me change."

"I promise."

He left with a heavy heart. Dr. Lara met him in the hallway.

"Thanks for doing that. You're the only one that can get through to her."

"Whatever it takes, though I wouldn't mind finding that asshole who did that to her. I could put these claws to use for once."

Dr. Lara headed into Lisa's room at the same time Remi came rushing into the ward. The alarm on her face had his heart stopping. He knew something was wrong. Very, very wrong.

"Is Lily okay?"

"She's fine. Shaken up, but fine." Remi lowered her voice. "They took the Horn."

"What?"

"The Caoránarch hit the clinic hard. Lily said she was so focused on protecting everyone she forgot about the Horn. By the time the chaos had settled, she realized why it had shown up, and by that time the Horn was gone."

"Let's go."

The Kamikaze Kids rig was waiting for them outside. Ansel ran sirens all the way to the twelfth ward.

"Help the wounded," Remi said to the EMT team.

The enclave looked like it'd been hit by a cluster of bombs. The sheet metal walls had been torn asunder, with gaping wounds in them. People were crying in pain everywhere. He saw numerous bodies as he rushed towards the clinic, which was at the center of the enclave.

They found Lily kneeling over a young woman with dark gray skin and curled horn nubs on her forehead. The blank stare was a clue to her condition.

"They took the Horn."

"Who?" asked Damon.

"When the Caoránarch hit the enclave it was pure chaos. The residents put up a good fight, but even they were outmatched."

"The demon dragon took it?"

Lily's mouth came to a point.

"I saw men with antlers."

"Any you recognize?" asked Damon.

"Their faces were obscured by enchantment, but I saw which way they went and I can follow the trail. They left a swath of faez residue behind them a mile wide."

"We should go right away," said Remi.

"What about the wounded?" asked Damon.

"Damon's right," said Lily. "We can't leave them like this. Too many will die."

"Too many will die if we don't get the Horn back right away. Come on, you two, you know exactly what Dr. Decker would say about triage. Staying here is the wrong choice."

Damon hated that she was right, but he couldn't leave.

"You're right, but we can't," said Damon.

Lily put a hand on Remi's shoulder. "I'm not leaving either. I promised Dr. Marcie that I wasn't just joining the clinic because I didn't have anything else to do. We'll help them and then we'll head after the Horn. The trail won't go cold in that time."

"What if I can get people to replace us?" asked Remi.

"As long as they're being cared for," said Lily.

Remi disappeared back to the front of the enclave. She returned shortly after.

"There are at least five EMT teams on the way. They were just getting off their shift, but they've agreed to come here instead. Now can we leave?"

Damon shared a look with Lily who gave a short nod.

"Come on," said Remi. "Ansel will drive us."

TWENTY-THREE

The rig drove the entire way with its sirens. No one spoke as Lily steered the driver as she sniffed out the trail left by the Caoránarch and the antlered men.

"We don't know it's him," said Remi at one point, receiving a frown from her friend.

"It's him. It has to be Aleksandr. Think about it, Remi."

She did. It wasn't that she disagreed. Everything fit. From their first year with the White Worm, to his cosplaying as the Wild Hunt at his Society retreat, to his expertise with magical plants. Everything made sense.

"It means he was the one that put my parents on the path to getting killed. He was the one that changed my life. Everything. I don't know if I'm ready to deal with that."

"You'd better figure it out soon, we're almost there," said Lily.

It hadn't taken long after they left the twelfth ward enclave to figure out that they were headed to the Society of the White Hart. Between the antler helmets and the general direction of the faez trail, it'd been pretty obvious.

Ansel dropped them off two blocks away. Remi sent him back to the others.

"What are we looking for again?" asked Lily.

"Oh yeah, you weren't here last time. It's the Ane's Chic House, which is at 180 Crowley Avenue, right between the One Spell and the Hi-Lonesome Boutique. It's protected by a powerful Look Away enchantment."

"I can fix that," said Lily, and she put an enchantment on their eyes that helped them see past the illusion.

The front door was a carved darkwood with a relief that displayed the badge of the Society. Illusionary windows covered the brick walls.

"What do we do?" asked Damon. "It's not like we can go in the front door. It's got to be guarded."

"We'll try the service entrance."

With Lily's seeing spell, they found the illusionary brick wall. The back entrance looked less imposing than the one on the street.

"Now what?" asked Damon.

"Not excited about going in there without some serious protections. Grimm is a patron, and I'm sure the others in there are no joke. I'd sooner tangle with a bar full of drunken Fomorians," said Lily.

Remi bit her lower lip.

"Then we wait until he's gone," said Remi. "We have to sneak in and steal the Horn back. He's clearly brought it here."

"That's great," said Damon. "But even if he's not here, this place is sure to have a metric ton of wards protecting it. We can't go waltzing in and definitely not looking like ourselves."

Remi snapped her fingers.

"Exactly. I know what we need to do, or who we need to see. Come on."

When they reached the sidewalk, three black SUVs were waiting outside. To their surprise, Aleksandr appeared along with another man that Remi didn't recognize.

"That's the mayor," whispered Damon.

"What are they saying?"

Damon waved her off, so she slipped behind the wall. When she heard a door close, she punched Damon in the arm.

"What did they say?"

"I was going to tell you." He sighed and hung his head. "It's not good. The mayor was saying that he's not going to run next term and will endorse Aleksandr."

"With the Horn, the mind-control parasites or however he's corrupting them, and now the mayor's endorsement, he'll be a shoo-in to win, and then he could do just about anything," said Remi.

Once the SUVs were gone, they hurried to a different corner and called a taxi. The entire ride to the eleventh, Remi formulated what she was going to say. She hadn't spoken to Warnock since her once-parents had disappeared into an abyss inside the Veil. It was bringing back gut-wrenching emotions she thought she'd gotten past.

The regular bartender was working behind the counter at the Charm & Hammer. He started to speak, but she pointed a finger at him and he held his hands up.

At the bottom of the stairs past the secret door, Remi barged into Warnock's office. The dreadlocked owner was sitting on a couch with a beautiful woman with two different colored eyes and platinum hair weaved into a beehive.

"What's going on?" asked the woman.

Warnock stood, an angry retort on his lips, but then he stopped and his expression broke. He leaned over to the woman.

"I'm going to need a bit. Head into the bar and have a drink."

The woman huffed and stormed away on her high heels.

"Remi..."

The softness of her name broke down her defenses. She hadn't planned on thinking about her parents but standing before one of their oldest friends sent her thoughts tumbling.

A blustering sob shot from her lips and before she knew it, she was surrounded by Warnock's comforting arms. The tears flowed like rivers, even when she told herself she needed to stop and focus on the problem at hand.

Some time later, and after a quick introduction to her friends who had been standing in the back quietly, he led her to the couch and handed her a box of tissues. Then he went to his little bar and poured a round of whiskeys for all four of them.

"Does this mean what I think it means?" asked Warnock when he sat across from her.

Remi nodded.

"Was it the Big One?"

"It was."

He leaned back in the couch, shaking his head, which made his dreads dance around his face.

"I knew that shit would get them in the end."

"They're not my real parents," she spit out.

"What?"

Warnock leaned onto his knees.

"They're not my parents. They admitted it once I figured it out."

"Wait? You were there?"

"I was."

"The job?"

Remi squeezed back her emotions.

"We pulled it off."

Warnock leaned back with a whistle.

"You were always the best of them."

"But they weren't my parents."

He shrugged.

"The problem now is someone stole it and we need it back."

Warnock tilted his head.

"You know they were always working for some heavy hitters. It might be time to step away and cut your losses."

"We know, but we don't care," said Remi. "This is too important."

"Every job seems important, but you have to know when to walk away."

"This isn't one of those times, Warnock. Bad shit is going to happen if we don't get it back. Real bad. The Patron of Arcane Phytology is behind it. It seems he's been behind a lot of stuff for a long time."

"How bad?"

"Apocalyptic. With the artifact he has, he can do just about anything he wants."

"Then maybe it's a good time to get out of Invictus. I've got good friends in other realms. You all could come too."

"No," said Remi, right away. "I'm not running from this. We're the ones that made it possible, so we have to stop it."

Warnock snorted softly.

"You really did it. You really did."

"What?"

"Changed your life. Got out of their shadow and made it your own. I'm proud of you, Remi. So for that reason, and that reason only, I'll help you, if it's in my power."

"We need disguises. Not rubber mask, or makeup bullshit, but the real heavy hitting magical face changing stuff."

"And what makes you think I have that kind of materials on hand?"

"Because you were never an idiot like my parents. You were always prepared and knew when to walk away. You even knew enough to get out of that game," she said, gesturing to their surroundings.

He raised his glass of amber liquid.

"You know me well."

Warnock disappeared into a hidden hallway. A few minutes later, he came back with three golden masks.

"These are very pricy. I want them back."

"Thanks, Uncle Warnock."

He walked them to the secret stairs that led to the old bar.

"I'm so sorry about your parents."

"They were your friends too."

"But they were your parents. I know, I know. But in their own weird way, they were. They made you who you are."

"Do you have any idea...who, like, might be..."

Warnock gave a tight shake of the head.

"Sorry, Remi."

"I had to ask."

TWENTY-FOUR

Back at the service entrance, Lily waited with her friends for someone to come out. It took longer than they wanted. Damon kept arguing to go in, but even Lily knew that was a bad idea.

Finally, two workers came out in their black pants and white button-downs. A quick spell incapacitated them, placing them in a semi-comatose state that could be used for minor surgeries. Bill Taster and Molly Tuttle were the names on their badges.

"You two go in," said Lily. "They're each about your size and I'm afraid I can't shake my accent. I'll grab a third if one comes out alone, but we can't wait."

They used the golden masks to capture the faces of the unconscious workers. Once they had them on, Lily couldn't tell that it was her friends, especially after they'd donned the workers' outfits.

"Don't take stupid chances," said Lily, pointing directly into Remi's chest where the employee badge was located. "And let me put these on you, so I can find you when I get inside."

Using a couple of four-leaf clovers one of her patients had given her last week, Lily put an enchantment on them that would help her locate them inside the Society building.

Once her friends went in, Lily stayed outside with the two unconscious workers behind the smelly blue dumpster. Twenty minutes later, a group of four workers headed out, talking of hitting the local smoke bar. When she heard one of them mention they were the last of the shift change, she knew she had to take a chance.

Lily waited until they were outside on the sidewalk to follow them out. She lurked behind at a distance, until they stopped at a traffic crossing and then she hurried up, and keeping the golden mask held against her chest, triggered the face-stealing spell.

Then as the light changed and everyone moved to cross at once, she let her legs clip the woman next to her, and they tumbled to the concrete together.

"What the hell?" asked the girl as she struggled to disentangle herself.

"Oi, sorry, I've made an ass of myself."

"Damn right you have," said the girl, scowling.

When they were getting pulled to their feet, Lily shoved the girl's badge into her pocket.

"Sorry, I'm so embarrassed."

Lily ducked her head and went the other way, perpendicular to the direction of the Society workers.

She circled around the block, proud of her lift until she returned to the hidden alleyway to find out that the face on the mask didn't match the badge. She'd somehow grabbed the guy's face rather than the girl that she thought she had.

"Great, my badge says Denise White, but I don't look like her at all."

The other problem was she didn't have the white button-down or black pants, but she hated knowing that her friends were inside risking themselves while she was outside.

Lily stood by the workers' entrance, psyching herself up to go inside despite having mismatched disguise and badge, and not wearing the right uniform.

"You can do it, Lily de Meath. You've Greenwalked to the Court of Summer and survived a Tomb in the Veil. Surely this can't be as bad."

She'd just about convinced herself to go in when she heard the scuff of footsteps.

"Hey, you're the bitch that ran into me. And you've got my badge!"

The girl reached into a pocket, producing a plastic whistle. Lily did the first thing that came to mind, and blasted her with a force bolt. The impact threw the girl five feet onto her back, landing hard onto the concrete, while the whistle tumbled out of her hand.

"I'm sorry, I truly am, but I had no choice."

Lily repaired the girl's bleeding head before dragging her behind the dumpster, stealing her clothes, and redoing the mask spell. Once she had the right face, she headed into the back entrance.

The doorway led to a locker area next to a bustling kitchen. She peeked through the gap to see a half dozen cooks working the stoves and chopping vegetables. The smells were divine. She saw one chef throw a lobster into a pot while another was plating a tray of appetizers.

When the kitchen was at peak chaos, Lily swooped through and grabbed the finished tray and quickly scooted through the swinging doors while a chef yelled at her. But she knew there was no way he would follow and cause a scene.

The plush carpeted hallway led two different directions. She followed the quiet murmuring of conversation until she reached a grand hall. The amount of darkwood, mahogany, and dead supernatural animals was staggering. She'd stepped out next to a stuffed camazotz, or death bat, that loomed menacingly over the party.

Milling about the large area were at least two dozen men and women, with others seated at the little corner areas enjoying appetizers and drinks. Lily was certain someone would see her and know that she wasn't who the badge said she was, but then an older man she thought might be a famous thunderball player strolled past and snatched a handful of treats from her tray.

Lily scanned the room for her friends, but she saw neither Remi's nor Damon's disguises. There were other rooms, so maybe they were there. So she strode into the space, keeping her head down, but watching with her peripheral vision.

§

Damon couldn't believe the people who were at the Society hall. In the first five minutes since he'd taken a tray of champagne into the open sky room, he'd seen at least three patrons and a half dozen other famous people that he hadn't realized were members of the Society of the White Hart.

The ceiling had been replaced with an illusion of a brilliant night sky. The Milky Way rotated slowly, with the occasional shooting star descending past the horizon. Damon had to remind himself that he wasn't new and shouldn't be gawking at the sights.

He tried to stay moving, getting close enough to the knots of people that they could scoop off a glass, but not so close that they might notice he was in disguise. He hated the feeling that he was always a minor mistake or fated chance away from being discovered. Damon didn't know how Remi could have done this as a career before Aura Healers. The anxiety alone was worse than even the most difficult patient.

When his tray only had two glasses, he stood against the wall and examined the other exits, thinking about places the Horn might be hidden. Before he'd entered the Society, he was certain that they were all in on the heist, and they'd be celebrating their victory, but listening to the conversations proved that most were blissfully unaware.

Aleksandr had probably corrupted a smaller subset of the Society, though Damon doubted that would last long now that he owned the Horn. A simple request would produce an elixir that could enslave the rest of them. As far as he knew, the city could have already been taken over and they were just there to witness his ascension.

Damon spotted an unmistakable blonde coif of hair wander into the chamber and head straight for a slight, gray-skinned maetrie in the corner. Patron Celesse D'Agastine. The head of the Honorable Order of Alchemists. He wanted to listen in on the conversation, especially when he saw how heatedly she spoke to the older maetrie, but she turned and strode out before he could get up the nerve.

"What are you doing here?"

The voice came from his right. He'd been so focused on the famous patron, he hadn't heard someone come up from behind.

"Working, what does it look like?" he said in a forced whisper.

The woman on his right was wearing the same outfit.

"What's wrong with your voice, Bill?"

He tapped on his throat and gave a shrug, which brought a furrowed brow. The woman looked ready to lay into him until someone waved her over since she had a full tray of drinks.

Relieved to escape, Damon wandered into the hallway, but headed away from the voices. He found a closed door and peeked through it to find a stairway going down. Damon gave the air a big sniff, catching a whiff of potency. It was the Horn. And it'd been used. He knew it from his own experience.

Damon thought about going down alone, but he knew it'd be better if he found Remi first. She knew how to bypass locks and other arcane protections. But where was she?

§

The moment she stepped into the Society building, Remi knew what she needed to do. She dug through the lockers, popping the locks easily, until she found a clipboard. The list on the paper looked like an inventory, which was exactly what she'd been looking for. She'd figured at least a few of the workers would have more responsibilities, including the managing of the staff or inventory.

Remi shoved the clipboard under her arm and headed into the carpeted hallway. The air she cultivated was one of deference but responsibility. She had to look important enough not to be bothered by the members, and the other staff. It didn't matter that Molly didn't have that position for real. Sometimes people were temporarily deputized when another worker was missing, or during emergencies, and the clipboard was the best disguise possible.

But what she didn't have was a map of the interior.

Remi kept her head down as she wandered through the halls until she spotted an electrical panel behind a painting in a side room that looked meant for staff.

The panel wasn't a map, but it gave her a list of the rooms and their electrical needs. She flipped over one of the lists and copied the information. A quick glance showed that the two biggest power needs were in the kitchen where all the appliances were and another location noted as "Stag Office."

Remi thumbed through her phone until she found the spell she was looking for. It was an old list from back when she'd been determined to go after the Horn, but before she knew where it was located. But those spells she'd prepared would come in handy now.

She practiced the words and gestures three times before deciding it was safe to try. The spell would turn on or off a set of electrical circuits after a certain amount of time. Remi set the spell to cut the electricity to the Stag Office in fifteen minutes.

If she wasn't in the room and ready, she figured she could swing back and release the spell before it triggered. Now she had to find the place.

Remi kept to the outer hallways, peeking into doors, receiving a few glares for her interruptions. The place was larger than expected and she was getting nervous about the timer when she spotted Damon in disguise at the end of a hallway, gesturing hurriedly.

"I think it's down here," he whispered, keeping his head on a swivel.

"Have you seen Lily?"

"I don't know."

"Blood and bone, you're right. If she's here, we don't know what she looks like. We'll have to go down alone."

Remi gently shut the door behind them and padded down the stairs, which led to a branching hallway.

"We've got four minutes to find the Horn."

"Four minutes? Why?"

She jogged ahead, putting her ear to the first door before trying the handle. A quick pop with her picks had her peeking into the storage room.

"It's not this way," said Damon.

He tapped on his nose.

"Lead on."

He took her the opposite direction. She knew the place as soon as she saw it. The badge of the Society had been etched into the solid darkwood door.

"It can't really just be in here, can it?"

Remi examined the frame for traps or hidden runes. She breathed faez over the surface, looking for sparks or faint illumination.

"He wouldn't expect us to hit them back right away. There's a chance we might be able to grab it before they realize they should protect it better."

Once she was mostly sure that the door wasn't warded, Remi tested the handle finding it unlocked, which made her more nervous than if it had been.

On the surface, the office looked like it belonged on the top floor of a corner corporate suite for the CEO. The first thing Remi saw was framed pictures of Aleksandr Grimm with famous people, including other patrons, heads of major corporations, and political figures. Then she noticed the little trinkets and artifacts displayed in glass cases around the space. There was what appeared to be a shrunken iridescent wing covered in strange writings in one and a set of four hooves in a smooth wooden bowl in another. A thorny crown with black flowers had a position of prominence in the corner while a curved dagger covered in runes that she couldn't make out from across the room made its home on the opposite side. There were at least a half dozen more, but she didn't have time to investigate them, nor were her thoughts inclined in that direction.

"We handed it to him on a platter."

She hadn't meant for the desperation to come out in her voice, but she couldn't deny it. They'd deluded themselves into thinking they could protect the Horn. Even if they got it back, she worried they'd never be able to protect it in the long term.

"It's behind this," said Damon, surging towards an unassuming door in the far corner.

"Don't!"

He froze before he touched it.

"Sorry."

Unlike the door to the office, this one was covered in overlapping wards that would take longer than a few minutes to unravel. She wasn't even sure if she could get past it with a full hour and additional resources.

"Not good?"

With a hand on her hip, she gestured towards the barrier.

"It's right behind there and we can't get in."

"Could I just throw a shoulder through the door and grab it?"

"I didn't look long, but those wards aren't kids' stuff. You'd likely end up dead or grossly transformed. Dammit. We're so close."

"What do we do now?"

Remi put a hand on her forehead.

"We have one small chance. The power to the office is going to go out in ninety seconds. If we're lucky, the wards are connected to the electrical system and we'll have an opportunity to get through it and grab the Horn."

"And if not?"

She exhaled through her nostrils.

"Then we're probably leaving this place in handcuffs."

Remi tapped her foot while they waited. Sixty seconds.

"Someone's coming," said Damon, grabbing her arm.

"Shit."

As big as the office was, it didn't provide many places to hide. They threw themselves behind the desk and hoped it wasn't anyone who'd be staying long.

The door creaked open. Remi heard footsteps on the plush carpet as she held her breath.

"Remi? Damon?"

They both popped up to see a strange woman with Lily's voice.

"Oh, thank the trees that I found you. Aleksandr is back. We have to get out of here. I heard them say they were going to check on their 'little project.'"

"How much time?"

"They're coming. Now. We have to get out."

Remi eyed the barrier.

"Let's go."

They ran down the hallway, but when they heard voices, Remi tried to route them into a side room. It was locked. The picks flew into her hands and she was working the tumblers as Aleksandr's distinctive voice grew louder.

The moment the lock clicked, they slid through the opening and closed it behind them gently right when Aleksandr and his companions came around the corner.

She checked her watch. Thirty-two seconds. Right about the time Aleksandr and his crew would be settling into the office.

"As soon as we hear the door close, we have to get out. Fast."

Her friends nodded.

She risked a peek into the hallway to see the office door closing.

Remi sprinted towards the stairs, thankful for the thick carpeting to hide Damon's heavy footfalls.

They were halfway to the locker room when her phone buzzed softly, announcing the moment the power was cut in the Stag Office.

Then a stern-looking woman with her hair in a severe bun and wearing the same black and white uniform appeared in their way.

"Molly, Bill, Amanda. What is the meaning of this? You were supposed to be off shift over an hour ago. I'm not paying you for this crap," she said with her hands on her hips.

At that moment, the lights flickered twice and an alarm chirped once. The widening of the supervisor's eyes was clue enough.

"Run," said Remi, bursting past the woman, who tried to grab Lily, but she put a shoulder in her chest, knocking her onto her rear.

They hit the outer door, but it was locked with magic. Remi felt the vibration as soon as she touched the surface.

"It's warded."

She barely had time to get the words out before Damon barreled into the door. The explosion of magic and splinters threw her into the lockers.

Remi shakily climbed to her feet to find the door hanging on its hinges and an unconscious Damon, undisguised with no sign of the golden mask nearby, lying on the concrete outside.

"Wake up, wake up!"

With Lily's help, she hauled him to his feet groggily around the time that an older gentleman in a tweed jacket appeared in the destroyed doorway. He took one look at them and a spell leapt to his lips.

Lily was faster, hitting him with a hex that sent him tipping over like a stiff board.

"We're never going to make it out of here," said Lily as they positioned Damon on their shoulders.

Other members of the Society would be right behind. There was no way they could carry Damon out without getting caught.

"I have a bad idea."

Remi shifted away from Damon as the ritual sprung to her lips. Without a barrier or any of the other protections, opening a way to the Veil would be extremely risky and she wasn't sure she could get them back into their world. It wasn't difficult to move into the Veil, but only the imprints of the dead could easily return. But she was willing to risk it rather than be caught by the Society.

She ignored the shouting and brief battle at the doorway as Lily fought to defend the opening from the Society members. Remi worried she'd fumbled the ritual in her haste until she spotted greenish mist forming around her feet.

When she opened her eyes, she saw the featureless landscape ahead and grabbed the unstable Damon, who'd not fallen, but appeared drunken in his weaving. Lily grabbed his other arm and they hurried into the Veil, leaving the scene of the Society building behind. Two members stumbled outside the moment she cut the link to their realm.

"Where are we going?" asked Lily.

"As far as we can until something finds us," said Remi.

But as soon as the words left her lips, the mournful howl of a hound reached them and sent shivers down her spine.

"Hurry."

They stumbled across the uneven landscape, crushing old bones and lost memories until Remi felt they could go no further.

"It's right there," said Lily.

The hound was closer than she thought and moving fast. She let go of Damon and began the ritual again. She didn't know if it would work. Punching a passage back to their realm was exponentially more work.

Remi ignored Lily's play-by-play of the hound's approach as she poured all of her faez into the ritual, drawing on her strange powers and hoping it would be enough. It felt like trying to pry open a door using only her fingers while a team of elephants was leaning against the other side.

"Remi, hurry!"

She kept working, pushing her fingers into the gap, knowing if the ritual rebounded on her, dying to the hound would be the least of her problems. A low, rising moan issued from her lips as she put every ounce, every cell, every part of her soul into opening the barrier.

The cry of victory died on her tongue the moment she opened her eyes to see the hound right on them. Remi grabbed one shoulder while Lily grabbed the other and the three of them threw themselves through the portal.

As they flew back into their world, Remi remembered that they would be in an entirely different location. She saw the bright lights of a speedy vehicle as they landed on the asphalt. Tire screeches followed by tortured brakes had her throwing up her arms.

The truck missed them by mere inches, and before the next would have to swerve, they hauled Damon onto the sidewalk while heavy honks disapproved their surprise arrival.

"We're about four blocks away," said Lily when she spotted a glass gondola passing overhead.

Remi waved her arm at an approaching yellow taxi, sending out sparks when she wasn't sure it'd seen her. They climbed into the back and had the driver take them to the enclave.

"You okay?" she asked Damon after checking the dilation of his eyes.

"Blistering headache and all my bones feel like jelly, but otherwise, I'm fine. I figure the twins have sustained worse hits in lacrosse."

Remi leaned back into the seat as the weight of what had happened shifted onto her shoulders.

"Did you really do what I think you just did?" asked Lily.

With her eyes closed, Remi exhaled deeply.

"Yeah. I just wish we'd been able to get the Horn."

TWENTY-FIVE

After the failed trip to the Society, Lily and her friends stayed at the enclave all night healing the wounded. Lily couldn't help but think their injuries were her fault. She saw the same in her friends as they ignored the calls from the hospital about their absence.

It was early in the morning. A nimbus formed on the horizon and they were sitting on the upper level of the old factory drinking coffee. They hadn't talked about the Horn since they'd arrived back at the enclave.

"It's not like we'll ever get another shot," said Remi with her feet hanging over the edge. "They'll never leave it unguarded again."

Damon stared at his phone, which had Dr. Broomfield's name on it.

"I guess working at the Institute was never going to happen anyway."

"If we don't go back, can they really unlink us from our Patron?" asked Remi.

"Unfortunately yes," said Damon.

Lily was half-listening, but mostly she was thinking about Aleksandr Grimm. When she'd found her friends, the scent of the kalkatai had been strong. She took two things away from it: he had something to do with what had happened in the Summer Fae, and he was no longer concerned about hiding it—otherwise, she would have smelled it on earlier meetings.

"What if he killed Oberon?" she asked suddenly.

"Oberon? Oh, the King of Summer Fae," said Remi, shaking her head. "Is that even possible?"

"Theoretically anything can die. It's just the Fae Lords are really hard to kill. No, it seems more likely that fooking eejit did something to Oberon which made the corruption possible."

Remi squinted at her.

"You sound like you're working towards something."

Lily searched her own thoughts, which included what the Bhróin, or fairy lover, had told her in Hog's Breath about cutting out the corruption like a tumor.

"Aye, I guess I am."

"Care to share with the rest of the class?"

"What if, and I know this sounds like mad bonkers shite, but what if we went back to the Summer Fae?"

Remi sat up straighter.

"Why would we do that?"

The deep exhale came unconsciously as if her body was trying to get rid of the bad idea before she could speak it.

"I can't shake the time I went on my Greenwalk and ended up in the Court of Summer where the odd chaos-shaped hole tried to trip me up and keep me there."

"And?"

"What if that thing is the corruption? What if we need to cut it out like a bad tumor?"

"A hole?"

Lily frowned. She didn't want to tell them about the Bhróin, but needed to get through to them what she'd learned, which until recently hadn't made much sense.

"It wasn't quite a hole and I wasn't really there, so it was hard to see it truly. Not with my Medb-blessed eyes. But it felt like a cage, holding back a world of miseries. The more I think about it, the more I worry that it's the source of all our troubles."

"I don't know, Lily," said Damon, shifting his mouth to the side. "You really think this one little thing could affect so much?"

"The bloody Horn isn't that big either."

"Good point."

"Theoretically, because I think it's a terrible idea," said Remi, "what would it take for us to go to the Court of Summer in person? Besides, you know, a complete lack of common sense and no fear of impending death."

Lily snorted softly.

"Aye, it'd take those things, a lot of luck, and some friends who don't mind if they never return."

"I could bring my sword," said Damon brightly.

"I thought you said you were shite with it?"

Damon shrugged.

"I am, but they wouldn't know that. Might be big and scary enough to scare off some of the stuff in the Fae."

"I don't think it's going to scare off the murderous, horny satyrs. Might even get them excited," said Remi, smirking.

"I don't know, is this a bad idea?" asked Lily.

Remi tilted her head.

"I wouldn't mind seeing Coraline again."

"Why's that?"

Remi lifted a shoulder.

"Don't know. I just, you know..."

"I did like her," said Lily.

"Me too," said Damon.

"Does that mean we're going?" asked Remi.

Lily looked out across the city. It was a big place, full of millions of people. She didn't know what Aleksandr had in mind for the Horn, but it was likely to be terrible.

"We *were* the ones to bring the Horn back."

"Yeah," said Remi. "It's kinda our fault. If you think we can fix it in the Fae, we should."

"If we could get Oberon back, maybe he could help us with Aleksandr," said Damon.

Lily couldn't explain it, but she felt like going to Summer was the right choice. They'd been avoiding the source of her problems, and maybe it was time to confront it head-on.

"Aye. To the Summer Fae."

"How are we going to get there? Lady Nimueh?" asked Remi.

Lily thought about it and shook her head.

"I think we should have a long talk with Dr. Marcie. I have a feelin' that she or someone in the enclave can help us get over."

TWENTY-SIX

The enormous sword felt strange strapped to his backpack like a pair of skis on a mountaineer. Damon had never worn it in that way, but it seemed like the best solution given the need to bring all their food and water with them. He'd considered not worrying about it, since it was unlikely they were going to survive the trip, but he wasn't ready to give up yet.

"Is Dr. Marcie really going to be able to get us into the Fae?" he asked Lily.

His Irish friend had borrowed some clothes from her sister, Alice, who'd brought them along with other gear for the trip.

"Aye, she says as much."

As if summoned, Dr. Marcie appeared in her white jacket and double braids. She had a dour look, and Damon supposed it wasn't just because of what had happened because of the attack.

"The Elder is ready."

The procession felt doomed. They arrived in the back of the factory, the air thick with smoke, making his eyes burn. He'd been warned about the old shaman, but seeing her with his own eyes was frightening. The huge shape loomed out of the smoke, lips burnt and lined with scars. She looked like a living mountain beneath her furs. He felt her power intuitively. The sword bristled in her presence.

"Three creatures of the Fae, on a quest to save it from itself," cackled the old shaman.

"Thank you, Elder, for this chance to make things right," said Lily, inclining her head with Neko at her side.

The Elder shaman spat on the floor.

"It would be better if I let your cursed realm die, but I'm told by my friends here that you've done our people a great service at cost to yourselves. And I pay my debts as I know you do too, witch."

Lily gave no hint of reaction at the intended slight.

"Thank you, Elder," she said, rising.

"Before they go," said Dr. Marcie, reaching into an inner pocket of her white coat. She pulled something small out and approached Lily. It looked like two bones fused together into an "X" but the centers had been bored out and replaced with iron. Damon could feel the item's power even without trying.

"This is a gift from the other shamans and myself."

Lily wrinkled her forehead.

"What is it?"

"A Fomorian weapon. It was made during the great battles when King Nuada was alive. In your tongue it would be called a Crux. It's made to channel power into a form that hurts Fae creatures."

Lily flinched when she accepted it, but then ran her fingers over the bone.

"Thank you, I'll return it after we're finished."

"I have another gift," said Dr. Marcie, gesturing them forward. "It will help you on your journey."

The spell was in a language Damon didn't recognize. If he had to guess, it was a native tongue, but he wasn't familiar with the languages of the tribes, and it felt beyond old. Ancient perhaps. As Dr. Marcie chanted, Damon saw her in a different light, but not what or who she really was beneath that form. Maybe horns. Maybe fangs. It was hard to tell. When she was finished, his entire body tingled as if it'd been coated in faez.

"It is time," she said.

"Where will this portal take us?" asked Remi.

The Elder coughed, sounding like gravel being crushed by steel.

"I cannot send you to the Court. Even still there are lingering magics that protect that cursed place."

"That's okay, we have someone else to see first. She lives further away in the mountains."

Remi went on to explain the waterfalls and other features, until Lily stepped forward and said something that got the Elder laughing.

"It shall be so."

The Elder's ritual felt more primal than any magics he'd ever witnessed. The foot stomps left his body ringing, even though the impact hadn't made any noise. The old Fomorian shaman threw ochre dust from her pouch and sliced her gnarled hand through it.

He felt her power when the portal opened. The tearing of the barrier between realms made his ears hurt even though there had been no noise. The air looked like the ripples of heat on a desert highway. He could see the waves of dark green beyond. This would not be an easy passage.

"Quickly."

Grabbing Remi's hand, he hurried through the ripple. The passage was like being tossed off a mountain. The instant vertigo and rush of descending had him crying out until he landed in the dense forest. To his relief, not only was he intact, but he was with his friends, unlike the previous time when they'd landed apart.

"I can't say I ever want to do that again," said Damon, swallowing back bile.

"We should move quickly," said Lily, who was unusually terse.

The tortured, compact forest seemed alive and unwelcome. Branches seemed to get in his way, or grab his clothing even though he was certain that he'd slipped past. It was as if the corruption knew they were there to cut it out and was trying to slow them down.

"I hate this," Remi said suddenly, grabbing a branch and snapping it with her bare hands. "I feel like I'm in some weird haunted house."

Lily led them through the undergrowth, while Damon stayed at the rear, checking their surroundings, and especially the canopy of trees. During one section, they heard the wild satyrs hunting and whatever they caught met a quick death with a high squeal and then unnerving silence.

The sound of falling water had Damon hopeful they were near their destination, but then they came upon the misty air and found that it wasn't the waterfall they'd seen near Coraline's house.

"Let's take a break," said Lily, slipping out of her pack.

Their clothes were covered in green smears from the trees. Foreheads were beaded with sweat from the humidity. They washed their faces in the water and snacked on food they'd brought from their realm.

"In the Greenwalks of my youth, these lands were a beautiful dream. Both garden and forest at the same time. An Fae álainn. Welcoming and free. Now it feels like we're an unwanted tumor."

"How much further to Coraline's?" asked Damon as he sat with the sheathed sword in his lap.

"I—"

The words died on Remi's lips as her chin lifted and her gaze roved into the trees. Damon spun about quickly, knocking over his water, to find a heavily clothed and masked shape watching them from above.

"You shouldn't have come back," said Coraline with her mask pulled down.

"We've no choice," said Remi.

Coraline gestured frantically.

"Hurry, hurry. This is a bad place. Grab your things. We have to go before it returns."

The meaning of the warning was undefined, but that didn't stop Damon from hopping to his feet and quickly putting his gear on. They followed Coraline through a previously unseen path. A few minutes after they left the waterfall and pond, they heard grunting and gnashing, which made Coraline lead them faster.

In the hour they followed Coraline, Damon sensed a more frantic demeanor and noticed her clothes had been heavily patched in several points. The Fae had not been kind to her since they'd seen her nearly a year ago.

When they finally reached her branch-height pathways, the tension in their guide seemed to drop, and then when Coraline removed her gloves to spell them through her viny barrier, he saw the thinness of her hands.

Once they were inside the cave, Coraline slowly removed her layered clothing until she revealed a woman emaciated and haunted with the pain of survival. The shadows around her eyes were cavernous.

"You shouldn't have come back."

TWENTY-SEVEN

It wasn't until they arrived at the cave-home that Remi realized she'd been looking forward to this moment more than any others. The reasons didn't make sense, but she couldn't deny the feelings she had. Those thoughts were lost the moment Coraline revealed herself from beneath the overlapping fabrics.

"Are you okay?" asked Remi, surging forward.

The gaunt cheeks and cracked lips were answer enough.

"Please, let me get you some food," said Remi, digging into her pack and quickly handing two food bars over.

Coraline stumbled to the table and collapsed on the chair.

"How did you find us?" asked Lily while their host devoured the food bars.

"The Fae has grown more wild and dangerous since you left, and the plants have been less generous with their gifts, or turning poisonous. I've had to go farther and farther to find edibles, which has put me at constant risk."

"That doesn't explain how you found us," said Lily suspiciously with her hand on Neko's back.

Coraline stared back at the Irish witch.

"You stumbled over my alarms. I was out foraging when I heard them. You're lucky I did." She jutted her chin towards the tea pot. "You're welcome to make some with your own water."

Damon grabbed the pot and put it over the fire, adding a few logs to get it burning again.

"Why are you here?" asked Coraline with hurt in her eyes.

"We're headed to the Summer Court," said Lily.

Coraline sat back in her seat and glanced to each of them.

"You're serious."

"As a grave," said Lily.

"You're fools."

Remi crouched by the chair.

"We have to stop the corruption or the entire City of Sorcery is at risk. We need your help getting to the Summer Court. You're the only one that knows the dangers of the corrupted Fae. We came here first for your help."

"Going to the Court would be suicide," said Coraline. "The Caoránarch would get you before you got remotely near."

"The Caoránarch?" asked Remi. "That can't be possible. We've seen it in the City of Sorcery. It tried to kill me on the streets."

"I don't know or care which one is real, but I'm certain the one here can kill you quite easily."

Remi pulled out a chair and sat on it.

"That doesn't make sense."

Lily tilted her head.

"The one in our realm had a habit of disappearing in odd places."

"Real or not," said Coraline, "you should go back. I can't help you. I've survived this long, I'm not about to throw it all away on a foolish quest for an impossible task. Face it. The Summer Fae is no more. What it is now, I can't say, but it'll be my grave eventually. Just not today."

Remi had been so excited to see her again, but the heartbreak in her tone and in the weight of her shoulders was painful to watch.

"Millions of lives are at stake."

Coraline picked up the food bar wrapper and crinkled it in her hand.

"As you can see, I've barely been surviving here. Worrying about a bunch of people I haven't seen in decades and who never came for me when I went missing isn't high on my priorities."

The finality of her comment made it feel rude to continue the course of the argument.

"Then we'll only stay here to recover and head out shortly," said Lily, inclining her head. "We wouldn't want to inconvenience you."

Coraline closed her eyes against the comment as if she were warding it away. Remi reached out, almost taking their host's hand.

Instead, Remi joined her friends near the fire.

"What do we do?" asked Damon quietly.

"It's her choice," said Lily. "We'll have to find our own way. Until then we should get some rest. Once we return to the forest, I don't think we'll get any more."

When Remi looked back, Coraline had turned her body away from them as if it were too painful to see other people. The urge to interact with their host was strong, but she didn't want to bother someone who clearly didn't want them there, so she moved to her pack to grab some food for herself.

Kneeling down by the cot to unzip the pack, Remi spotted the board of Courts shoved under the bed. The pieces were lying loose on the floorboards as if the entire game had been shoved beneath it in haste.

As Remi reached for the board, intending to ask Coraline if she'd like to play another game, she spotted the colorful box she'd seen last time further beneath the bed. Acting on instinct, she pulled it forward, mesmerized by the two tiny handprints on either side.

A feeling in her chest coiled tighter, the wellspring of hidden secrets driving her forward to unlatch the box. The lid clicked open, briefly revealing a faded child's blanket before Coraline appeared above her, slamming the lid down.

"What are you doing? I offer you sanctuary and you dig through my things?" asked Coraline angrily.

The older woman stood above her, dirty blonde hair lazily spiked from frustration, rather than styling. The bags beneath her eyes big enough to sleep on.

But Remi wasn't ashamed.

The lightning bolt of truth had shocked her into immobility as she stared up at the painfully familiar woman. She wasn't sure how she hadn't seen it the last time, but then again, Remi had been sure she knew who her parents were. But there were similarities: the eyes, the slightly crooked shape of her mouth, and more importantly, the way she'd survived against all odds.

"You had a child."

Coraline's jaw pulsed with anger. She yanked the box out of Remi's hands, clutched it to her chest, and marched to stare at the wall. A sob slipped out as she slapped a hand to her mouth.

"The Wildes stole her from me. They took her, leaving me with nothing but my memories. Every single day I regret letting those thieves into my house."

The admission brought the heads of her friends up. She could see it in their eyes, but they kept their mouths shut to let the scene play out.

"Archer and Greta are dead."

Coraline half turned.

"How?"

"In the Veil."

"Did they have anyone else with them? A young woman?"

Remi bit her lower lip.

"Yes."

"What happened to her?" asked Coraline, turning completely.

"She lived."

Coraline put a hand to her mouth.

"I'm her. I'm the girl they stole. I'm your daughter. Mother."

Remi didn't remember rushing forward to meet Coraline, but then she was locked in an embrace, sobbing and squeezing, caught between the bliss of reunion and the ache of missing time.

"How could this be?" asked Coraline, wiping away tears with the back of her hand.

Remi led her mother to the table. A cup of tea appeared in her hand, brought by her friends, who were clearly trying to stay out of the way. For the next many hours, Remi told Coraline everything she knew, including the story of the Horn. She left nothing out, because after all, this was her mother. The woman she'd been unknowingly waiting to meet her entire life.

Getting to talk to Coraline, and piece together the frayed fabric of her life, helped give sense to her unusual upbringing. The Wildes had stolen her from Coraline because she was a human child born in the Fae, which they thought would help them with the challenges of the pendant. It's why they'd raised her to be a thief. She was a tool like any other, trained for one specific purpose.

"I'll help you," said Coraline, later in the night after many rounds of discussion, and after Lily and Damon had reluctantly entered the conversation and added what they knew of her life. "I can't bear to let you out of my sight again. So yes, I'll help you reach the Court of Summer."

TWENTY-EIGHT

Not long after they left the safety of Coraline's abode Lily worried that they'd never be able to reach the Court of Summer. Three times that first hour, they barely avoided a pack of wild satyrs. The first two times, it was Neko's senses and Coraline's cunning that kept them from being caught. The third time was pure luck when the pack sensed easier prey in another location and went whooping after it.

Between the constant dangers, Lily watched the interactions between Remi and her mother, Coraline. In retrospect, it made sense, even if the physical similarities hadn't been that obvious. But now they were reunited, Lily didn't want either of them to get hurt. It would be heartbreaking for Remi to lose her mother, or the other way around, after the long unexpected reunion.

When Coraline held her hand up, everyone froze, dipping down to be less visible. She'd sensed something in the trees by the tilting of her head. Lily couldn't see it, but she wasn't as experienced as Coraline with the corrupted Fae.

Eventually, she rose, and they followed her across a clearing, avoiding one of the mud pits that were a frequent obstacle. Lily was so focused on the ground, she didn't see the pixie until they were almost beneath her.

The slight Fae creature with wings had been bound to the trees with rough vines, pulled tight enough to break flesh, while the translucent wings had been burned to crinkly nubs. The pixie's eyes had been gouged out. Other signs of torture were evident all over her nearly naked body. While this pixie was much smaller than the Clover sisters, Lily couldn't help but think of them as the same.

"What did this?" asked Remi.

Coraline shook her head.

"I don't know. I've seen something like this once before. I try to stay to my territory where the packs of wild satyrs are the worst of the dangers."

Damon pulled out a knife and cut the pixie down. They laid her in the high grass. Neko sniffed the body, but recoiled and never went near it again. Without a shovel, they couldn't easily bury the dead pixie, so they found a few rocks and set them on her chest.

"I'm sorry we couldn't give you a proper burial," said Lily.

Later on, at the crossing of a stream that was coming down from the high places, they found two more small bodies nearly torn to pieces. Brownies. The small Fae creatures usually kept to the trees. There'd been one that had lived near their home in Ireland that Lily liked to bring gifts during the holidays.

"Whoever is doing this is a monster. Brownies are the gentlest of Fae beings," said Lily.

"Keep that sword at the ready," said Remi.

After they left the bodies at the stream, the scent of burning wood had everyone on high alert. The trees grew wilder, growing in odd angles, and with strange flowers sprouting from their limbs. Malformed insects crawled over the bark. A black beetle longer than her hand fluttered its wings only to reveal a gooey interior.

The further they went, the more Lily was afraid that they'd never make it near the Court. Coraline had said it would be multiple days of travel through the trees until they could reach one of the wider rivers where she hoped they'd be able to find a boat that could take them swiftly towards the Court.

When the light grew dim, Coraline had them climb high into the canopy. One benefit of the twisting of the trees was that they were easier to sleep in. Coraline showed them how to tie themselves down so they wouldn't fall during their slumber.

The forest grew nosier as it darkened until it sounded like a warzone, with screeches and other wild noises happening all around them. At one point, not long after dusk, something was chased to the branches right below them. It died with a high-pitched yell and then silence.

It took many hours for Lily to finally sleep. As a child she'd always dreamed of getting to visit the Court of Summer, but this trip was the nightmare version of it.

In the middle of the night, she woke suddenly, worried that a creature had snuck into their midst, but realized that she'd heard Remi and Coraline quietly talking on their set of branches.

Content that nothing was wrong, Lily stared into the bright swatch of stars in the canopy of night. The patterns and shapes were unfamiliar, but pleasing all the same. For a short time, Lily forgot that she was in the corrupted Fae, until she fell asleep again.

In the morning, they found splatters of blood on the branches one level below. No one spoke as they descended to the floor of the forest. They knew it would be a challenging day. Until they could get onto the river, they'd be exposed to whoever or whatever had been killing pixies and brownies.

The previous day, they'd been working their way down the valley from where Coraline had made her home. The mountains narrowed to a low pass they would have to cross to reach the river where they hoped things would be easier.

The black smoke trailing into the sky was their first and most obvious sign of a problem. The second was the way the trees stayed silent upon their passing.

As they crossed a ridge, they saw what lay ahead. The trees along the pass had been cleared away and a great fire burned at the top.

It was no ordinary fire.

The flames burned in alternating purples and greens like a mixture of bruising and gangrene. Looking at the bonfire made Lily nauseous like when she'd seen the chaos-shaped hole at the Court of Summer.

"It's a fooking disaster," said Lily.

"I could never in a million years believe I'd see an open pyre in the middle of the Fae," said Coraline, eyes rounded.

"What are those creatures? Damon, can you tell what they are?" asked Remi, squinting.

The handsome werewolf peered forward at the shapes moving across the blasted ridge.

"I see pixies and satyrs and other beings, but they don't look like they should. Extra wings, hunched backs, bent spines. They look like muta-tions of the real thing." Damon sucked in a breath. "Oh, no. I see the one who's in charge. A dryad I think, but she's bound by a greenish-purple aura. She's the one giving the commands to burn."

"A dryad burning trees of the Fae? It's worse than I thought," said Lily with a hand to her mouth.

"I'm sadly not surprised," said Coraline. "How do we get past them?

They block the entire pass, and without the tree cover, there's no way to sneak."

Lily checked the sky. They were hours away from evening.

"I know a spell. Something my Mhamó taught me when I was only knee high. It helps with passage through the Fae. She taught it to us in case we ever had to visit and got lost. It would help keep the beings of the Fae from finding us until we can make our way to safety. But we'll have to wait until it's dark."

Given that they'd seen creatures moving into the forest, they climbed into the highest canopies and made camp for the day. Coraline and Remi spent their time chatting quietly with each other. It looked like they were teaching each other spells.

Lily used the time to scout the way ahead with Damon. They found a branch big enough to hold both their weight.

"Some of the Fae are clearly being held as slaves. The most normal looking ones are being forced to haul the wood to the pyre," said Damon.

"What about the dryad?"

He frowned.

"She looks formidable. I don't know what's with that aura, but I saw part of it whip out like a tendril and injure one of the others. They rolled around on the ground as if they'd been burned."

"Anyone else to watch out for?"

"The satyrs are the muscle. They look like they've been jacked up on roids. I saw one break a trunk as big as your thigh in half with his hands. The pixies with the three and four wings are the scouts. I've seen them disappear into the woods and reappear with small creatures in their grasp. The rest are either slaves or more muscle. Is your spell going to get us past them?"

Lily sighed.

"Under normal circumstances, I would say yes, but I fear that the dryad is a bigger problem than we're prepared to handle. Either way, we'll find out tonight. Let's get some rest."

They prepared to sleep when it was still light. Neko would keep watch given their nearness to the camp. Lily found it hard to sleep at first, given the smell of smoke, but eventually she found slumber.

TWENTY-NINE

Remi woke to the sounds of struggle. The last thing she remembered, she'd been lying on her side, waiting for sleep to come. Then she was aware that she was awake and that someone was grunting nearby.

A hand grabbed her leg, and she quickly shook it off.

She looked down to see a pair of iridescent wings holding a pixie aloft as she tried to grab her ankle. The Fae creature only had one eye, and fangs stuck past her thin lips.

When the pixie realized Remi was awake, she reached into a pocket and blew on a handful of black dust. Before the cloud could overwhelm Remi, she pulled the quick release on the knot that was holding her to the tree and rolled off the branch.

She landed ten feet below on the next level, hitting hard enough she worried she'd broken a few ribs. As the pixie flew after her, Remi rolled onto her back and blasted the creature with a force bolt, sending her spinning away.

Disoriented in the dark, Remi heard more wings and grunts. Backlit by the starry sky, she watched as two sets of pixies carried unconscious shapes away from the trees. Realizing there was nothing she could do for her friends if she was caught, Remi leapt down to the next level, barely landing where she'd planned and grabbing the trunk to keep from going over.

Voices followed her through the trees. They were searching for her. Seeing she was unlikely to evade them for long, Remi started a Veil ritual. The words fell over her lips as she hurried to complete it. As the sounds of her pursuers condensed around her location, she pushed herself into the Veil.

With the cold fist of the land between the living and the dead holding her fast, she watched through the hazy barrier as the misshaped pixie landed not far from her location, but could not see her as she wasn't completely in the Fae.

A quick bark from below had the pixie darting downward in pursuit.

She heard others crashing through the trees. The sounds drifted away until she could only hear the beating of her heart.

Movement to her left had Remi freezing, thinking she'd been spotted. She turned her head as slowly as possible until she could see a faint shape peering at her through the foliage.

A ghost in the Fae.

Remi couldn't believe it. She knew it was possible as the Veil touched nearly every realm, but she'd thought the Fae beings too long lived to leave leftover souls.

The slender form covered in a dress made of bark revealed that the apparition was a dryad, and the burns on her arm suggested her death had been recent.

Remi ended the spell before anything noticed her in the Veil. She hadn't completely gone over, but had shifted halfway as Dr. Morsdux had trained her.

When she was certain she was alone, Remi let out a round of curses, slamming her feet and spinning in a circle.

They'd taken her friends. Her mother. She was alone in the Fae. A dangerous place even in the best of times and now the corruption had made it unlivable.

Finished with her outburst, Remi slumped against the trunk. She sensed the ghost dryad hadn't left, but she was too emotionally eviscerated to care.

Eventually she'd have to climb back into the trees to grab her backpack, which was tied to the trunk, but then what? She couldn't imagine taking on the entire camp filled with jacked-up satyrs and malformed arsonist pixies.

When Remi lifted her head, she saw the ghost dryad had moved nearer. Remi had never seen a dryad up close. She was more alien than expected, with elongated eyes and movements that suggested a tree in the wind.

"Yes, I can see you," she told the ghost when it tilted its head.

The ghost crouched beneath a gnarled bush, holding her knees with her arms like a child hiding after it'd gotten in trouble.

"They took my friends." Remi barked out a laugh. "Not that you care. You're already dead."

The silence felt crushing.

The dryad stared at her with what appeared to be sympathy, but Remi thought she might be projecting her own feelings onto the ghost.

"Did you die because of the corruption?"

The ghost dryad nodded her head once.

"I'm sorry."

The hand gesture was unrecognizable to Remi, so she just shrugged.

"What's your name? Some ghosts can talk. Can you?"

A quick shake of the head.

"Then I'll call you Willow. You move like one."

If Willow didn't like the name, she gave no indication, and eventually moved closer until she was only a few feet away.

"I'm guessing you're stuck like this because they burned your tree or something."

Willow nodded angrily.

"Yeah, I—"

The sounds of heavy footsteps crashing through the trees had Remi freezing. Satyrs probably. But there was no time for another Veil ritual.

Remi looked for a place to hide but the undergrowth wasn't thick enough. She heard at least three satyrs headed in her general direction. Panic set in as she decided between running, climbing, or just freezing in place and hoping they didn't see her.

Then a fourth option presented itself.

She had no idea why she did it. Instinct mainly. But it seemed like something that should be possible.

Remi shifted into the same spot as Willow.

It wasn't just an overlap. Remi slipped into the ghost as if she were a skin to wear.

The cold, alien sensation made her gasp loudly, which brought grunts and the hurried approach of the satyrs.

Three towering muscle-bound satyrs with thick beards and wild eyes crashed into the tiny clearing. One of them stopped two feet from Remi's left. Her heart was in her throat, but she was also caught in the strange thoughts of the dryad.

Tree-Heart. Wind-Talker. Life-Water.

Their meaning washed over Remi as she waited to be discovered. The satyr turned as if it sensed her unconsciously.

A grunt and the pack hurried deeper into the forest.

Remi's entire body collapsed with relief. She'd been sure she was caught. She moved out of Willow's space to reclaim her thoughts.

"I'm sorry I did that. I hope you don't mind."

Willow put a translucent finger to her mouth that Remi interpreted as *quiet*, like a librarian warning a loud customer.

Remi mouthed, "Thank you."

With the satyrs gone, Remi ascended the tree to get her backpack. Once she had it, she used the far branches to scout the pass.

The bonfire was burning higher, sparks twirling lazily into the night sky like fireflies.

In front of the grand pyre, there were three new piles being created, each with a central pole sticking out, and each one with a faint figure suspended on it.

Remi knew exactly what they were. They were going to burn her friends and mother.

"How do I get them back?"

A cold hand touched Remi and she nearly slipped off the branch. She found Willow lurking nearby. The ghost dryad gestured towards the ridge and tapped on her chest and then pointed at Remi.

"You want to help?"

Willow nodded.

"Do you have something in mind?"

Another nod.

Willow reached out until their hands were overlapping. The cold was bracing but bearable. Remi stayed silent and let the apparition do what she wanted.

Then she shifted overtop.

The first time when the satyrs had arrived, the movement had been out of necessity and her mind was occupied by getting caught.

This time she was focusing on nothing else.

The shock of overlap made her gasp. Not only could she sense Willow's thoughts, but she could feel her connection to the tree. The trees were an extension of her, and they were in pain. Great pain.

Remi looked at the great pyre as smoke coated the inner parts of her nostrils and ash caught in her throat. It was like having been burnt over a large part of her body with nerve endings constantly firing.

"Blood and bone. No wonder a piece of you stayed here. This is so much pain. Oh, Merlin, how do you stand it?"

She wanted to shift out of Willow, but clearly the ghost was trying to teach her something.

The intention came without words. A feeling Remi suddenly had, so she let Willow take control of her body.

When they walked towards the tree, Remi feared that it was a trick and the ghost dryad was going to fling her off the side, but then Willow sprinted into the trunk.

Remi's mind had no way to describe it at first. She was in the tree. She *was* the tree.

It was all too much.

She felt herself slide through the roots: jumping through loamy soil, mineral-infused rocks, and the ashy tasting wood. Part of her disassociated and curled into a ball until it was over.

When she opened her eyes, she was no longer in the forest, but crouched by a pile of fallen trees, dragged into a pile by industrious satyrs. The scent of burning wood was powerful—and disgusting. Remi almost threw up before she realized it was Willow's feelings.

The ghost stepped out of Remi, letting her collapse onto dirt.

"It's awful."

Willow nodded, her lips squeezed into a knot.

Remi checked back to the forest behind. She could see where she'd been only a few moments ago. They'd traveled by tree. She couldn't say she ever wanted to do it again, but it'd gotten her past the guards and workers.

They were off to the side. A staging ground of materials to burn. Remi crept around until she could see the top of the hill. Backlit by a raging inferno were three new piles each with a central pole where her friends and mother were suspended. Bound and gagged, they were forced to watch as pixie slaves dragged more fuel to the pyre.

She was about to risk running to the piles to free them when Remi sensed a terrible presence. She felt her before she saw her.

A dryad.

Except she was nothing like Willow.

Tall, sensual, and brutal. A nimbus of overlapping greens and purples whipped around her like a raging storm from a lost realm.

Remi had never quite known what Lily had meant about the chaos-shaped hole until now. She felt its destructive power. Whatever had taken control of the dryad was more alien than the Fae.

Primal madness.

It was like seeing into the heart of an imploding star.

Remi shivered as she yanked herself behind the woodpile, fearful of being spotted.

When the corrupted dryad spoke, it was like the air itself was being rended to create the sound. Remi cowered behind the pile, hands to her ears. The language was nothing like she'd ever heard, yet she could understand it.

"I am Raz'rushite Sila. You will burn."

Between merging with a dryad ghost and having another speak in a language not meant for physical mouths, Remi had a searing headache.

She crawled back to the edge.

Her mother was on the far side looking beat up from their capture. Lily and Damon looked no better. She could see no sign of the Shining

Sword.

A procession of torch-bearing pixies came forward, each one standing before an unlit pyre. The torches were thrust into the piles, which caught flame immediately.

"Can you get me to the back of the pile?" she whispered to Willow.

The ghost nodded.

Remi stepped into Willow. This time the sensation wasn't as jarring, but it still felt like she'd put on a chilled wetsuit made of smooth bark.

The shift through the fallen trees was no less disorienting, especially with some of them on fire. Remi could smell the smoke of her own flesh, which she realized was Willow's rather than her own.

But that would change quickly if she couldn't get her friends and mother free of the flames.

Remi scrambled up the back of the pile to find herself behind Lily. The rising smoke obscured her from the host of corrupted folk in front of the piles.

Realizing she didn't have a knife, Remi converted her fingernail into a makeshift blade with a spell from the hospital and sliced through the ropes.

"Don't let them know you're free yet. Not until I get the others."

Lily turned her head and nodded.

Climbing over the jagged wood took time and the flames were growing higher. By the time she reached Damon's spot, she could barely see her mother. She cut his ropes, told him the same thing, and hurried to the next.

Then a great cry went up.

Remi looked up to see she'd been spotted.

Misshapen pixies with three and four wings rose into the air, shifting through the smoke to attack, but the heat and fumes made it hard for them to reach Remi.

"Mom, I'm coming!"

Bright flashes of sorcery exploded behind her as Lily and Damon leapt into the fray.

Remi scrambled up the pile, but the heat was growing unbearable and the pixies were making it hard to climb without getting grabbed. She punched one that got too close and blasted another with a force bolt.

Then a kick to the face had her falling, rolling backwards down the broken branches and trunks.

A scream from the pyre had Remi more frantic than before. The flames were high enough that she could barely see Coraline attached to the pole.

Pixies grabbed for her arms.

She looked up in hopes that her friends were able to save her mother but they were barely holding their own against the satyrs and the corrupted dryad.

The flames overtook Coraline.

A great swirling bonfire.

A miniature tornado extending into the sky.

A hole opened in Remi's chest where her heart had once been.

In a fit of desperation, she stepped into Willow who had stayed near throughout the fight.

While her eyes and senses burned from the smoke and fire, she reached out to the wood using the dryad. The pain and confusion along with the grasping pixies made it hard to find what she was looking for but eventually she found it: the central pole.

Remi knew what she was asking was like telling someone to break their own arm, but her rage and overwhelming need overcame any instinctual resistance.

The central pole where her mother was attached and consumed by flames snapped at the base.

For a terrifying moment, she thought it would tip forward into the heart of the bonfire, but at the last moment it fell backwards, tumbling down the pyre over broken branch and jutting log.

Remi reached her mother as herself, fearful of what she would find. Coraline was battered, burnt, and unconscious—but alive.

She dragged the pole away from the flame, checked to make sure Coraline was stable, and then once she was certain that she would survive, stepped back into Willow.

Remi had always wondered what Damon's rage was like. She'd always been a cooler head, even at the worst of times, but this was different. She'd almost lost the mother that she'd only recently rediscovered. To lose her again would have been to lose herself.

She channeled that feeling into rage.

And it wasn't just her rage, but Willow's too, at the loss of her home and friends, and her entire realm.

The burning pyre exploded forward.

Wood flew in all directions, taking down streaking pixies and crushing satyrs that had gotten too close.

Remi had never felt so powerful.

And so out of control.

It was freeing and horrible and joyous all at the same time.

Consumed by bloodlust, Remi barely remembered smashing the corrupted dryad beneath an enormous severed tree trunk. She scattered the pixies and decimated the satyrs until there were no more of them to destroy.

THIRTY

Black smoke rose into the morning sky as the great pyre burned to ashes. Damon leaned on the Shining Sword. The battle had gone long, with mad Fae creatures throwing themselves at his weapon. He was no master, but it hadn't required skill, only the willingness to kill.

The scattered bodies left him feeling like he'd betrayed his oath as a healer. Damon knelt to rip a piece of leafy cloth from a pixie that had died to an eldritch blast. Her eyes stared at the empty sky, so he used his forefinger and thumb to shut them forever. The cloth cleaned the weapon of blood, but left a stain on his heart.

"Are you done?" he asked Lily.

The Irish witch, smudged with soot and burning internally with anger, looked like a Fae goddess after a long war. Lily gazed across the battlefield looking for more foes, then eventually nodded and let her shoulders dip slightly.

"I think we've killed the last of those mad buggers."

Damon nodded.

"The corrupted dryad was driving them to destroy their own land. I think their minds snapped the moment she died."

Lily turned her head towards mother and daughter, sitting against an unburnt pile of trees. Remi was cradling Coraline in her arms. She'd been injured during the pyre and rescue, but was looking more recovered after being healed.

"How do you think she did that?" asked Damon.

"I don't bloody know, but I'm glad she did. Or we wouldn't be alive."

The vision of Remi standing atop the pyre flinging burning tree trunks heavier than a small car across the hilltop was imprinted in his mind. She'd looked like vengeance personified.

Neko came jogging up to Lily in the form of a great wolf rather than his changeling self. He'd been hunting the corrupted satyrs and pixies that had fled. Lily crouched down to commune with the big beast.

"We have visitors," she said, rising.

Damon reached for the hilt of his weapon, but let his fingers skip off the top when he saw them.

A line of Fae Folk ascended to their location led by a small curly-haired gnome in a fancy waistcoat that was burnt at the edges. His face had deep cuts along the jaw that hadn't quite healed. There were sprites, and brownies, and other strange creatures that looked like living parts of the forest that Damon had no name for.

"What is purpose human child?" asked the gnome in halting English, glancing back to his friends for support.

He stood back a ways as if he hadn't yet decided if they were danger-ous or not. A smaller woodland being that looked like living grass hurried to the gnome's side and whispered into his ear. Gestures were made to-wards the sword, which brought increased chatter amongst the crowd of

Fae Folk.

Damon heard the sword's name, Claíomh Ag Lonrú, repeated multiple times until the gnome spoke again.

"Are you of King Nuada?"

"I am his descendant and Keeper of the Sword."

"Why not bound?"

Damon's cheeks burned.

"I don't know how," he said even though it wasn't entirely the truth since he'd tried before unsuccessfully.

Connor had explained the process before he disappeared. It should have been simple.

"If King's heir has returned, are you here to free Oberon from curse?"

Lily responded in Gaelic, which brought a response from the gnome. The two conversed for a bit before Lily turned her head, remembering that he was standing nearby, and switched into English.

"He said that something changed recently. That's why they'd come out of hiding, because they believed that Oberon had returned. Unfortunately they did so only for some of them to get captured by the corrupted dryad."

"Oberon has returned? That's great news. Right?" asked Damon, tilting his head at her odd expression.

"He says they aren't sure. That something doesn't feel right and that they could be wrong about Oberon. It's a feeling, not a fact. I'm inclined to believe 'em. This whole thing sounds like bollocks. Not the gnome, but what's going on. If he was back, there's no way that this shite could happen. Not the Oberon I grew up hearing about, anyway."

Lily spoke to the gnome again. After a minute of back-and-forth, she turned to him.

"He wants you to know that bonding with the sword should be simple. The rituals are usually easy, but are sometimes different depending on the warrior. But he was clear that you need to open your heart to the sword. Then you won't look like a child playing with a toy." Lily grinned. "His words, not mine."

Damon rolled his eyes.

"I'm aware."

Lily shifted her mouth to the side.

"I thought you'd been training?"

"I have, but as one of the masters told me, I don't have a warrior's heart. I fear I'm not the right person."

"The willingness to wield it is all it needs," said Lily.

Damon nodded to the Fae Folk.

"What will you do now?"

"Bury the dead," said the gnome. "What is you do?"

Damon smiled.

"What will we do? We're headed to the Court of Summer."

The gnome's eyes went wide and then he repeated it to his friends, which caused a tizzy. They looked like he'd just said he planned on blowing up the moon.

"It's not safe," said Lily in translation. "What are you thinking?"

"We need a guide."

Lily nodded.

The conversation went on for a while. There was a great disagreement between the Fae Folk.

"I, sorry. We cannot take you. Danger bad and the way is not same as before. Strange tides change all, even the land."

"Strange tides," repeated Damon with a sigh.

The Fae Folk scurried backwards making hand gestures and hissing with displeasure. Damon thought he'd said something wrong until Remi limped into the clearing.

"I can lead us."

"You can?" asked Damon.

He thought he saw a shimmer appear briefly by her side. A small shape that he couldn't quite decide was a small tree or an actual being.

"I can."

The Fae Folk continued to chatter, clearly upset by Remi's presence.

"What are they saying?" asked Remi.

Lily swallowed.

"They name you Bhean an Bháis, or Lady of Death. They saw what you did to the corrupted dryad and they're afraid of you."

Remi glanced back to her mother, who was drinking water near their pile of gear.

"They should be."

He saw something had changed in Remi. She looked like she was wrestling with new information about herself.

"I require something of you, gnome," said Remi, jaw pulsing.

When the gnome didn't answer, Remi gestured to Lily.

"Tell him."

Upon hearing, the gnome flinched, but he nodded quickly as if he feared to be slow. Damon didn't entirely understand why they were afraid of Remi and not him or Lily, but he wasn't entirely sure how she'd rescued them alone either. Or did the thing she'd done at the height of battle.

"What is the request?" asked Lily.

"I want him to care for my mother, Coraline. She's recovered from her injuries, but needs rest. I can't risk her again either. If they have a place they call home, I want her taken there, and if not, for a party of them to take her back to her place."

After the translation, the gnome spoke with his friends. The conversation went back and forth before the gnome answered. Damon had the feeling that they felt they couldn't refuse the request.

"They accept."

Remi closed her eyes and exhaled through her nose.

"Thank you."

Then she turned and limped back to Coraline. Lily shared a shrug before telling the Fae Folk to rest for now and that they'd be leaving for the Court of Summer shortly.

"What was that about?" asked Damon.

"I don't think she wants to lose Coraline again."

"Yeah, I suppose you're right. She just seems a little different, is all."

"Weren't you different after the massacre?"

"I was."

Lily frowned.

"You should bond with the sword. We need all the luck we can get for the journey."

Damon let the Shining Sword rest on his shoulder as he headed away from the burning hilltop. He wanted to find a more appropriate spot for the ritual than the battlefield of the dead.

He had to go a ways to avoid the decimated landscape. When he reached the forest, he pushed through the overgrowth until he found a clearing that if he squinted reminded him of the Fae that he'd heard about, except as soon as he knelt down, tiny insects started attacking his exposed neck. A quick spell dispersed them.

The sword was cool under his fingertips. He could sense its power even as it felt distant.

"I know I'm a healer, not a warrior, but I need to be able to use you. Please, let me bond with you so we can get to the Court of Summer and end the corruption, however in the seven hells we're supposed to do that."

Damon felt no response from the Shining Sword. In fact, he didn't even feel its power anymore. It was just a two-handed sword. A beautiful and deadly weapon, but useless in his hands.

He stayed in the clearing for a while longer, but eventually gave up.

Whatever trick was required to bond, he was incapable.

When he returned to the camp, Lily looked up from digging into her pack and he gave her the thumbs-up. Damon hated lying to his friend but they were already in a tough spot. No reason to bring her down with bad news.

THIRTY-ONE

The other side of the pass was a valley cut through the center with a growing river. By the time it slipped around the hills leading into the plains, it looked like a raging beast, white with foam. Not the tranquil watershed that Lily knew from her Greenwalks.

The journey was difficult and fraught with danger, but Remi seemed to anticipate the problems as if she had supernatural senses, or the power of foresight. During one section, a wild pack of satyrs came up the path unexpectedly, but Remi had them shift into the undergrowth and vines suddenly grew up around them, creating a cocoon that hid them completely.

The reason for her newfound powers was unknown. The only hint Lily got was the occasional double image of another being overtop. She imagined that it was a result of her Veil powers, which made Lily wonder who her friend really was, or if she even knew.

It took two days to cross the long valley and reach the plains. They slept in protected domes of undergrowth that felt like tents. Remi spoke little. She seemed to be having internal conversations constantly and reacted at a delay when spoken to.

Damon wasn't much more talkative. He spent the time touching the Shining Sword absently or muttering under his breath. Lily hoped the distractions wouldn't impact their mission.

Once they reached the plains, they traveled along the river, which had combined with two other smaller flows. Remi called it the Abhainn Bhán, or White River, though she didn't explain how she knew its name, nor how she pronounced it perfectly.

About half a day later, they came upon a vine-choked settlement on their river bank. The wooden walkways had been upturned with jagged, broken planks sticking up making passage treacherous. A statue in the central glade had been knocked down and the head was missing.

The great hall had holes in the ceiling and the interior smelled like satyr musk. A bloated rotting carcass covered in maggots lay at the foot of the thorny throne. When Damon nudged it with the toe of his boot, the ribs collapsed and a hiss of greenish-purple mist slipped out and disappeared into the surrounding trees.

Lily could see the former majesty in tattered banners and ornate wooden bowls but it was fading quickly. The corrupted forest would claim the hall within a few years.

"This was a river lodge from where they would hunt," said Remi as she closed her eyes in pain.

"Remi..."

"We should move on. It's not safe here," she said.

"I saw docks further up the river," said Damon.

They found a boathouse and docks in a protected cove, though the high water had destroyed parts of the structures. The tip of a grand barge stuck from the water, exposing a horse galloping. The smooth wood appeared shaped rather than carved.

"That would have been nice," said Lily.

"I'm not sure," said Damon. "That river looks treacherous."

Neko gave a short bark at the entrance to the boathouse. Inside, they found a smaller barge that looked untouched by the corruption. It was in the shape of a unicorn with the horn sticking from the prow and could hold a dozen people easily.

"How do we steer it? It's meant to be propelled by poles, or magic, but we lack both," said Damon.

"I don't know any spells for working boats," said Lily.

They both looked to Remi, who was standing still, mouth moving absently. A translucent shape shifted away from her before disappearing across the river.

"It might take a moment."

Lily looked after the apparition.

"Maybe now is a good time to tell us what's going on?"

Remi rubbed her temples with both fingers as she leaned against the wall.

"It takes so much concentration..."

"What does?" asked Damon, reaching out, but Remi flinched away.

"I'm sorry. I need to focus. I can't lose myself."

After they'd eaten, the apparition returned, disappearing right into Remi, which made her stiffen and gasp aloud.

"She says she found us help getting down the river. Once we push into the center, they'll do the rest."

"Who?"

Remi lifted both shoulders and climbed into the boat. She immediately sat on the bench near the back and crossed her arms.

Damon gave them a good push to get them moving, then used one of the long poles to help them into the current. Once the river caught hold, it spun them and tried to bounce them off the bank, but Damon slammed the pole into the side and deflected them enough they were yanked into the center still spinning.

"Remi..."

She held a hand up.

"Remi, we're not stable."

A huge submerged tree was floating towards them. The massive knot of roots looked like it could pierce their hull. Lily leaned against the side and prepared to blast it with force, when the boat shifted.

The sudden movement was disorienting until the barge was righted and faced downstream. Lily still worried about the huge tree, but realized they were moving faster than the current. She leaned over the side to see a pair of green-haired women pushing the barge using their webbed feet.

"What are they?" asked Damon when they returned to the center of the barge.

"Asrai," said Lily.

He leaned closer.

"I'm not sure I completely understand what's going on with Remi, but I'm grateful."

"Aye. I as well. I just hope she's okay when it's over."

The journey along the river was swift and long. They spent three days on the water with the asrai propelling them the entire time. Remi dozed in back without much conversation, and Damon seemed to be pining for interaction with her, so Lily spent her time staring at the passing forests.

It'd always been a dream of hers to visit the Summer Fae in person, but not this way. The lands were choked with foliage where sunlit-filled glades were the norm before. The Greenwalks had reminded her of the Irish countryside, except more manicured and exquisite, enough that one could ride or walk for days under idyllic conditions. Sleeping on soft grass.

Eating from the trees and bushes.

But not this. Nothing like this. This was a travesty. The land had been sapped of its vitality. Twisted until it was a grotesque caricature.

She remembered her first Greenwalk as a child, when she got to watch a nereid bathe in a moonlit pool beneath a shimmering waterfall. They'd not seen the moon since they arrived in the Fae. The days were overcast and the nights dim.

On the fourth day, the boat docked against the opposite shore. Damon tied it off against a vine-choked tree. The nereids disappeared into the foamy waters, but Remi wouldn't move. There was no visible sign of the translucent form that had surrounded her.

"Remi," said Damon, shaking her unconscious form.

"She wore herself out. You'll have to carry her."

"Is that ghost still with her?"

"It doesn't look like it."

He glanced over his shoulder.

"Can we get through that without her?"

There were spells that could detect ghosts and apparitions, but Lily didn't want to insult their guide.

"It might be around helping us. Either way, we have to go."

With Remi slumped over Damon's shoulder, Lily took the lead. The way was choked worse than deep jungle. She leaned on the wisdom of her elders, using green lore and tree-speaking to get them past the unruly foliage that clearly didn't want them. The plants begrudgingly parted, though not without their price. Branches snagged their clothes, or tripped their feet. A few times when they rested too long, they found vines had coiled around their ankles like hungry snakes.

After a morning of constant struggle, Lily collapsed against a tree, pounding her fist against the bark, only to have it go through the outer husk. A cloud of biting insects burst forth, which took a few minutes of frantic flame to eliminate.

"I can't do this much longer. This whole mission is a bloody slog. The Fae has gone to shite. I feel like we haven't gone but a few city blocks from the river."

Damon's mouth twitched.

"I can hear it still."

"Bloody hell."

A vine tried grabbing her ankle, so she stomped on it out of frustration, letting out a little scream when a thorn scratched her thigh in retribution.

"We can't stay here and wait for Remi to wake up," said Damon, flinching away from a curious branch.

"I know, I know."

"What about Dr. Marcie's gifts?"

"I don't want to use the Crux. It would feel, I don't know, wrong. Sacrilegious."

"Do you want to get stuck here?"

Lily grumbled and reached into her pouch. The Fomorian weapon felt light in her hands. Too comfortable for her taste. She would have preferred if it'd rejected her.

Accessing the artifact's magic required communing with the item. She held it out with her eyes closed. The familiar smells of brimstone lurked beneath the surface but so too did the scent of petrichor: rain on warm rocks. She saw towers of stone and great ziggurats built on unrepentant lands.

The lands of the Fomorians were brutal and volcanic, with the ground opening up and swallowing unlucky tribes whole. Then she saw the way they harnessed the magic of the stones, pulling themselves out of barbarism to create the loose bonds of civilization. The environment meant that life was fragile, but they managed to survive long enough to learn how to slip into other realms.

"Lily—"

The name was spoken with need. She opened her eyes to find the trees had decided they were easy prey. At least three vines had wrapped around her midsection and Damon was wrestling with one trying to steal Remi.

Lily would have preferred to spend more time getting to know the Crux, but they needed its ancient magics now. Adding her own faez to the object helped her tap into its powers. Without thinking about how it came about, she pushed the stones in the earth up until they were jabbing their sharp edges into the roots of the trees. The vines hissed and slapped at their arms and faces, but when Lily pushed harder they retreated.

"Is that you?" asked Damon, gesturing towards the pieces of rock sticking up from the soil.

At first their progress was halting. Lily felt like she was only using a fraction of the Crux's power. When she tapped into the elemental fire, the hot stones moved the trees out of their way faster than the sharp edges. Lily hated hurting the trees but they weren't the ones she knew from her Greenwalks. They hissed and snapped like serpents.

Before long, the trees were parting long before they reached them, providing a jagged pathway. Progress was swifter the rest of the afternoon until the shadows lengthened and she knew it was time to camp.

Without Remi's invisible friend to provide safety, and the blood thirst of the trees, Lily leaned into the Crux for shelter. She managed to create a ring of tall stones, pulled from the earth, and infused them with fire to keep the treacherous vines from sneaking through the gaps.

"This will have to do," said Lily.

She meant to sit down but her knees gave out and she collapsed to the soil. Using the Crux had taken a lot out of her, even as it'd gotten easier as the day went on.

"We're a sorry lot," said Damon as he gently laid Remi on the ground.

He stretched his back and neck, looking haggard from carrying Remi for the entire day.

"You rest first," said Damon. "My exertion was physical."

Lily could barely keep her eyes open. Now that she was no longer concentrating on the Crux, she could feel the ailments of her physical body closing in.

Sleep came like a thunderbolt. When she awoke it was dark. Damon was watching. He nodded then turned to his side and was snoring within moments.

Lily could have never imagined she'd be in the Fae surrounded by a protective stone barrier made from Fomorian magics. Occasionally, she heard the sizzle of wood-flesh that had gotten too close to the stones. The stone ring had an added benefit of providing warm air for a cool night.

The next day was the same as the last. Lily wasn't entirely sure they were headed in the right direction, but she followed her heart and hoped that would be enough.

Sometime in the afternoon, they found a strangely unaffected glade. Angled beams of sunlight illuminated the circular space. Lily let the magic of the Crux drop, feeling less drained than the previous day.

"Something's coming," said Damon, setting a partially conscious Remi on the grass. She'd been slowly waking up, eating and drinking small amounts, but looked too tired to move on her own power.

Lily put the Crux back in her pouch. She wasn't sure why, only that it didn't feel right.

Her instincts were rewarded when she saw the majestic creature push through the foliage. Lily almost couldn't believe it. A full-bodied white hart with a rack larger than she'd ever seen. The fur seemed to glow with inner light. This wasn't just any white hart, but The White Hart. The one that the Wild Hunt would pursue through fields and glades, and after slaughtered, would reform the next day. This was a primal force deeply connected to the Summer Fae. It had yet to be corrupted by the kalkatai, which gave Lily hope that there was still a chance to fix the realm.

The buck bent one knee and bowed its head towards them, snorted, and jerked its head in the opposite direction.

"It wants us to follow."

Lily didn't realize who was speaking until she saw that Remi was sitting up.

"So you're seeing this too?" asked Damon.

"It's not an apparition if that's what you're wondering," said Remi.

The White Hart sauntered towards the trees, which parted, allowing it passage.

They hurried towards the gap, which closed after they entered. The next few hours, or days—Lily couldn't be quite sure—they followed the White Hart through the Fae. Time lost meaning in the wake of the ancient creature. Passage had a dreamlike quality until they stopped at stone steps that led to a vine-choked archway.

Lily found herself aware again, and refreshed. Despite moving her body without rest, she felt like she'd gotten a chance to slumber on soft grass for days. The White Hart bowed its head and before she could thank it, disappeared into the forest.

THIRTY-TWO

The moment the White Hart disappeared, Remi felt some of her previous tiredness return, though it was a shadow of the former exhaustion.

"Did that really happen?" she asked.

The Irish witch shook her rainbow locks.

"I can scarcely believe it myself. I think some part of the Fae is still trying to be saved."

"Do you think that means that Oberon is alive?"

Lily's mouth pinched to a point.

"Where are we?" asked Damon, pulling vines away from the archway, which broke away easily, some disintegrating into dust.

The stone steps went up through the gap, bound by columns reaching as high as the trees. After spending many days with Willow, Remi could sense the condition of the trees. They were barely alive. Black rot was everywhere. She slapped an insect against her arm only to find that it was misshapen, with five wings and too many legs to count. Another insect that looked like a striped worm drunkenly flew by in a zigzag pattern.

"It's here."

Lily's brow was knitted. She nodded.

"Aye, I can feel it."

"What?" asked Damon, checking back to them both.

"The corruption," said Remi.

"The chaos-shaped hole," said Lily.

Damon looked through the darkened archway.

"Oh, that's what that is."

Lily reached into her hair and pulled out the white rat, which transformed into Neko. The changeling shook his hairless back while his tendrils twitched nervously.

"I bet this place was beautiful before," said Remi.

"Come on, we should get moving. The longer we stand here, the more I fear for our safety," said Lily.

The vines and branches that choked the pathway were easy to clear, unlike the deeper portions of the forest. Damon stopped at a few columns, cleaning them off to reveal frescos of idyllic scenes of Fae Lords hunting, or lounging on barges.

As they climbed the steps, a high-pitched whine taunted her hearing, making her squint. Her friends were also affected, Damon more so due to his superior hearing.

At the top, an enormous statue greeted them. The greenery had fallen from most of the figure, a sign that the rot was at its worst. The figure wore a helm of antlers. A nest had been built between the tines, but it was falling apart, half covering the statue's face. Damon used the sheathed sword to knock the debris away, which brought audible gasps.

"Blood and bone. Is that who I think it is?"

The similarity was unmistakable. Remi couldn't believe that they'd known Oberon this entire time.

"It's not possible," breathed Lily. "Not bloody fucking possible."

"Yet there he is," said Damon.

Remi swallowed. The piercing eyes, the stern jaw, even the height and squareness of his shoulders were the same.

"How can Oberon be the Patron of Arcane Phytology? Or is it a coincidence that he looks like Aleksandr Grimm?"

"That's him for certain," said Damon.

"It would make sense he's the head of the plant hall, I guess. But what does that mean for us? For the Fae?" asked Remi.

"I think the answer lies ahead in the Great Hall."

As they strolled across the dirtied marble floors, Remi could imagine the festivities before the corruption. Fae lords and ladies swirling together in dance, laughing, drinking, enjoying the bounty of the realm. Now it was a husk of its former self, a carcass rotted until only the bones remained.

When they stepped into the grand inner chamber, the keening grew so loud that it was like having needles stuck into her ears.

"Merlin's tits, what *is* that?" asked Remi.

"It's the kalkatai," said Lily.

Upon a dais, an enormous throne lorded over the space, choked with old vines, crumbled and black. It looked like it'd been caught in living webs made of plants and in the darkness lurked a pulsing heart.

"That's it. That's the corruption. The one that I saw in my Greenwalk," said Lily with her arm outstretched.

Neko was growling, tendrils undulating angrily, his head low.

Remi found it was hard to even look at it. The chaos-shaped hole seemed a fitting description as it absorbed any attempt to categorize or label it. The edges burned with sickly greens and pale purples like the solar ejections of a failing star.

Nausea rose up, forcing her to swallow back bile. Her instinct was to run.

"We shouldn't be here. It's trying to get in my head," said Lily, bent at the waist. "I don't know what we were thinking. We can't stop that."

Remi took a few more steps towards the throne. Each one felt like the first step off a high cliff. She wanted to shout, pull her hair out, curl into a ball.

By instinct alone, Remi reached out with the senses she'd developed from Willow and her time in the Veil, like feeling the intensity of a fire just by the heat it was giving off. The thing at the throne, the chaos-shaped hole, it was dense beyond meaning.

Then she realized what the noise was. Screaming. The voices of millions caught in perpetual destruction. If she didn't know that it was impossible, she would have thought that it was an entire realm squeezed into a space the size of her fist.

A booming voice from behind startled them.

"No living or dead can touch the Thrice-Cursed Stone. I should know, because I dared to test it."

Aleksandr Grimm stood at the entrance to the great hall in the fitted suit she'd seen him in last, the black-and-gold Horn of Bran Galed clutched in his fist. He was tall and fell, the twisted might of the Fae carried on his broad shoulders with a perverse darkness in his piercing eyes. He wore no glamour, nor did he hide his power, which was marbled with the perversion of the Thrice-Cursed Stone.

"Bend your knee and serve me, or I will smite you from existence."

THIRTY-THREE

It was him. Oberon. King of the Summer Fae. And also, Aleksandr Grimm, Patron of Arcane Phytology. Damon could hardly believe it.

But as he looked at the tall Fae, Damon saw how they'd been deceived. Glamours had hid the signs of corruption, the angled cheekbones that were common with the Fae, and the patient darkness in his stern gaze.

Damon stepped in front of his friends, holding the sheathed Shining Sword before him like a ward.

"Run. Get out of here. I'll protect your exit."

"What? And get devoured by the forest," said Remi. "No, I think this is the end, one way or another."

He half-turned.

"Remi..."

"She's right," said Lily. "This whole situation is shite, but it's the hand we've been dealt."

Damon unsheathed the sword, which glowed faintly in the dim hall. Oberon smirked at the reveal.

"The three of you have been quite resourceful. First forcing me to destroy the White Worm, then thwarting my favorite assassin, and then stopping Balor. I would have been quite cross if you hadn't also brought me the Horn, which I thought was out of reach, but now it will solidify my plans."

"Balor?" spat Lily. "How could you conspire with our lifelong enemies?"

"Have you no shame, holding one of their artifacts in your possession while you dare to accuse?" Oberon chuckled. "Balor of the Evil Eye was never in my charge. I was aware of him through the Society of the White Hart, and I had an inkling of his plans, but I saw they would help me with mine, so I let his unfold."

"Your plans?" asked Damon.

"Why, control of the Hundred Halls. Is there a greater prize in all the realms?"

"The mayor," breathed Damon. "You're a shoo-in to win the next election if he steps aside and endorses you. But how does that help you with the Halls?"

"Because many see that young Head Patron as too inexperienced to contain the chaos that besets the city. Since the Infernal Invasion, the city has been in constant unrest, the fault of which is laid at her feet."

"Chaos of your doing," said Damon.

"Yet the blame falls on her. I needed to destroy faith in your systems and structures. I needed people to mistrust mages with all their power and lack of responsibility. You'd be surprised how many people believe the Head Patron caused the invasion so she could take control of the Halls herself, which is only helped by her rule-breaking past. She may be seen as powerful, but she's also seen as cunning and not worthy of trust.

"Of course, that was my plan before I was able to acquire the Horn, thanks to you. Now, it will be simple to convert the other patrons to my point of view until I've enough to topple her rule and assert myself as the logical successor."

"But why?" asked Damon. "You're the King of the Fae."

"Because the Halls have grown too powerful, too dangerous. You weak-minded mortals meddle with forces you don't understand. You open portals to places that could bring down all the realms. So I sacrificed my realm to fuel my conquest."

The colors of his eyes flashed sickly green at the same time as the chaos-shaped hole near the throne. His friends had seen it as well.

"You didn't sacrifice it," said Damon. "You're being controlled by another, just as you seek to control the Halls."

Thunderclouds of anger crossed Oberon's gaze. The trees shook and rotting leaves tumbled into the hall.

"I am in control of my own destiny, and yours, it seems. Which ends today since you lack the sense to submit."

"Never," said Damon, knowing that his friends would agree.

With the two-handed sword between his hands, Damon grunted and advanced on the Fae King. The shining weapon flashed as Damon raised it high, preparing to smite Oberon with a heavy blow.

Oberon barely reacted.

As the deadly edge flew at his head, he casually raised his arm, catching the blade in his fist.

"You dare to attack me with my own weapon? I was the one who imbued it with its power. I am its master. Not you!"

A twitch of the arm and Damon was thrown across the hall to crash into an old bench. The wood exploded into dust, insects bursting and attacking him ferociously.

Damon let his rage consume him as he tossed the blade away and transformed into a huge gray wolf, knowing that his hybrid form wouldn't be enough. As the crackle of eldritch energies filled the air, Damon leapt at Oberon, who swatted him away with the Horn of Bran Galed to land on the stone steps.

§

The moment Oberon stopped the Shining Sword with his bare hand, Remi knew they were in trouble. She reached for the Veil, searching for ghosts that might be able to help her against the Fae King, but there were none nearby. The awful artifact at the base of the throne was probably the cause for their absence.

But she had other tricks.

Remi chanted the ritual that would open the barrier between the Veil and the Fae. She had no protective wards, but anything that might come through would be equally as dangerous to Oberon. When the ritual completed, green mist wrapped around her ankles and spread out across the great hall, creating a spectral field in which she could work.

She chummed the waters with copious amounts of raw faez, the golden sparkles making her nose itch. Immediately, the grotesque howl of a single hound answered. It sent shivers down her spine, but she continued feeding the Veil with unspent magic while Lily and Damon battled Oberon.

A dark, loping shape moved through the Veil towards her. It was moving fast. Remi prepared to jump out of the way, hoping to be like a matador with a charging bull. If she timed it right, the hound would speed past and find the Fae King as its prey.

"Remi!"

She almost turned too late, finding the towering figure of Oberon over her. She saw a ghostly helm over his head, antlers as wide as a long bow stretching out. His eyes crackled with sickly green energy, and overlapping him, she saw the Caoránarch.

Newly grown thorny vines sprung from the earth, wrapping around Remi like a nest of serpents. The sharp tips shred her flesh, spilling droplets of blood as she screamed.

The Veil hound was nearly upon them, but she could no longer hold the barrier open under such duress. The green mist sucked towards her and disappeared, leaving nothing but broken stone and pain in its place. As the vines continued to grow around her, obliterating her vision, Remi feared the Court of the Summer Fae would be her tomb.

§

In a thousand, thousand lifetimes, Lily would have never imagined that she would be battling Oberon, King of the Summer Fae. They stood no conceivable chance to defeat him. They would have found far easier targets in the former Head Patron Invictus, or one of the ancient dragons that were known to lurk in their realm.

Normally, she would have relied on plants and hexes in an all-out battle, but Oberon was immune to them both. Lily produced the Crux, the Fomorian artifact, and channeled her magic through it. The twisting of elemental earth and fire, born of a volcanic realm, made her choke on the black smoke and brimstone. She fought through the discomfort, squinting from the heat, and sent a deep stone up through the earth, knocking Oberon from his feet before he could hurt Damon again.

The Fae King quickly found his feet, and after tossing the Horn to the side, directed his anger towards her. He wrapped the specter of the Wild Hunt around him, ghostly antlered helm scraping the walls, as he pulled a fell blade from nowhere.

Oberon attacked her with the ferocity of a falling comet. Lily barely got the Crux up to deflect the shadowy Blade of the Wild Hunt. The impact blew her backwards, tumbling past Remi, who was deep in a Veil ritual.

Her bones ached from the blow. She felt like she'd been in a dozen car crashes one after another. Lily crawled to her knees to see both Remi and Neko being consumed by thorny vines.

Lily poured her magic into the Crux, willing it to unlock its magics. This time, she exposed herself to the Fomorian artifact, knowing any hesitation would cost them. In the blink of an eye, she witnessed its creation, born in the belly of a volcano: the shaman who had donated its bones being stripped of flesh by the all-consuming fires. She saw how it was used in the wars against the Fae, except the seelie lords were the ones on the offense, riding their ghostly horses through stone villages, slaughtering Fomorians en masse.

Seeing how they'd been treated, and how the Fae had lied about who was the aggressor, Lily embraced the Crux. She felt it unlock, and power flooded into her veins like hot lava. It was almost too much. The stifling heat and pressure was intense, but she channeled it through the artifact, sending a stream of flaming liquid at the Fae King, much as Balor the Evil Eye had done to them.

Flame and smoke filled the chamber amid screams from her friends. Lily used the artifact like a fire hose of lava, spraying it towards the Fae King, who deflected it with his arm, but was unable to press his advantage. She'd always thought of Fomorian magics as a perversion of nature—fiery destruction rather than living growth—but as the magic flowed through her, she saw how it was equal to the enchantments of the Fae.

But as powerful as the artifact was, it was no match for Oberon, King of Summer. He waded through the flame, closing the distance, bringing her end painfully near.

She could no longer see her friends amid the black smoke though she could hear Damon's growls and Remi's cursing as she climbed free of her cocoon of thorny vines.

"We have to get that bloody artifact out of here! I'll keep him distracted," Lily shouted.

She backed up, keeping the flow of flame pointed towards Oberon, even as the Crux grew hotter in her fist. The skin on the back of her knuckles had already begun to bubble from the heat.

"Come on, you corrupted fool, follow me," she muttered to herself.

The spray of lava was catching everything in the great hall on fire. Flame licked up the walls and spread amongst the old wood and dead vines.

"Bloody hell, what am I doing?"

THIRTY-FOUR

The burning vines screamed and pulled away from Remi, tearing her skin, but giving her enough room to crawl free from the plant mass. Black smoke burned her eyes and lungs as Lily battled Oberon in the lower part of the chamber. She'd heard her friend's instruction to get rid of the artifact, but how could she accomplish that?

Remi limped to the throne, which remained untouched from the destruction. The fire had gotten into the walls and was climbing towards the ceiling.

As she approached the chaos-shaped hole, the high-pitched keening that had made her squint before returned. Even looking in its direction made her sick to her stomach, but she persisted, taking step after step until she was only a few feet away.

She finally could see what was lurking in the nest of vines beneath the throne. It looked like dark quartz, but as she peered closer she saw how the colors shifted from green to black and back again, inky tendrils lifting from the surface like coronal plasma ejections from the sun.

The artifact whispered to her: promising power and the end to her pain, even as she heard the screams beneath the din. The urge to hold it against her chest and experience annihilation made her reach out against her will. She felt the artifact drag her forward, fingers digging through the vines...

Damon grabbed her arm.

"What are you doing?"

The sight of a naked Damon in the middle of the burning hall broke her out of the trance.

"I don't...know."

"Don't touch it. I know that much, even if I don't know what it is."

"It's in my head," she said, squeezing her eyes shut for a moment.

"I hear it too. It's whispering sweet oblivion. But you can't touch it. I remember what Oberon said. *'No living or dead can touch the Thrice-Cursed Stone. I should know, because I dared to test it.'*"

Remi checked back to the battle between her friend and the Fae King. The flames and black smoke hid the details but she could hear the shouts and painful destruction of the great hall.

"The Thrice-Cursed Stone," said Remi, wishing she knew something of the artifact before them. But she'd spent her time in the Halls studying how to heal people, not deal with artifacts that were strong enough to warp an entire realm.

A rising scream that ended suddenly had them turning their heads. The geysers of flame that had signaled the battle between Lily and Oberon were no longer there.

"He's coming," said Damon.

"I have an idea, but I'm going to need time."

"I can't stop him."

"You'll have to think of something," she said as she opened her mind to the Veil.

§

Naked and covered in splatters of burnt flesh from the sparks, Damon collected the Shining Sword from the hall floor. He searched his mind for a way to defeat Oberon, but he knew that way was madness.

He wasn't a warrior. The attempts to train with the sword had proved that much. Better it'd gone to someone else, but here it was in his fist, as the one who created it approached.

The antlered Fae King appeared out of the swirling smoke. He snapped his fingers and the flames that were consuming the great hall collapsed as if they'd been doused in water.

"I took care of your friend, now it's your turn."

Lily!

"Please, don't you see what that artifact is doing to you? It's warped your mind. You've destroyed the very realm you were meant to protect."

Oberon hesitated as if his deep mind was answering the question, but then the crown of his head was ringed in sickly green flame. His eyes glowed with madness.

"You cannot stop me, and once I'm done here, I will return to your realm and take control using the Horn."

Despair punched a hole in Damon's chest as he thought about how easily Oberon would dominate the Halls. But then he had a hopeful thought: if he were so powerful, why did he come back to the Fae, unless they could somehow endanger his plans? Otherwise, he would have stayed in Invictus and let the artifact or the wild lands take care of them.

He had no idea how to stop Oberon, but maybe he didn't have to. Remi had a plan. He just needed to give her time.

Before Oberon could reach him, Damon drove the tip of the Shining Sword downward and bent his knee until it hit the floor.

"As King Nuada's heir and the warden of the Shining Sword, I, Damon Wolfhard, do renew my bond with Oberon, King of the Summer Fae."

The pledge halted Oberon's progress forward. The Fae King paused, first in confusion, then in laughter.

"Finally came to your senses. Better to be alive on the side of the victor than to die fruitlessly. Rise, Damon Wolfhard, Heir of King Nuada and champion of the Claíomh Ag Lonrú. Rise and serve me."

Damon cautiously regained his feet, keeping his right hand wrapped around the hilt. He felt a strange energy enter his body. It was both enlightening and fulfilling. For the first time, he felt his purpose in life. Foolishly spending his time helping others in the hospital had been nothing but a distraction. This was his true mission: to serve the Fae King.

"What do you command me to do?"

"Kill your friends."

§

Within seconds, the swirling green mist wrapped around Remi's ankles. She feared that the Veil hound might be lurking nearby, but didn't sense its presence.

This time, instead of chumming the waters with faez, Remi called out with her entire body and mind, vocalizing for the sake of balance.

"Stranger! Please hear me and heed my call!"

She repeated the phrase three times before she remembered that she knew his name from the ghost drummer.

"Devlin! Please, we need your help, or the realms will fall like dominos."

She felt his presence before she saw him. A dark, brooding figure shifting across the landscape without the act of movement. Within a few blinks, he was standing before her, just beyond the barrier between the living and the dead.

"You should not have called me. I cannot save you."

"I'm not asking you to save me."

He flinched at her response, but she couldn't understand why. Then Devlin searched the space nearby.

"What have you done?"

"It's not what we've done, but the King of the Summer Fae. He's been corrupted by this awful artifact, the Thrice-Cursed Stone, but neither the living or the dead can touch it."

Devlin stared back at her.

"I see."

"You have to take it. It's warped Oberon's mind and turned him against his own nature. I'm not even sure the Veil is safe if he gets control of the Hundred Halls in this state."

"What do you want me to do?"

"You said it yourself, you're no longer living, but you're not dead either. You, and you alone, can touch the Thrice-Cursed Stone without being affected."

"And what would you have me do with it?"

"Take it to the Tomb and keep it safe."

His lip curled in disgust.

"I can smell the Horn nearby. I should take it back instead."

"Please..."

Devlin, the Stranger, stared at her forlornly. She couldn't understand the reason for his emotion, nor why he continued to help her after all she'd done against his wishes until she was hit by an epiphany.

"You know my mother, you know Coraline..."

His eyes rounded with surprise.

"You've met her?"

"You're my father, aren't you? Don't lie to me. Not now."

Devlin's mouth wrinkled with pain.

"I was forbidden to, but I—"

The upward flicker of his gaze was the only warning Remi had. She threw herself to the side as the Shining Sword slammed down into the spot she'd just been standing.

A naked Damon approached with the sword in his fist, eyes glowing with sickly green light. Behind him, the tall antlered figure appeared out of the smoke. Oberon's gaze flickered to Devlin, who was not yet in the Fae, but standing at the barrier between realms.

"Whoever you are, you made a mistake coming to her aid. Your defiance ends now!"

A voice called out from behind.

"Oberon!"

To Remi's surprise, a battered and burnt Lily appeared out of the gloom. She looked like she'd been pulled out of a burning building the moment before it collapsed. The edges of her curly rainbow hair were crisped and soot covered her face as she looked barely well enough to remain standing.

But none of that was as important as what was in her hand.

The Horn of Bran Galed.

"Your reign ends now. The liquid in this Horn will give me the power to destroy even you. There's nothing you can do to stop me!"

Hope bloomed in Remi's chest. The powerful artifact had gotten lost in the battle, but Lily had found it and a way to turn the tide against the Fae King.

Lily lifted the Horn to her lips.

And it was snatched from her grip by Oberon, who darted to her side faster than a blink.

"I'll show you the meaning of power."

Remi saw their end coming quick. Once he drank from the Horn, he would kill, or enslave them with the Thrice-Cursed Stone. They'd lost. So close to the end.

Then she saw the smirk on Lily's lips. A tiny little curl at the corner, that Irish grin in the face of certain death.

"Take the stone!" she yelled at Devlin. "Now!"

The brooding figure reached into the chaos-shaped hole, releasing the dark quartz from its nest as sickly green and purple tendrils flickered over his form without affecting him. He nodded and disappeared into the Veil.

When she turned back to Oberon, he had a hand to his throat. Whatever liquid Lily had tricked him into drinking, it was affecting him severely. He gasped and punched himself in the sternum. The spectral flames whipped around his head, growing thinner by the second. Damon was equally injured, on his knees as the sickly green light fled his muscled body.

A booming crack in the roof of the great hall had them throwing themselves out of the way as the structure collapsed. Smoldering wood splintered in all directions.

Through the gaps in the walls, Remi saw the forest shake as if it were in the middle of a hurricane. The ground rumbled and birds took to the sky in great clouds.

"We have to get out of here!" screamed Lily.

But there was nowhere to go. The entire realm was going through a great upheaval as the Horn did its work on Oberon.

"Remi..."

The familiar voice had her spinning around to find Devlin standing in a portal of his own making.

"Bring me the Horn."

Lily scooped the artifact from the ground and handed it to Devlin.

"Grab your friend, I'll give you passage back to your realm."

With Lily's help, they lifted the naked Damon by each arm and dragged him through the shimmering field, collapsing on hard concrete in the middle of a light rain.

Battered, burnt, and exhausted from the travel through the Fae, Remi was almost too tired to lift her head to find out where they'd landed until she heard the sweet sounds of an approaching siren.

"We're back. We're at Golden Willow."

THIRTY-FIVE

The frenzied squeaks of a frightened Neko emanated from her burnt hair. Lily took in her surroundings, finding against expectations that they were at Golden Willow. Which was good, because she'd sustained a lot of burns in the fight and needed more than the care she could easily give to herself.

"I know, Little One, I know. That was too close."

She'd managed to rescue the changeling from the vines before she stumbled onto the Horn. Neko was injured too, but he healed quicker than she was able to.

"I think we've been spotted," said Lily.

"Kinda hard not to with this tall, handsome, and very naked fifth year at our side."

Lily raised an eyebrow.

"He's a real stunner."

"Where are we?" muttered Damon on his hands and knees. "And did anyone grab the sword?"

"No, but it doesn't matter now. We're home."

He groaned and put his fingertips to his temple.

"That was awful. I was an observer in my own body."

The approaching ambulance slowed, which brought laughter from Remi. Lily thought she might have gone mad until she saw who was leaning out of the window.

"Was there a fire nearby? And did your boyfriend get his clothes burnt perfectly off?" asked Vasquez, smirking.

"Got a jumpsuit in his size?"

A few seconds later, Paxton threw an EMT jumpsuit out the window and the ambulance continued to the ER entrance with its sirens off.

A few pedestrians gawked as Damon climbed into the jumpsuit, but it was much better than the scene he'd cause once they went inside. They headed to the side entrance.

"Do you think it worked?" asked Remi with her hand on the door. "I thought the Horn couldn't fix a corrupted realm."

"It can't, but it can fix a person. Oberon is the embodiment of the Fae realm." She glanced upward. "Should I even be here? I kinda forgot that I quit."

"I did too."

Damon was tugging at the crotch of his jumpsuit, which was a size too small.

"If you don't like the fit, you can always change and turn it into shreds," said Lily.

"It doesn't feel good either," he said, tugging at the fabric around his crotch.

Inside the hospital, Lily led them limping towards the main entrance.

The smell of antiseptic and lemons was soothing to her exhausted mind, which felt strange after a childhood in the forest, but despite the struggles, she'd come to love working in the hospital.

"Where are we going?" asked Damon.

"To find out if it worked."

Coming around the corner, they ran into Boon, who was walking briskly and typing into his phone. He had a sucker in his mouth, which slipped out the moment he laid eyes on them. The candy exploded on the tile.

"You're back? And are you all okay?"

"This might seem like a strange question, but how long have we been gone?"

His eyebrows went up and down in thought.

"Nothing is strange when it comes to you three. A month. It's March already. Where have you been and why do you look like you escaped a burning building? Except you, Damon, why are you wearing EMT clothes?"

"Because he was naked when we got back," said Remi.

"Damn, shame I missed that," said Boon, winking.

"It's a long story, and right now, we're too bloody tired to tell it, but we need to check on something."

"What?" he asked with a furrowed brow. "Don't you need medical care first? We're not far from the ER."

"Not yet," said Lily with a grimace. The burn on her left thigh felt like fire, but there were more important things. "Dr. Broomfield. Know where he's at?"

"Are you crazy? Didn't he threaten to call the police on you before you quit? And things have gotten worse since you left. Weird too. Like half the class has been talking about quitting."

"Like what?" asked Damon.

"We don't have time," countered Lily while grimacing.

"Are we sure that's a good idea?" asked Remi. "It's not like we ever saw the weird green light in his eyes."

"Weird green light?" asked Boon.

"Call it a hunch."

Boon checked his phone.

"He's probably at morning check-in."

"Thanks, Boon. I have one more favor to ask."

"Anything."

"Can I borrow your phone? I'll give it back in a little bit."

"Sec," he said, typing furiously and then hitting send and handing it over. "If you get any strange messages..."

"I won't read them, Boon."

"Thanks."

As they headed to the Curse Ward, Lily dialed her sister. The phone rang and eventually went to voicemail, which didn't surprise her. The Mists required late nights. She left a message.

"Not awake?" asked Remi.

"Probably. She could have spent the night at Mag's too. I'd hoped to know before we talked to Broomfield. We'll know either way soon enough."

To their surprise at the nurses station, they found Dr. Paddock giving terse instructions to the staff in his typical tone-deaf style. The pulsing jaws and shared eye-rolls went unnoticed by the doctor.

"Where's Broomfield?" Lily asked one of the nurses, receiving bulged eyes for her unexpected arrival.

"Healer Lily...I wasn't expecting to see you again. Are you okay? Do you need care?"

"I wasn't expecting to be here. And no, not yet. Please."

The nurse looked them over with a narrowed gaze.

"He was in the cafeteria having breakfast a short while ago as he does right before staff meetings, but then he fell over and they rushed him to a room. He's doing fine, but he seems a little out of it. He's saying shit that nobody can understand."

"What about?" asked Remi.

"Excuse me," said Dr. Paddock as he shoved his clipboard under his arm. "I don't believe the three of you work here anymore. Would you please excuse yourself from the hospital before I call security?"

"We won't be in your hair any longer," said Remi.

A smattering of laughter behind cupped hands spread through the group as Dr. Paddock glowered. As they moved away, the nurse mouthed the number of Dr. Broomfield's room. They went around the long way so Dr. Paddock didn't think they hadn't left.

Dr. Broomfield was sitting up in bed when they arrived. His hair had gone completely gray and he had his hands clasped in front, with fidgeting thumbs rubbing against each other. His eyes widened with fright when he noticed them in the open door.

"If you're going to do it, make it quick. I won't struggle."

Lily shared worried glances with her friends.

"What do you think we're going to do?"

His mouth worked but no words came. He looked like he was in existential pain.

"I don't know, but I deserve it. The things I've done, please..."

The normally stern doctor broke down with his face in his hands, sobbing uncontrollably. Lily strode to the bed and slapped his hands away from his face. He was startled. Surprised. Looked ready to bolt.

"Don't you dare think that way, you bloody eejit. You were out of your fooking mind because Aleksandr Grimm had stuck his greedy Fae fingers in there and scrambled your brain like eggs."

"Grimm?"

"Yes, Grimm, you eejit. But he's not just the Patron of Arcane Phytology, he's the bloody King of Summer Fae. Oberon. His Majesty and all that. But his mind was gone too. Taken over by some awful artifact."

The news seemed to be too much for their head instructor. His mouth wrinkled in horror as he stared out the window.

A subtle knock announced they had a visitor. Dr. Fairlight was standing in the doorway with a pinched expression. Her eyes flickered to Dr. Broomfield and then back to them. She nodded towards the hallway and closed the door behind them.

The bags and dark circles under her eyes were worse than Lily had ever seen. She looked like she'd been crying.

"Are you okay?" asked Damon.

"Better now."

Her eyes flickered to the door.

"Did Broomfield do something to you? Because if he did, it wasn't him. He was being controlled."

Her nostrils flared as she crossed her arms.

"It doesn't make it any better."

Lily shared another glance with her friends. Clearly some bad things had happened while they were gone.

Heavy steps had them turning around to find a cadre of Invictus PD coming around the corner. Lily froze. She hadn't expected Dr. Fairlight to call the cops on them. The head of Golden Willow pushed through the group and introduced herself to the officers.

"Are these the problem?" asked a mustached officer with his hands on his belt.

Dr. Fairlight glanced to them with her mouth set in a grim line.

"No. He's in the room. Dr. Broomfield. He's the one that needs to be taken into custody."

Lily watched as the officers marched into the room and after reading him his rights, hauled the doctor out of the building. When the show was over, Dr. Fairlight turned back to them.

"I assume the three of you will be resuming your roles in Aura Healers and Golden Willow?"

They shared shocked glances before nodding.

"Good. I'd hate to lose three excellent Healers. Now please excuse me, I have some other problems to deal with before my head implodes from this migraine."

After she left, the three of them huddled around.

"Poor Dr. Fairlight. Whatever happened while we were gone must have been bad," said Damon.

"More importantly, does this mean...?" asked Remi.

The answer was interrupted by Boon's phone.

"Alice?"

"Branch and bough, you're alive. I thought I'd lost you, sister."

The tremble in Alice's voice made her heart tear.

"I'm not that easy to kill. None of us are."

"What happened?"

"A long story for another time, but how are you? That's what's more important."

She didn't want to tell her yet, not until she knew for sure that it'd worked.

"Are you sure you didn't do anything?"

"Why?"

"Because about a half hour ago, I was lying in bed with Mag and suddenly I was in awful pain. I ran to the bathroom and boked up this black tar crap that won't even flush. That's why I missed your call. We're going to have to pay for a plumber. That's how bad it is."

"How do you feel now?" asked Lily with her heart in her throat.

"I might need to boke again, but otherwise, feeling better than I have in years."

The tension broke in Lily's shoulders as she put a hand to her fore-head.

"Oh, thank Medb."

"Not Medb, I imagine, but you. What did you do, Lily?"

"Do me a favor and find out how the rest of the clan is doing. I have a few things I need to do around here first."

After she hung up, Remi tilted her head.

"What do we need to do first?"

Lily collapsed to one knee and pulled up her shirt where the heat from the battle with Oberon had bubbled her skin.

"If I don't get this taken care of right bloody now, I'm going to pass out."

THIRTY-SIX

The runed circle around outside of the patient's room pulsed faintly, a steady pace that was soothing as Remi sat on the edge of the bed and watched Ms. Dar speak quietly with the apparition on the other side. The ghost had been her sister, who'd died tragically when she was much younger from a serial killer in the eleventh ward.

"It's done," said Ms. Dar.

The older woman's brown skin pinched and wrinkled around her mouth as she gave her sister's ghost a feeble wave. The ghost, still in the bloom of youth and wearing a flowery dress popular in the previous century, returned the gesture and faded backwards into the Veil, disappearing into the faint green mist.

Remi dismissed the spectral field with the flick of her wrist. The cold mist that had been swirling around the tile and beneath the bed rushed back into the realm between the living and the dead.

Tears dribbled down the old woman's cheeks. Remi collected one hand within her own, giving a gentle squeeze for reassurance.

"Inaya said it hurt a lot, but it was quick, and there was nothing I could have done. She'd been sneaking out to meet a boy who didn't show up that night and she decided to walk home. She wouldn't tell me what happened after that..."

"I'm sorry, Ms. Dar, that sounded difficult to hear."

The old woman thumbed away a tear.

"This sounds selfish, but I worried that it was my fault my entire life. I thought I'd done a poor job as the older sister. My parents were always telling me, keep an eye on Inaya, she's a wild one, if something happens to her, it's your fault. But now I know it wasn't. I'm sorry, Inaya. I wish I could have saved you."

Ms. Dar turned her head away, so Remi gave her hand one last squeeze and let herself out of the room. The runes could be cleaned up later. They were harmless without her connection to the Veil.

"How do you think it went?" asked Dr. Morsdux, who'd been watching remotely.

"She got the closure she wanted." Remi furrowed her brow. "But there was no guarantee that was going to happen."

"Would your opinion about the experience be different if that hadn't happened?"

Remi cupped her chin.

"I think she needed the truth so she could die in peace, even if that truth wasn't what she wanted to hear. I would do it again. She deserved that much."

"For what it's worth, I agree," said Dr. Morsdux with a tilted grin. "Which is why I'm going to bring our findings to Dr. Fairlight this week for official approval of the program. Assuming you're still up for it?"

Remi thought about her past, the lies from her "parents" and how it'd twisted her life into something unrecognizable compared to the one she had now. They'd kept so much from her. It wasn't until Remi had learned the truth, that she'd come from a union between Coraline and the being from the Veil named Devlin, that anything in her life had made sense. So she understood Ms. Dar's need for the truth to facilitate her closure. Remi felt like she was finally able to reckon with the person she was. Her only wish now was that she could talk to her real parents again.

"Yes, but only for the Hospice Ward. I don't want to turn into a three-penny séance service. This is just to make sure they pass into the Veil safely and with the peace that I hope they deserve."

"I've made note of that in my findings."

"Thank you, Dr. Morsdux." She paused, feeling heavy from her thoughts and the time spent on the borders of the Veil. "Are you still, you know, thinking about...?"

"Not right away, a few years as we discussed, but I think it's time for me to pass the torch."

A little panic set in as she thought about being in charge of an entire ward.

"A few means like five or ten years? I haven't even graduated yet."

A wry smile appeared on his lips.

"I won't leave until you're ready."

"Thank you." She checked the time. "May I be excused for a bit? I have some things I have to discuss with, well, you know."

"Of course. Give Healers Lily and Damon my regards."

Remi touched the plaque on the way out of the Ward. The brass letters were comforting under her fingertips. Heading up to the rooftop only brought back the memories of her trip to the Summer Fae. She'd kept herself busy since the return to ward away thoughts of the struggles and the final battle. While they'd ultimately been successful, she was still haunted by the destruction that the Thrice-Cursed Stone had caused, and that they hadn't heard anything about the aftereffects of their fight with Oberon.

Damon was sitting on the picnic bench with a Mage Blast Purple Passion energy drink cupped between his hands. He opened a cooler and handed her one, Ruby Red, her favorite. She leaned on his shoulder and enjoyed the light breeze brushing through her hair and the sounds of distant sirens as she sipped the chilled beverage. The whirl of a helicopter was receding and she hoped whoever it was going to fetch would be okay until it got there.

"Is this where all the cool kids hang out?" asked Lily when she appeared.

She dug an Energy Emerald out of the cooler and took a spot next to Remi, cracking the top with a wrist twist, which brought a faint squeak from her curly auburn hair. Since the burn recovery, she hadn't been able to dye her hair while the healing elixirs were repairing her skin.

"I'd feel a lot cooler if I hadn't had to assist a disimpaction this morning. You'd think as fifth years that we'd be over that kind of stuff," said Damon, before he threw back another gulp.

Lily chuckled and held out her bottle.

"I had a sanguine tumor explode on me this morning when I tried to apply a counterhex to it. Got some in my mouth too. Lovely fooking stuff."

"That bloody sucks," said Remi, holding back a grin.

"Totally bloody sucks," said Damon. "Really bloody."

Lily chuckled and pulled the sleeve of her scrubs past her elbow.

"Piss off, you fooking eejits. I've got these damn runed patches I have to wear for the next week. Supposedly going to make my piss smell like burnt toast."

Remi held up her drink.

"I helped a dying woman talk to her sister who'd been murdered by a serial killer last century. Her death had been haunting her since forever."

"Ouch, you okay? I think I'd rather deal with hardened fecal matter than that," said Damon.

"It was the right thing, even though it was hard to hear."

Lily bumped into her.

"Speaking of the dead, you seen that handsome, brooding father of yours since?"

"No. I opened the barrier to the Veil a week ago and tried to talk to him, but there was no answer."

Technically, it was the third time since she'd returned, but she didn't want them to know how desperate she was to reconnect with at least one of her parents.

"That sucks," said Damon.

"At least I know *who* my father is. I can understand if he doesn't want to reciprocate. It's not like he's free to come and visit, being a creature of the Veil now."

"What about Coraline?"

"When things are settled down, I want to go back and see her. I have a lot of questions."

"Hey," said Damon, his joyful expression falling to disappointment, "have you heard the news about Dr. Fairlight?"

Remi turned towards him.

"She's giving up her position and taking a leave of absence."

"Wow, but also, not surprised, given everything that happened recently," said Remi, shaking her head.

"What a shit show," said Lily.

"I also heard that Broomfield tried to hang himself in jail with his blanket. After what he did, mind-controlled or not, I can't imagine having to live with that."

Remi shuddered. The reports of what had happened after they left were horrific. Half of which was only still being uncovered. The investigation would probably last for the rest of the year.

"Not to be callous about his situation, but what does that mean for you?" asked Remi.

Their relationship had been on hold since they'd come back, mostly due to a lack of time and dealing with the repercussions of everything that had happened. Even before they'd left for the Summer Fae, they'd been dancing around the topic of what happened with them once their time in Aura Healers ended. At the time, he was slated for the Institute while she was thinking she'd end up staying at Golden Willow. While a long-distance relationship wasn't out of the question, it certainly wouldn't be easy.

"I don't know. He hadn't given his recommendation yet, but maybe now that's a good thing. His reputation is tarnished beyond recognition. At this point, I don't know what I'm doing in two months after we graduate. I'll probably stay here until I figure it out."

Warmth rose to Remi's cheeks. She bumped into him playfully and smiled when he glanced over.

"What in the bloody nine hells is that?" asked Lily, sitting up tall.

Damon stood, which blocked Remi, so she climbed onto the picnic table to get a better view. She rubbed her eyes the first time, thinking she was hallucinating.

"Is that what I think it is?" asked Damon, wrapping his arm around her thigh.

Remi scrunched up her forehead.

"What do you think that is?" she asked.

Clopping down the street leading to the front entrance of the hospital were a pair of enormous elks with racks wider than a city bus, pulling an ornate carriage that looked like it was made from tightly woven vines with bright flowers covering the outside. It looked like a traveling garden.

"I think we should go down," said Lily.

Their brisk pace turned into a hurried run as they sprinted down the stairwell and through pristine white -tiled hallways of Golden Willow, passing staff and patients who gave them a wide berth.

Remi burst out of the front with her friends behind to a crowd that had formed at the appearance of the elk-drawn carriage. The elks and carriage were even bigger than they looked from above, with the racks nearly scraping the high port.

"Blood and bough," she muttered.

The crowd was busy trying to take pictures, but were cursing about their faulty phones. Remi had a pretty good idea why they weren't working.

When the crowd wouldn't part, Damon stepped in front, politely maneuvering people out of the way. An older man refused to budge until Damon revealed his claws and then there was no more resistance.

The three of them stood side by side a few strides from the carriage door. The intricate woven vines created fractal-like shapes in both the woody material and the spaces between. The vines that made up the door retreated into the rest of the carriage, while others formed a stair step to the road.

From the open space, Remi was expecting the handsome Fae King's alter ego Aleksandr Grimm, or one of his heralds or members of the Summer Court. She almost didn't recognize Morwen when she first stepped out of the carriage. She was the same eternally cute pixie with her hair in a faux Mohawk and wearing flowing robes the colors of summer, but she was radiant like the sun. A woman in the back of the crowd fainted.

It wasn't just Morwen, but Talwen too, who followed her sister out of the carriage, looking resplendent, rather than the run-down pixie with darkened eyes that she'd been when they'd last seen her.

Morwen strode forward with the grace of a Fae Queen...until she reached them, raised her arms, and threw herself around Remi with a squeal.

"I can't believe you did it!"

Remi hugged the pixie back, smiling at Talwen, who'd rolled her eyes at the outburst. Morwen proceeded to hug each one of them, while her sister patiently waited for the greetings to finish.

"I know I'm supposed to be all formal and stuff, but I couldn't help myself."

"What's this all about?" asked Lily.

Remi knew that Lily had been talking with her sisters in Ireland regularly, and asking when they could come visit, but they'd been unusually tight-lipped, which Lily had interpreted as a sign that Medb had given them instructions. If Alice weren't in town, Remi suspected Lily would have returned to Ireland to see her family.

"What do you think, silly?"

"No one's been telling us anything. Does your appearance in this carriage mean that the Summer Fae is fixed?" asked Damon.

Morwen lifted her shoulders playfully.

"I can't tell you anything, except that you've been cordially invited to a celebration in three days' time. A carriage, which I hope is akin to this one, so fade, it has vines that you can drink from that taste like watermelon soju, but anyway, what was I saying? Oh yes, there's a certain someone who'd like to see you again and thank you for everything you've done. Me too, in fact, not that it means as much."

"It means just as much to me," said Lily, beaming a smile.

Morwen gave the Irish witch a curtsey.

"I can't stay long, trust me, I want to, but you don't get opportunities like this very often. But we'll talk again in a few days. I can't wait to see you all."

"What should we wear?" asked Lily.

"Oh right," said Morwen, turning to her sister, who handed over three small flower buds.

"This one is for you, and this one is for you, and the last one is yours."

Remi stared at the petite closed flower bud in her palm. She felt it shiver on her flesh, the tremble of magic waiting to be unfolded.

"Don't wake them until it's time. Anyway, gotta run, meter's running and all that. See you soon!"

After another round of hurried hugs, the sisters disappeared into the cavernous interior of the carriage as vines reformed to create the flowered door. The enormous elks surged forward, ducking their heads as not to damage the lights under the high port, and then went back the other way. The carriage disappeared through a shimmering mist, leaving the three friends, and the assembled crowd, stunned in silence.

THIRTY-SEVEN

The appearance of the Fae carriage three days previously, on top of the upheaval in the staff and the rumors of where the three of them had been during their absence, had made them into minor celebrities in the hospital. Damon couldn't go anywhere without nurses or even patients whispering to each other behind cupped hands.

He was relieved when the day finally arrived. Damon wished he still had the Shining Sword, but he'd left it in the Court of the Summer Fae.

When it came time to wake the magic in the flower bud, he breathed golden faez into his palm. The sparkles made his palm itch and then the bud trembled like a leaf in a storm until it bloomed into a light purple hooded flower that he recognized as wolfsbane.

The transformation continued as thin vines exploded from the base of the flower, wrapping around his wrist and forearm, startling him to step backwards, hitting the bed with the back of his legs before falling into his piled laundry. For a brief moment, he feared the flower had been a trick, but then he saw what was happening. The vines were weaving a suit around his body. He'd been naked except for his boxers when he'd started, but wondered what would have happened if he'd been wearing scrubs.

In the span of a few minutes, the vines created a fashionable, elegant suit made of green and brown vines with accents of purple wolfsbane throughout. The shoes that grew on his feet were cushioned with fungus.

When he examined himself in the mirror, Damon didn't know what to think. He didn't recognize himself. The clothing made him look Fae-like, especially since his cheeks had grown a little gaunt from the long year.

Damon turned heads when he entered the hospital proper. He was always used to a little side-eye from the ladies, or occasional man, who appreciated his athletic form, but this was different. Even the orderly in white clothes mopping the floor let his jaw drop when he saw him.

By the time he reached the front of the hospital, he had a little follow-ing, mostly women and a few curious kids.

"I feel like the Pied Piper," he muttered to himself.

When he stepped outside, he found Lily already waiting. The mass of curly auburn hair was a dead giveaway, but if she hadn't had that, or a transformed Neko at her side, he might not have recognized her.

The magical flower bud had wrapped her in a dress made of emerald silk covered in pink flowers. The designs suggested Celtic symbols, which gave her a witchy feel while still being elegant. She turned when she heard him clear his throat.

"You look stunning," said Damon, bowing at the waist.

Lily put a hand to her mouth.

"You almost gave me a pang of desire," she said with a wink.

"I'll take that as a high compliment." He turned to Neko, who'd chosen a sleek white fox as his form. "And you look smashing as always,

Neko."

The changeling bent his forelegs in the semblance of a bow.

"I take it your dress didn't come from vines?"

Lily splayed out the lower half.

"The bloody silkworms gave me a start. I thought it was a trick until they began weaving my dress around me. The bog rosemary is a nice touch. They were plentiful where I grew up and are great for healing."

"I had the same..."

He didn't get to finish what he was saying because Lily's jaw dropped as she faced the entrance. Damon turned to find the most beautiful woman he'd ever seen strolling through the parting crowd.

The dress Remi wore defied understanding: a mix of mist and shadow, summer green and eclipse black. It wrapped tightly around her body, yet breathed with her movements. Each step produced a puff of shadow, which created a pseudo tail. Her hair was its same messy style, but it matched the dress in ways he'd never thought possible.

"Please don't look at me like I'm an animal in a zoo," said Remi, fidgeting with the front of her dress and glancing askew.

"Blood and bone," said Damon. "You'd make Celesse D'Agastine jealous."

Remi recoiled with her cheeks turning crimson.

"Damon..."

Lily shook her head.

"He's right, Remi. I didn't know you had it in you."

"Really?" asked Remi, staring down her chest at the unusual dress.

"I think the mix of Veil and Fae really bring out who you really are."

A cheer from the crowd, which had grown to a few hundred in the short span, announced the arrival of the carriage. It was the same as the one that had brought the Clover sisters, yet seemed grander. The elks had to bow their heads to fit under the high port, and when the door unraveled to form stairs that led into the carriage, the crowd applauded.

"I feel like a princess climbing into the pumpkin," said Remi as she went up the steps.

Damon went up last, giving the crowd a wave before disappearing inside. The benches were made of velvety mushrooms, and as mentioned by Morwen, there were curly-Q vines that looked made for drinking.

When the carriage surged into motion, Damon reached out and clasped hands with Remi.

"You know you two can never get married now," said Lily with a smirk.

"What?" they both responded.

Lily laughed heartily with her hand on Neko's white back.

"Because you'll never have a wedding outfit as beautiful as the ones you're wearing."

"Yours is gorgeous too," said Remi, reaching out.

Lily lifted both shoulders.

"Oh, it is. It's right fooking gorgeous, but it's also practical. These symbols make this dress into a potent arcane focuser. My Lord Oberon has gifted me something priceless."

Damon was about to ask when they would get to the Fae, when the air crackled with eldritch magics. They peered through the gaps between the vines to see a shimmering appear ahead of the elks. The transition to the Summer Fae was smooth as silk with none of the normal vertigo that came with travel between realms.

The carriage appeared in a green glade, moving swiftly across a stone path that led along a serene river that tumbled playfully over small rocks and boulders while tiny glowing shapes flitted between the trees.

"Is that...?" asked Damon.

"The river we traveled? Yes," said Remi.

"Oh, bloody hell," said Lily with her face pressed against the front.

"It's all back. It's really back. I think I'm having a fooking heart attack."

Damon climbed onto the front with Lily and Remi to see what lay ahead. The last time they'd been in the Fae, it'd been a tortured forest of gnarled trees covered in choking vines that had made them fight for every foot of passage.

None of that remained.

Tall trees resplendent in their summer leaves rustled in the soothing breeze. The carriage passed beneath the canopies on the way to a grand hall higher upon the hill. Flags and banners marked their path and as they turned, the stone path widened, and hundreds of faerie—pixies, dryads, gnomes, goblins, satyrs—lined the way, cheering as they passed. The carriage anticipated their desires and created windows on either side for them to watch and wave at the crowd.

"I see Willow! I see Willow!" exclaimed Remi.

"Who?"

"The ghost dryad that helped us reach the Court. I'm glad she's alright," said Remi, leaning back into the carriage to thumb away tears.

The vehicle stopped at the base of the steps that would lead up to the grand hall. Damon led his friends out of the carriage and even he found himself blushing from the attention.

Without talking about it, they held hands with Damon in the middle and Remi on his right. They ascended the stairs with patient steps, taking in every moment.

Damon could still see bits of the corruption in the faeries in the form of extra wings, or scars on their lithe forearms, but they were minor compared to the previous damage and appeared to be on the way to healing completely. He imaged that Oberon had focused his attention on the area around the Court, and that further out the corruption would still be present.

Halfway up the slope, the crowd changed to the tall Fae with elongated features, angled ears, and piercing, ageless eyes. They were alien and aloof, but managed to portray a begrudging thanks with their inclined heads.

When they reached the grand hall, trumpets sounded, making Damon's heart thunder against his chest in remembrance of their last battle. He had a moment of panic as he remembered how easily Oberon had taken control of him once he'd pledged himself to the Fae King and that the vow was technically still active. Would Oberon decide that he would stay much like his ancestor King Nuada? He hoped not. His duty was in the hospital, not the Fae.

Damon didn't even realize who he was seeing in the crowd gathered along the side until Remi gave his hand a squeeze. Both his parents and the twins were in the great hall, wearing clothes of similar design, though less grand. Nat's dress looked militaristic while Talia's was more old Hollywood. Their parents looked like they might explode from excitement, waving enthusiastically like children.

Based on the gasps of his friends, he knew his family weren't the only ones in attendance. Then he heard Remi sob, so he knew exactly who she'd spotted. Coraline had her hand to her mouth, holding back emotions from a spot just past his family. Damon half-expected to see Devlin, but then again, he was a creature of the Veil. He might not have permission to leave, even for an event like this.

Lily's entire family of witches had a place of honor up near the throne. The older de Meaths stayed in back, while her sisters stood in a line, oldest to youngest.

Biddy had changed much since the last time he'd seen her—of course, the Fae magic helped. She had the same trademark severe bun and emerald green dress, but the silken threads and blue highlights softened her edges, along with the proud smile she wore as she beamed at Lily.

Damon recognized the others from pictures, or Lily's descriptions of them. Evangel, with her golden blonde hair, was astonishingly beautiful, looking as angelic as her name, only eclipsed by the next, Nyx, who was as close as possible to the Fae Lords and Ladies without being a caricature of them. Then came Zella, who was a multi-sport star in Ireland, in an appropriate tracksuit-like outfit. The next was Kerensa, the sister with the wicked tongue and bright red hair that reminded him of bright plants that used the color as a warning to stay away. Last was Alice—young, beautiful Alice—who'd somehow stepped out of the shadows of her famous family, wearing tight clothing and eye makeup that made her look like a hired assassin.

The distractions of the guests allowed him to reach the back of the great hall without reacting to the figure on the stage. Damon released their hands and together, they bowed to their host, the Summer King of Fae, Oberon the Oak Father.

In the final battle, Damon had seen Oberon in all his fury wearing the ghostly antlered helmet of the Wild Hunt with the spirit of the Caoránarch rallying through him. He'd been frightening and fell, and the corruption had only made him worse.

This version of him was nothing like that one. In fact, he seemed more like Aleksandr Grimm than even the grandiose statues of his former glory. He beamed a fatherly smile at the three of them, holding his hands out in welcome. He'd chosen an understated outfit and wore a simple crown of thorns, yet the contrast with the elaborate outfits of his Court made him stand apart even more. Or maybe the experience with the kalkatai had humbled the great King.

The haunting ethereal music that had been playing in the background faded to silence as Oberon raised his right arm.

"Beannachtaí laochra an chroí! Welcome, Damon Wolfhard, Remi Wilde, and Lilith de Meath. My heart soars at the sight of you."

"That's my brother!" yelled Talia, receiving bulged eyes from the nearby guests, but the interruption turned to laughter when Oberon smiled.

"A fine lineage, you should be proud. All of you." Oberon faced each of the three families in turn. "Because standing before me are the three people, and one changeling, that saved me from that cursed kalkatai, the corruption that I had foolishly allowed to infect my mind, and thus endanger all the realms in turn. I owe a debt, *we all* owe a debt to these three. Our Champions of the Fae!"

Thunderous applause followed. Damon's entire body tingled from the attention, which went on far longer than he was used to. In fact, he blanked out for a bit when Oberon told the story in great detail, including how Lily had tricked him into drinking the cure from the Horn.

"Remi Wilde, please come forward," said Oberon.

The panicked look she gave him as she approached the throne was as endearing as it was believable. This was unfamiliar territory.

She approached with a bowed head, bending her knees slightly when she reached the throne.

"As a Champion of my lands, I ask what you would like as your boon?"

"My boon?" asked Remi.

At first she was stunned by the offer, but then a mischievous grin formed at the corner of her lips.

"Can I ask for anything?"

Oberon leaned his head back and burst into laughter, prompting the rest of the assembled to follow. When everyone was silent again, he grinned.

"Within reason, Ossarii, or Trickster of the Veil."

"My boon is simple. I want my mother to be able to come back home."

The tall handsome Fae King regarded Remi with slitted eyes and mirth on his lips as if he'd anticipated this request.

"It shall be done. I give permission to travel freely between our two realms for the both of you. But I have another gift. Please come forward."

The root ball was no bigger than a fist and covered in fine root-hairs and green sprouts. He leaned over and whispered in her ear as he handed it over.

When she turned again, Remi beamed at her mother at the side of the crowd. It was clear they were barely restraining the urge to run into each other's arms. Remi returned to his side, clutching the root ball as if it were made of pure gold.

"Lilith de Meath, please come forward. Neko, too."

The Irish witch was now intimidated by the circumstances. She strode to the dais with the white fox changeling at her side, chin lifted and proud. Oberon bowed to them both.

"Little One," said Oberon, clearly addressing the changeling. "For your bravery and steadfastness in support of your mistress, I give you my blessing and name you a member of the Summer Court. May your lineage grow long and fruitful."

Neko gave a little bark of happiness that brought smiles from the crowd.

"And you, Lily," said Oberon with a wry grin. "A witch for the ages. The de Meath family has long been a faithful friend of the Fae, under the watchful eyes of the warrior Medb, but this service goes beyond expectations. What boon would you ask of me?"

Lily paused and after a moment of reflection, said, "May I speak my request in private, King Oberon?"

His eyebrow arched elegantly.

"Of course. But since I must give you something now, so my kin do not think me miserly, I will speak to a certain leannán sídhe upon your behalf. I promise my negotiations will be beneficial for you both."

The exclamation that slipped from Lily's lips betrayed the importance of the gift, even though Damon had no idea what it meant. Had she bargained with another powerful being to find the cure? Damon suspected that was the truth.

"Damon Wolfhard, please come forward."

The call made his heart jump around in his chest like a jackrabbit. He'd never been so nervous in his life, but kept his chin high as he strode towards the throne.

Having met Aleksandr Grimm multiple times as well as battled the corrupted Fae King, the face of Oberon was familiar, yet he couldn't help but feel small compared to the ancient being. Oberon winked when he reached the dais.

"Damon Wolfhard, heir of King Nuada, and Champion of the Claíomh Ag Lonrú!"

Damon bent onto one knee.

"I'm afraid, King Oberon, that I left the sword here upon my last visit."

Laughter followed his comment like the rising of birds. Oberon smiled.

"It's lucky for you I'm a forgiving sort," he said, gesturing to the side, where an armored Fae warrior brought the Shining Sword to the King. "Kneel, Damon Wolfhard, and be officially named the Keeper of the Sword!"

A hitch caught in Damon's throat. He couldn't believe he was about to say what he was, but he knew it was the right thing to do.

"My apologies, King Oberon, but I must decline."

Shocked murmurings traveled through the crowd like an earthquake, followed by anxious silence.

"I am not a warrior. I know that now. I am not the right person to be Keeper. I put forth my sister, Natasha. She has a warrior's heart and the arm to wield it."

He turned to see his sister's jaw nearly hitting the floor.

"What...?"

Without missing a beat, Oberon nodded and turned towards a stunned Natasha.

"Natasha Wolfhard, please come forward."

His younger sister shuffled forward, suddenly shy, her cheeks blooming crimson. She gave him a "what the hell is going on" look when she reached his side, making him laugh, because it was the first time in a long time he could remember that she seemed both surprised and disarmed.

"Do you, Natasha Wolfhard of the Clan Zev, agree to become the Keeper of the Shining Sword, the Claíomh Ag Lonrú, the famed treasure of the Emerald Isles, and representative of your family at my side during the Wild Hunt?"

Natasha swallowed, then managed a firm answer.

"I would be honored."

"Kneel."

King Oberon placed the beautiful runed two-handed sword on each shoulder.

"You may now rise as Keeper of the Shining Sword!"

The crowd cheered when she reached her feet. King Oberon handed her the weapon hilt first, which she took, and after giving Damon another pained look, made her way back to the rest of their family while staring at the weapon in her fist.

King Oberon smiled down at Damon, once again suggesting that he'd anticipated that wrinkle, but then again, he was a powerful Fae and had honed his expressions over many millennia. Damon was foolish to assign human emotions to one as powerful as him.

"Since my Champions are both modest and wise, I must force upon them gifts befitting their station. As you stated before, you are not a warrior. You are a healer. Therefore, I gift you the healing touch of the Fae."

A warm sensation burned into his forearms. Damon pulled back the sleeves of his jacket to find Celtic knots on his flesh. One for each arm.

Damon bent at the waist and returned to his friends. He was dizzy with excitement and curious about how these new powers would manifest.

King Oberon spoke in a Fae tongue to his kin, before turning back to the humans.

"Now is a time for celebration! Do not fear to eat or drink, I had it brought from your world, so you're safe to enjoy the festivities today, though I wouldn't trust anything outside of my Hall."

The Fae King raised his fist and the crowd cheered.

"To our Champions!"

THIRTY-EIGHT

A whirlwind of faces passed by Lily, congratulating her, and she milled about the party until she eventually stumbled into the giggling knot that was her sisters.

"You always were an annoying shite, my dearest sister, so it comes as no surprise that you would ignore the common wisdom to save King Oberon," said Evangel, smirking.

Lily always felt insignificant next to her beautiful blonde sister who looked like she could have been kin to Celesse D'Agastine.

"I want to hear the story of the Bhróin," said Kerensa. "Did you really make a deal with one of the leannán sídhe? Knowing you, you probably marched in and demanded an answer without negotiating. What did you have to give up?"

"The virginity of your last boyfriend, dearest Kerensa. I figured it was safer to feed him to the leannán sídhe than let you flay him with your wicked tongue," said Lily.

Kerensa rolled her eyes and stuck out her tongue.

"Come on, sisters," said Zella in her emerald green pantsuit. "You know that leannán sídhe took one look at who she was dealing with and gave up. There's no one more annoying or persistent than the second youngest. Right, Biddy?"

The eldest de Meath had been standing quietly in back, but at her name, she slipped forward.

"I would let Lily annoy me to the end of days, because it would mean that I was near her."

Heat rushed to Lily's cheeks as she threw her arms around Biddy.

"Thank you," she whispered.

"Does this mean we finally get to see our dearest sisters again? Lily? Alice? Will you be returning home?" asked a dead-eyed Nyx.

Lily shared a smile with Alice, who'd been quiet mostly.

"The stars aren't as bright as in the City of Sorcery," said Alice. "And I've found a purpose I quite enjoy."

"Did you hear that, sisters?" said Kerensa, smirking. "She called us overbearing twits."

"I mean," said Alice with a single shoulder raised, "it does fit."

Kerensa threw her arms around Alice and kissed her on both cheeks.

"I'm coming to visit soon. I need you to show me where all the hot, stupid boys are."

"So you can flay them with your tongue? I suppose that would be entertaining," said Alice with a hand to her chest.

"What about you, Lily?" asked Nyx.

"I haven't decided," she said, which wasn't the truth and her sisters knew it, but they were kind enough to let her carry the fiction.

"Lily…"

The stiffening of her sisters could only mean one thing. King Oberon.

They parted and bowed their heads at his approach.

"Greetings, Ladies. May I speak with your sister?"

"For the price of a kiss," said Kerensa with her tongue between her teeth.

Oberon leaned over and gently pecked her cheek, which made her cheeks turn as red as her hair. Kerensa swallowed and allowed herself to be pulled away while gawking at the handsome Fae.

"We'll never hear the end of it now," said Lily.

The handsome Fae King held out his arm, which she accepted and allowed herself to be led through the crowd. The way parted before them, leaving her feeling like a member of the royalty. She knew she should be awed by his presence—which she was—but she'd also seen how even the most powerful beings of the realms were vulnerable. It worked the other way too. He knew that she'd seen him in such a state, which made what normally would be a formal relationship feel almost intimate.

Eventually, Oberon led them outside the Great Hall to an idyllic garden with ancient flower-covered statues. He released her arm and gestured towards a stone path.

"You wanted to speak to me in private."

Lily chewed on her lower lip.

"Forgive me, King Oberon, but when I was wielding the Crux, I saw visions of past battles between the Fae and the Fomorians."

"You did not like what you saw."

She looked away.

"I'd always been taught that the Fomorians had been the aggressors, but the vision showed me a battalion of Fae warriors charging into Fomorian villages and slaughtering them, children and all."

"Would you prefer a convenient fiction, or the painful truth?"

"I'm not a child."

"Nor have you ever been," said Oberon. "The truth is neither the Fae nor the Fomorians were innocent. But those were less civilized days. The past is not an easy place to visit."

"Our realms are more connected these days, shouldn't we make amends?"

"I can see why your elders called you difficult," said Oberon as they headed along the manicured path. "Should I reach out to Balor after he tried to destroy the hospital?"

"I'm not asking to offer an olive branch to Balor. He can burn in a pool of lava for all I care. But in the twelfth ward, there's an enclave where many Fomorians, and even some Fae and other non-humans, gather at the edges of society. My request is for you and your Society of the White Hart friends to charitably fund the enclave and especially the medical clinic run by Dr. Marcie."

"Dr. Marcie? Twin black braids and a tattoo of a deer on her fore-arm?"

"You know her?"

Oberon smirked as he glanced askew.

"Know? No. But one hears rumors."

That Oberon, the Oak Father, had heard of Dr. Marcie made Lily wonder who the woman really was. She'd suspected supernatural origins, but now she was sure Dr. Marcie was much older than she looked.

"It will be done," he said eventually.

Their stroll took them to a glade at the end of the path where a single Eó Ruis tree waited. The yew was young, with a trunk only as wide as a man's chest, but in time, it would grow to be wider than three arm lengths. Lily smiled thinking of the Eó Ruis near their home in Ireland.

"What do you think of the tree?"

"Was this planted after the corruption?" asked Lily.

His eyes glittered with thought. He was testing her.

"It was planted after the corruption," she said eventually.

"Do you notice anything else?"

Lily peered at the yew tree. It was young enough the bark was smooth and the trunk was round, but in time it would grow thicker and with deep crevices. In ancient times, people thought that the way to reach the Fae was through the woody folds.

"It seems...sad," she said, noting the droop of the leaves.

"There are many things my magics can heal. After our battle, and once I'd regained my own thoughts, I poured my skill into returning these lands to their former glories. Further away from the Court, the corruption still rules, but in time, I will root out those flaws."

"What does that have to do with this Eó Ruis tree?"

"Not all things can be healed so easily. People especially are vulnerable to the wounds of their secret desires."

Lily couldn't tell if he was talking about himself or someone else, but he clearly wanted to tell her something particular.

"Was it your secret desire to take over the Halls?"

Oberon broke out in laughter.

"Anyone that has lived as long as I have would covet such power. If only to keep it from being used against me. I won't be the last either."

"What about the one that gave you the Thrice-Cursed Stone? Or put it in your path?"

His flawless face wrinkled with darkness, reminding her of his terrible power.

"That knowledge seems to be lost to corruption. But I fear that whoever it was, their intent to introduce chaos to the Halls has not changed."

"What are you planning to do with the Arcane Phytology Hall?"

"It will remain. I will hand over day-to-day operations to one of the professors, which is not uncommon in the Halls. I feel it should continue as a place of study as a kind of penance for what nearly occurred."

Lily stilled, only because she didn't know what else to say to a being that had been around longer than most human civilization. He was clearly holding back his power as not to intimidate her, but that very restraint was a demonstration of his power.

"What is it that you want me to see?" she asked after a long silence.

"Here lies before you, Dr. Marcus Broomfield."

"The Eó Ruis tree?"

"This very one."

Lily regarded the tree anew. There was something so sad about the idea that the man had been so thoroughly broken that the only way to re-deem him was to turn him into a yew tree.

"Can he hear us?"

"No. Not yet, but maybe in a few hundred years."

Lily contemplated Dr. Broomfield's fate. To be turned into a yew tree in the Summer Fae might be considered by some a boon, but she did not see it that way. Then as she stared at the quiet shiver of the leaves, she had an epiphany.

"King Oberon?"

"Yes, Lily."

"Have the other yew trees of Ireland been created in the same way?"

King Oberon did not answer. He stared at the Eó Ruis tree with an elevated melancholy for a long time, until he half-turned, gave her a brief incline of the head, and headed back to the festivities.

Lily stared at the yew tree until the laughter and cheering from the party renewed her desire for company.

THIRTY-NINE

Standing in the Court of the Summer Fae, surrounded by pixies and Fae Lords and Ladies, with strange ethereal music drifting into the Grand Hall, Remi only had eyes for her mother. She clutched Coraline's arm close to her side, afraid to let go.

"What was that gift that King Oberon gave you?" asked her mother.

The root ball was in her pocket.

"We'll find out when we return to the city."

"We?"

Remi faced her.

"You're coming back, right?"

"Of course. I just wasn't sure you'd want me around."

Remi squeezed her lips tight.

"Why wouldn't I? You're my mother. My *real* mother."

"The one who couldn't protect you and spent her time lost in the Fae.

I want to come back, but I'm also scared. It's been decades. I suspect longer than I remember. Time is weird in the Fae. What if I can't adjust?"

"I'll help you. It was like that for me too. I'd spent my life around other criminals and people like that, and it took time for me to understand not everyone's trying to rip each other off. Coraline. Mom. Not only do I want you to return, I want to live together. If that's what you want. I'm graduating from Aura Healers soon and I'll be staying at Golden Willow in the Hospice Ward. There are some great places nearby that I'm looking at. One in particular if it's still on the market when we get back."

Coraline put a hand to her mouth as her eyes glistened.

"I don't know what to say."

"Say yes. Say you'll come live with me. We'll hang out, talk, play Courts while we drink coffee. Anything you want."

She put a hand to her heart as she nodded enthusiastically.

"I would love that."

"Me too."

A cleared throat had them turning to find Arthur and Emily Wolfhard approaching. He put his hand out.

"Remi, it's wonderful to see you again. Is this your lovely sister?" he asked with mirth in his eyes.

"It's my mother, but you already knew that," said Remi. "How is KC?"

"Hot, sweaty, and thankful that our daughters no longer terrorize the lacrosse leagues."

Arthur winked.

"You know Remi?" asked Coraline.

Remi put a hand on his arm.

"He spent some time in Golden Willow after he got sick from a deadly assassin."

A shout followed by clattering and then laughter had them turning to see Nat with the sword drawn while a group of Fae ladies were getting ready to throw another dragon fruit at her and Talia whispered in a Fae gentleman's ear.

"We can't take them anywhere," said Emily, exasperated.

"Do you live in the city?" asked Arthur.

"Uh, no," said Coraline. "I've been stuck in the Fae."

Emily punched her husband.

"Didn't you hear her request? She asked for her mother to get to leave the Fae."

"Of course, I knew that." He grinned. "My understanding is you were stolen by some other folks? Does that mean your last name isn't Wilde?"

Remi wrinkled her forehead.

"What is my last name?" she asked her mother, who wore a strange expression.

"Your father's last name was Remington."

"What? Devlin Remington? That makes me Remi Remington," she said, laughing. "Maybe I'll keep Wilde. Feels more fitting."

"Arthur, we'd better do something before the twins insult our host," said Emily, tugging on his shirt.

After they were gone, Coraline said, "They seemed nice."

"They're a great family."

"What about you and Damon?"

Remi frowned.

"I don't know. I'm staying at the hospital, but he hasn't decided what he's doing. If he goes somewhere else, then we'll be in a long-distance relationship."

"And if he stays?"

Remi clutched her arm around her chest. It was one thing to be in a relationship with him during school, but now that time was coming to an end, she was thinking about her future.

"We'll see," she said, lifting a single shoulder.

"Remi?"

"Yeah...Mom?"

The title felt unfamiliar on her lips, but also good.

"I see your friends beyond the Great Hall."

Through a side exit, she saw Damon and Lily looking over the valley. The light had dimmed to dusk and faerie lights glistened over the party, giving everything a glossy feel.

"I can stay with you."

"No, you go on. We'll have time enough in the city to catch up."

Remi kissed her mother on the forehead and joined her friends, slipping next to Damon as they stared across the valley and watched a gentle evening descend on the Summer Fae.

FORTY

No one knew where the old lime green couches that had been a fixture in their common area had gone, but the ones they'd found to replace them were as close to the originals as possible without magic being involved. Boon was holding court near the front, telling a story about the threesome he'd been involved with that weekend that had gotten out of hand when a miscast spell had given them twenty times the expected amount of lube.

Damon had come in late, since he'd been working with Dr. Lara, and joined Remi and Lily on the couch.

"Do we have any idea who's going to graduate us? Will we get an appearance from Patron Jennings?" he asked as he put his legs over Remi's lap.

He really needed to talk to her separately, but there was no chance with everyone in the room.

"No one will say, not even a rumor," said Remi. "Which makes me suspicious."

"I doubt Patron Jennings would show up now after his whole Hall went to shite with that Broomfield business. Damn near took down the entire Golden Willow organization. Probably going to send us off with a pat on the rear and a warm recommendation," said Lily.

An exclamation had everyone checking to the hallway where a bearded, semi-familiar man wearing an overstuffed backpack was peering through the blinds with an unnerving grin. He was extremely tan and fit.

"Is that...?" asked Sasha.

When the scruffy traveler pulled a bottle of whiskey from his bag as he strolled into the room, Damon broke out laughing.

"Dr. Decker!"

"It seems you malcontents managed to survive your five years of school. Who has a shit load of shot glasses? We have a graduation to celebrate."

Ethan went scurrying down the hallway in search of drinking cups while the rest of the class crowded around Dr. Decker. Peppered with questions, he managed to explain that they'd just returned from a multi-realm walkabout.

Around the time Ethan returned with a stack of small paper cups for the whiskey, a gorgeous woman with black hair pulled into a ponytail strolled into the room casually.

"I hear there are some celebrations in order," Dr. Martinez said.

Before long, Decker was pouring out the whiskey and everyone downed their shots.

"When did you get back?" asked Damon.

Dr. Decker checked his watch while scrunching up his face.

"This morning? It's morning, right?"

Dr. Martinez put her arm on his shoulder while grinning at the class.

"We had to come back for a few meetings with the hospital board of directors."

"Does that mean what I think it means?" asked Boon.

Dr. Martinez spread her hands wide.

"You're looking at the new Chief of Staff. Well, not yet. But soon, after I sign all the contracts."

After more cheering, another round of whiskey was poured.

"Don't be fooled," said Dr. Decker. "No one else wanted the job after what went down this year."

Dr. Martinez extended both middle fingers.

"Don't think I'll be giving *you* special treatment."

"Are you rejoining the staff too, Dr. Decker?" asked Damon.

"There seems to be an opening in the Curse Ward. None of you had anything to do with that, did you?"

"We were in the Fae," said Lily, batting her eyelashes.

Dr. Decker rolled his eyes.

"Yet, I still imagine that you had something to do with it." He turned to the others. "So where are the rest of you miscreants headed next?"

Damon knew most of where everyone was going after graduation. Boon had gotten a job at a medical research facility on the west coast, Ethan was staying at Golden Willow to become a doctor, Sasha had taken a position back in London at the prestigious Arcane Hospital, and the others were scattered around other facilities.

"What about you three? You've been unusually quiet."

"I'll be working at the clinic in the twelfth ward," said Lily.

"Clinic. There's no clinic in the twelfth," he said.

"You're welcome to help, Dr. Decker. The pay is shite, but the work is good."

"What about you two lovebirds?"

Damon shared a glance with Remi.

"I'm going to stay in the Hospice Ward, and Damon, well, he hasn't told anyone yet," said Remi with a furrowed brow.

"That's because I hadn't decided, until this morning." He offered a weak smile. "I accepted the job at the Institute."

Damon tensed up, expecting a rebuke from Remi, but she beamed a smile instead.

"That's great!" she said as she threw her arms around his chest.

Damon hugged her tight and then let go.

"You're not mad?"

"No, why would I be? That's your dream job."

"But I'm so far away."

"Not that far by train, and given how busy we were during school, I'll bet that we see each other about the same amount."

A coil in his chest loosened, making it easier to breathe again.

"I'm glad you kids are working it out," said Dr. Martinez. "But I should go get changed for my meeting. I don't think the board would appreciate the homeless-chic that's been my life for the last few years."

As the party broke up, Damon caught Remi to the side.

"You're really not mad?"

She shook her head.

"Hells no. You'd be miserable if I made you stay here. Go. The Institute is what you've been dreaming about doing forever. I'd feel terrible if I kept you from that. Besides, I've got a lot on my plate too with the Hospice Ward and figuring out how to live with my mom."

"How's that going?"

"Good. No, wait. Great. We've got a lot of fixing up to do in the house, but Coraline is having fun with it. Once we get things settled, we'll have you over for dinner. I know she wants to get to know you more."

"Me too."

Remi stood on her tippy-toes for a kiss.

"I have rounds with Dr. Morsdux. I'll see you tonight at the bar."

After she walked out, Damon found he was the only one left. The others had all returned to their duties. And while they'd be getting together for drinks and a party in the evening and then graduation in a few days, Damon was certain that it was probably the last time they'd all be meeting in the common room. In fact, by the end of the summer, this room would probably be given over to a new crop of first-year students. Bright-eyed, bushy-tailed, and in no way ready for what was to come. He knew he'd been that way when he came to the hospital. So many expectations had been squashed so quickly. Damon wished he could give them advice on how to survive their time in Aura Healers.

And maybe he could. Damon grabbed a marker from the board and in meticulous block letters wrote:

"Rule #11: The best way to survive is to stick together."

FORTY-ONE

Grinding saws filled the air, sending sparks over the covered pathway. Lily ducked through the temporary doorway to cross the open space where she could see the four-story building going up next to the old clinic. The steel girders looked out of place next to the ramshackle pallet buildings where members of the enclave cooked on open fires.

True to his word, Oberon had raised the funds from his Society of the White Hart members to build a permanent enclave in the twelfth which included a state-of-the-art medical clinic that would focus on the plights of non-humans. Lily was in current negotiations with Dr. Martinez about making the clinic part of the Golden Willow hospital system, but until they could agree on the funding targets, the deal was up in the air.

A towering hob with a runed metal leg beneath his left knee was pushing a wheelbarrow through the gap ahead of her. She smiled. He'd been resistant to accepting magic from her given her relation to the Fae, but after a conversation with Dr. Marcie, he'd been a willing participant.

"How's the new leg, Darak?"

The tusked hob gave her a wide grin.

"It's good. Like new. I work hard now," he said in halting English.

Lily gave him a thumbs-up and continued through the construction area. Moving everyone around was a constant challenge, especially since they were still arguing with the city about who owned the property, but lawyers that Aleksandr Grimm had sent them were making short work of the disagreements. They'd been told that everything should be buttoned up by the end of the year.

The clinic was surprisingly empty when she arrived. The desk attendant said they'd knocked out the rest of the cases that morning and more weren't due for another hour.

"They're in the garden."

The garden. Lily still wasn't sure how she felt about it. The addition to the enclave seemed more hassle than it was worth, but she wasn't about to disagree with the gift. They'd just have to find a way to keep up with it.

Lily cut through the construction area to the central space. When the project was finished, there'd be four major buildings surrounding a green space that had originally been planned as a place for the members to set up small pop-ups and other shops, but with the garden plan, they had to move it to the front area. While the outer location was theoretically better for gaining business, she knew that most residents in the city didn't like to see non-humans openly flaunting their existence.

The buzzing of saws fell away as she stepped through the heavy plastic sheeting. The garden was surrounded on three sides by tall wooden walls while the final piece was the building under construction.

The moment her shoes hit the lush grass, her concerns fell away, especially as she saw how the young Eó Ruis tree at the center was thriving. Standing beneath the canopy were two figures. The taller one in a pinstriped suit was gesturing in various directions while Dr. Marcie looked on and nodded.

"Healer Lily," said Aleksandr Grimm upon her arrival. "This is good timing. I was just explaining how this entire central area will be contained by a dome, just like Arcane Phytology. Once the other buildings are completed, of course."

Lily had to hide her mirth. Dr. Marcie had no idea that Aleksandr was actually Oberon, King of the Summer Fae, but she probably suspected something was unusual about him. But Lily supposed it went the other way too, since none of them knew who Dr. Marcie really was under that unassuming form. Either way, Lily was glad to have them both working together towards the same goals.

"That sounds lovely. Shall I break out the tea to celebrate?"

Aleksandr gave her a wry look.

"I only meant to stop by for a short visit, just to see how things were progressing. I have to get back to my Hall. Thank you for indulging me."

The handsome Aleksandr strode from the garden while fiddling with his phone. Lily wondered if he was doing that for their sake, or he actually had messages to answer. She wondered what the people on the other side of the texts would think if they knew who he really was.

"Something amusing?" asked Dr. Marcie with an eyebrow raised.

"Did your meeting go well?"

Dr. Marcie shifted her mouth to the side.

"I keep expecting there to be a price for all this largess. We went from begging for scraps to having millions poured into the facility. I just don't get it. What kind of blackmail do you have on Patron Grimm?"

"The same kind I have on you."

"What's that supposed to mean?" asked Dr. Marcie.

"Exactly what it sounds like. I'm not in charge of either of you. I'm a bloody healer, not an administrator."

Dr. Marcie narrowed her gaze before letting a grin spread across her lips.

"Come on, I have something to show you."

They took the longer way around the construction to reach the clinic due to a crane being moved into position. Dr. Marcie spoke quietly to the desk attendant before handing over a ring of keys.

"Are we giving birth today?"

"Not that I'm aware of," said Dr. Marcie, leading her through an unfamiliar hallway.

"Where are we?"

Dr. Marcie stood outside a freshly painted door. She opened it and stood aside.

"Your new office. We converted the storage area since we're expanding. You no longer have to share a room with me."

Lily's heart lifted into her throat as she examined the facilities.

"This is as good as Golden Willow."

"Better, because it comes with a top-notch healer," said Dr. Marcie. "I don't know how we got so lucky to have you, but I didn't want you to have second thoughts about coming to the clinic, not when, as far as I can tell, you could have the pick of jobs from anywhere in the world."

There were a lot of things Lily could tell her: that she wanted to be near her friends, or that the City of Sorcery was too important, or maybe that she realized that after everything that had happened, she couldn't go home again.

"Because this is where I'm needed most."

FORTY-TWO

The steamy mug of coffee warmed Remi's hands as she studied the game of Courts in the greenhouse. A light patter of rain on the glass provided a soothing song as she considered her next move.

"Your turn," she told her mother after moving a piece two positions forward.

Coraline had been examining a pink flower on a plant near the center tree, which was a spindly sapling that looked like a hunched old woman.

"Is it really safe to have a tree that can be a portal to the Veil in your garden? Won't it let spirits and other dead things through?"

Remi glanced up to see the faint apparition floating near the back wall. The woman had died to childbirth in the early 1900s after the house had been built. Remi assumed she'd been an avid gardener because the ghost was always staring at the plants.

"The dead things are already around us, if you know where to look."

Coraline made an exaggerated shiver.

"I don't know how you do it," she said, returning to the table. Coraline took a few seconds before she moved her Herald into a forward position.

"Blood and bough, you undid my plans with one move."

"You'll have to be better than that to beat me," said Coraline with a wink.

Remi sighed but she was smiling. Now that she wasn't a student, she had more time off, and spending the afternoon playing Courts with her mother in the garden was one of her favorite things to do. She looked forward to it every week. Eventually she knew she'd want to do other things, but for now, Remi was content.

"I guess it could allow Devlin to come visit easier," said Coraline with her arms crossed, staring at the sapling.

The idea that her mother might want to see the Stranger as much as she did hadn't crossed her mind. It'd been a few weeks since she'd tried to contact him.

"Mom," she said, enjoying the way the word felt on her lips, "Devlin doesn't need a nekyia tree to visit. He can do that all on his own."

"I don't know..."

"How did you two meet?"

Coraline didn't speak for a minute. Remi worried that she'd brought back a bad memory until her mother turned and she could see the wistful smile.

"Long before the corruption, when I was just a young woman around your age, I was taking a bath in a pool beneath a waterfall. Sometimes the satyrs might spy on me, but they were harmless then, and I generally felt safe. But then the air grew unnaturally cold and shadows intruded on the pool. When I looked up, I saw your father. I had no idea who or what he was, but I could tell he was lost.

"It seemed he was on his way to the Court of Summer as an envoy for his Mistress, but had not been able to find his way. I agreed to help him, but not until the morning. He stayed in my cottage. We talked until late in the night. I don't think he'd had a human conversation in centuries. But I got him on his way the next day until we found a traveling Lord who agreed to take him the rest of the way. And then, months later, you were born."

"That's it? You only knew him for a day?"

"I was a lonely young woman. He was too, really. Being a servant for the Mistress of the Veil is not an easy job, I imagine."

"Do you know how he came to be in that position?"

Coraline glanced away.

"Not really. The only thing he mentioned was that he was born in a time of death and that his Mistress took him in when no one else would."

Further questions were interrupted by the doorbell. Remi moved to the edge of the greenhouse to see a woman standing at her door without an umbrella.

"Who is it?" asked Coraline.

"A mage, that's all I know."

"This isn't about the former owner of the house, is it? You said it wouldn't be a problem."

"No, it's definitely not that. Oberon himself destroyed the White Worm. Let me go see what this is about."

Remi ran through a million possibilities on her way to the bottom floor, but she was wrong about every one of them.

"Head Patron Pythia," she gasped upon opening the door. "Please come in. It's all wet out there."

Remi felt foolish for saying that. Although Head Patron Pythia wore a trench coat, the petite young woman had not a speck of rain on her. A silvery sequined dress was visible through a gap in the coat.

"Would you walk with me? I'm headed somewhere else, but I wanted to stop by."

"Of course."

Remi hurried to the Head Patron's side, but was still getting rained on. The Head Patron adjusted a ring on her pinky finger, which extended the faintly visible shield above her head.

"There. That should keep us both dry."

A thousand questions ran through Remi's head but she kept her mouth shut because it was unusual for one of the most powerful people in the world to "just stop by for a visit."

"Did you enjoy your time at Golden Willow? My sister loved that place."

"Your sister? Aurelia? I didn't realize she worked there."

The Head Patron made a gesture with her hand.

"As an orderly before we joined the Halls."

"That's..."

She was going to say crazy but that seemed insulting given who she was talking to.

"Yes, to answer your question, in a strange way, I really enjoyed my time as a student in Golden Willow, but I'm also glad to be done. With the student part. But it's nice to be somewhere I belong."

"Yes, yes it is."

Remi took a look around to see where they were headed, but she saw no obvious destination as they were still in the residential neighborhood made up of old three-story shotgun-style houses.

"I wanted to thank you, Remi Wilde."

"Thank me? I don't understand."

"You and your friends solved a very thorny problem, one that was going to metastasize into something much worse."

"So you know who Aleksandr Grimm is?"

"I do now, thanks to you. We had a long talk a few weeks ago about what happened and how the end of the kalkatai came to be."

"Have you figured out who gave him the Thrice-Cursed Stone?"

The Head Patron paused.

"No."

"That's a shame," said Remi, though she suspected that Pythia knew more than she was letting on.

The rain picked up its pace, splattering their legs and creating big puddles in the street. When they had to cross, the Head Patron gestured with her left hand and the puddle was swept away in a mini-flood, leaving them a dry patch.

"There are schemes within schemes in the City of Sorcery. Squash one and three more pop up. It's tiring, which is why I appreciate that a long-shot prospect like yourself was able to take care of one."

"Long-shot prospect..."

The Head Patron raised an eyebrow.

"I wouldn't expect a person of your past to be confused about how they were chosen and why."

"No, not at all. I knew you were taking a chance on me when you did. I'm glad I was able to prove your point. I was really thinking about the fact that I'm not the only one. Right? You've taken chances on other students that might not have been able to get into the Halls on their own?"

The Head Patron faced her with a smirk. The youthfulness of her gaze reminded Remi that she wasn't that much older than she was, in mage terms anyway. Maybe her early thirties. If the stories were true, and Remi suspected they were, then she was one of the most powerful mages in the entire world. But that youth was probably why there were others trying to test her position. Remi understood that. She'd been underestimated her entire life. It made her want to support the Head Patron in any way she could.

"It's my job to find the best and brightest students for the Halls, no matter where they come from, or what their past circumstances. The dangers to the Halls multiply exponentially, but thankfully, so do our resources."

Head Patron Pythia glanced to an alleyway that ran between two three-story brick houses.

"Anyway, I'm here. I would have liked to talk longer, but I seem to have less and less free time these days. One day I'll figure out how my sister was able to dump this burden on me."

"It was good seeing you again, Head Patron Pythia. Thank you for taking a chance on me."

"No, Remi, thank you. While there are thousands of mages with more power than you, it's not the quality of your magic that mattered, but what's in your heart. I'm glad you were able to learn to trust others and yourself. It's that bond of fellowship that will keep our realm safe. Now if you'll excuse me, I must squash one of those other problems."

The Head Patron strolled into the alleyway as if it were a runway, then she slipped the trench coat off, revealing the silvery sequined dress and sleeves of tattoos on either arm. She winked and walked right through the brick wall as if it were mist.

Remi ran forward and placed her hands on the wall to find it was solid. Without the protective barrier, the rain pelted Remi, so she grabbed the Head Patron's trench coat and threw it over her shoulders. As she hurried back to her house a few blocks away, Remi found a ring in the front pocket. It was the pinky ring that had protected them from the rain. She slipped it on her smallest digit and woke the magic, enjoying the relief the barrier provided.

By the time she returned, Remi had a hard time convincing herself that the meeting with the Head Patron had been real. If it weren't for the trench coat and ring, she might have thought it a delusion.

"Remi, is that you?" called her mother from the kitchen.

"I'm back."

"Who was that? I wasn't expecting you to go tramping through the rain."

Remi slipped out of the trench coat and hung it on the rack in the corner. She admired the silver ring on her pinky finger.

"An old friend from the Halls. She helped me out when I first got there."

"That's nice. Maybe I can meet her sometime and thank her."

Remi grinned.

"She'll be back eventually. Hopefully not anytime soon, but she'll be back. I'm sure of it."

Remi knocked the last of the rain from her clothes and headed into the kitchen where her mother was starting a batch of chocolate chip cookies.

It was good to be home.

EPILOGUE

The first ward was the last place Marrigan wanted to be on this sunny September day. The choked noisy streets, cars puking their fumes into the air, and the general arrogance of the inhabitants—that they were the promised people of all the realms—pissed him off to no end. He had a mind to crack one of them suited arseholes right in the kisser, but it wouldn't be a right time to shine.

The note had told him to use the back entrance. He'd almost marched through the front until he saw the faez detectors right inside the glass doors.

"Bollocks."

A man in mirrored sunglasses and a curly-wired earpiece was waiting for him at the appointed entrance.

"Marrigan?"

He got real close to the man, sensing him tensing up. The guard wanted to reach for his revolver, that much was clear. Marrigan examined his teeth in the reflective glasses.

"Sorry, mate, got a piece of kale in my teeth. Shouldn't have been no green stuff in my burrito, but these trogs don't know how to leave well enough alone. You get me?"

"You're expected upstairs."

"You don't say," said Marrigan. "I came all this way just to pick my teeth in front of a wanker with a gun whose arsehole is tighter than the Queen's purse. You should have just said piss off."

Marrigan brushed by the guard to head inside. He paused with the door open.

"Elevator with the blue door. They'll bring you up."

"Thanks, mate, you ain't all that bad," he said with a wink.

The car went up forever, past the final numbers which meant he was on the highest floors of the building.

When he stepped out, two guards were waiting for him.

"You sorry bastards are multiplying."

"Raise your arms, Mr. Marrigan," said the first guard.

"I ain't a Mister, you twat-waddle."

The guard waved a wand around his body. The beeps increased whenever they were near one of his trinkets. A brief examination proved they were minor, nothing worthy of concern. Marrigan had left his more potent items back at the crappy hotel he had the misfortune of staying at.

"All clear," said the guard into his earpiece.

"Yeah, all clear," said Marrigan, grinning.

Sorry fookers didn't think to check for mundane solutions. In a world of sorcery, everyone was always thinking about magic and spells and faez. Sometimes a good bit of C4 was enough to make an impression.

The suite was filled with priceless art. Marrigan had a mind for museums. When you traveled all over the world and the realms hunting for artifacts and solving other people's problems, there was a fair amount of free time, and a good museum was better than the other vices that plagued his line of work.

"Aye, that's a nice Picasso, and there's a good looking Benoit, and a Nyong'o, quite lovely, if I don't say. *Shards of Light After the Fall* is a stunner. Your boss has an eye for the good stuff."

He was led to a room with a long marble table. The door was closed behind him. Marrigan pressed his face against the glass. The cars below looked like busy ants.

Turning back, he found a strange painting that immediately put him on edge. He'd never seen its like, with brooding blacks, browns, and greens depicting an olden town surrounded by dense forests, but the closer he looked the more horrors he saw, including a vendor pushing a cart full of severed heads—

"Do you like it?"

Marrigan reached for the knife in his hip pocket, but let his hand fall away the moment he realized who was speaking. A maetrie. A city Fae. Regret wasn't the right word for it, but he suddenly wished he'd done a better job of vetting. He hated being surprised.

"Is there a problem?"

"No," said Marrigan. "You caught me unaware, which doesn't happen very often. I like to think of myself as a survivor. Whenever something happens that catches me by surprise, I have to reevaluate everything."

He hadn't met very many maetrie in his life. The city Fae were rare outside their own realm, but their talent for cunning and destruction was unmatched. Despite his host being on the smaller side, Marrigan knew that he'd be a fool to challenge him.

"You didn't answer my question."

Marrigan glanced back to the odd painting.

"It's hiding something."

The maetrie's eyes gleamed with amusement.

"You're a keen observer."

"Not keen enough. I wasn't expecting a maetrie."

"Is this a problem?"

"No, not at all. Your money spends the same, but I like to know who I'm dealing with is all. Makes for smoother transactions."

The off-smile on his lips soured Marrigan for the deal. He liked to know that he was in charge of every situation, or at least equal in his mistrust, but here he felt like he'd been dropped naked into a pool of piranha.

"Do you have the item?"

Marrigan reached into an inner pocket and produced a small runed cube. He slid it across the marble table.

"It looks like Menes Codex."

"It is. I had it verified before I came here."

The cube disappeared into the maetrie's pocket. A stuffed envelope was slid across the table.

"The reward."

Marrigan weighed the cash in his hand.

"This isn't even half of it."

"No, it isn't," said the strange maetrie as he stared back with a queer smile.

Marrigan lifted his shirt showing the band of explosive taped to his belly.

"You can pay me the correct amount or we can both take a short and very fiery ride to the concrete below. I'd rather be dead than let someone rip me off. Sorry, mate. It's just business."

"If you detonate that, the only one that will regret it is yourself."

"There's enough bloody explosives here to put a hole in the moon. I know there are spells and such, but trust me, I know what kind of shielding is possible, and this is more than you can handle."

The maetrie snapped his fingers and an awful keening filled the air. Marrigan wanted to vomit as he leaned over the table, but he kept his finger near the detonation device. The noise went on until he was sure his head was going to implode. When it finally stopped, he was able to open his eyes again.

"What was that—"

He never finished his words because he could feel the absence of the explosives around his thick belly. Marrigan checked only to find his scarred flesh rather than the explosives he'd carefully taped on that morning.

"That's a helluva trick," said Marrigan begrudgingly. "But I still want my money."

The smirk told him that he'd passed some kind of test.

"The word is that you're an excellent artifact hunter and an even better problem-solver."

"Depends on the problem, but yeah, I get shit done."

"Good. I need more men like that."

"I don't work for others. I'm freelance."

"Everyone has a price."

Marrigan cocked a smile.

"I doubt you could afford mine."

A ring bounced along the marble and came to a stop near his hand. He knew what it was as soon as he saw it. He'd been searching for one for years.

"Is that...?"

"A Watcher Ring? There are only a handful in existence. Quite the item for a man in your line of work. Keeps people from easily spying on you with magic, tells you when someone's watching you in person, obscures your location, and a few other little tricks."

Marrigan stared at the ring resting on his palm.

"What is this then?"

"Call it a down payment on your loyalty. That won't be the only perk. I have more money and resources than you can imagine."

"And what are these vast resources being put towards?"

"Plans."

"Gotcha."

"There's a furnished apartment in the seventh for you, plus a weekly stipend, and access to more magic like that ring."

"And what will you have me do for all this largess?"

The maetrie set a folded piece of paper on the table. He gave it a backhand wave and the note slid across to Marrigan. On the inside of the folded paper was the name of a famous artifact that had been lost for centuries.

"First job. An easy one for a man of your talents."

Marrigan shook his head. He couldn't believe he was considering it, but it'd be nice to have resources backing him for once.

"Alright, I'll accept on one condition."

"And that is?"

"I need to know who I'm working for."

The smile could have swallowed him whole. The strange maetrie was suddenly next to him with his hand out.

"It's lovely to meet you, Marrigan. I'm Dominion Thule."

§ § §

ABOUT THE AUTHOR

Thomas K. Carpenter resides in Colorado with his wife Rachel. When he's not busy writing his next book, he's hiking, skiing, and getting beat by his wife at cards. He keeps a regular blog at www.thomaskcarpenter.com and you can follow him on twitter @thomaskcarpente. If you want to learn when his next novel will be hitting the shelves and get free stories and occasional other goodies, please sign up for his mailing list by going to: http://tinyurl.com/thomaskcarpenter. Your email address will never be shared and you can unsubscribe at any time.